MORTAL BITE

SHARON HAMILTON

ISBN-10: 1495389847
ISBN-13: 9781495389849

CHAPTER 1

Paolo Monteleone swirled the black cape around his body as he checked the guest chamber's full-length mirror. The fabric arrived at his knees and calves well after he stopped spinning, and then draped back away to sway a few inches from the floor. He could see his face in the polished sheen of his shoes. The tux and red cummerbund, an elegant presentation, belonged to his brother, Marcus, but it fit him perfectly. Marcus's man had done well. The costume was a fitting outfit for any good vampire gentleman.

It had been a year since he'd returned to Italy, repairing the damage he'd caused his brother and his new wife. A year of learning to be a father to his son, making amends to the other Monteleone family members who at first didn't trust that he wouldn't run off again and try to live as the mortal he wasn't.

When Marcus and Anne graciously invited him to join them in California wine country, Paolo immediately agreed. The change of scenery was doing him good. Tonight he was going to attend his first party without a member of his family.

The door burst open and Lucius, all four feet of him, raced straight for Paolo. The boy wore his Superman cape and red boots—rain boots, to be exact—with all the pride of the superheroes he loved to emulate.

Paolo bent over and lifted his son, pressed the flesh of this little superhero to his chest and nuzzled just under the boy's right ear. The fresh smell of his mortality was the most satisfying moment of Paolo's day. Eventually, Lucius would have to make the choice whether to remain mortal or become golden vampire. But not yet. Not until he was of age.

"And just where are you heading out to? Anne taking you trick-or-treating? It's not Halloween yet," he murmured affectionately into the side of the boy's face.

Lucius drew back and his dark eyes flashed at his father, which always managed to melt Paolo's heart.

"I'm going with you to the party, father." His coppery brown eyes and pink cheeks made him look sweet despite the heavy, jagged, and uneven eye makeup he must have applied himself.

"Lucius, you could hurt yourself putting all that kohl around your eyes. You should have asked your aunt for help."

"Well, Anne and Marcus…" the boy paused and blushed. "They're busy all the time."

"Ahhhhh," Paolo said. He envied his brother and his long-awaited fated female and their new baby. The fact that Marcus found Anne after three hundred years of searching meant there might still be hope for him. Not a fated female, but someone to love and be loved in return.

A shadow suddenly covered his heart, and gave him a chill. He composed himself and addressed his son.

"Lucius, time enough for parties when you're older. This one is for grown-ups only. Not for…"

"Kids," Lucius finished with resignation. "But I *want* to go. You will protect me, father."

Indeed he could. Not an hour went by when Paolo wasn't fearful of the fact that Lucius, still mortal, could die, and Paolo, vampire, would be left to grieve for all eternity.

"I'm sure cook will find you something sweet in the kitchen. I think she made a berry pie." He winked as he set his son down, while he savored the change in the boy's face.

"Berry pie? Whoopee!" Lucius zipped out of the room and down the hall, down the massive wooden staircase yelling "Berry Pie!" at the top of his lungs. It echoed throughout the whole mansion, brightening a home that hadn't held the sound of a child's voice in over a century.

Then Paolo heard the carved wooden doors to Marcus and Anne's suite open. Marcus, dressed in a long paisley velvet robe, ambled across the landing to stand at his door. He was barefoot.

"That should get you the attention you deserve," he said as he sauntered into the room. "You'll be fighting the ladies off you tonight, brother. A real feeding frenzy."

Marcus was in a jolly mood, and comfortable, even though he was probably naked beneath his robe. At seven o'clock in the evening. After, no doubt, making love to his beautiful wife for most of the day—between the infant's feedings, of course.

Paolo forced his mind out of his brother's private bedroom activities "Your hair." He touched the back of his head, indicating Marcus's bed head

Marcus patted down the errant strands and rocked back and forth in his bare feet. "We didn't get much sleep. The baby was up half the night last night, and today, well…"

"No doubt harkening back to our dark vampire ancestors."

Marcus smiled and looked at the floor like he actually believed his lie had worked.

Paolo leaned into Marcus and whispered, "If I had a beauty like Anne, I'd never leave my bed either. Your secret is safe with me, although I've heard the staff gossip."

"Gossip? About what?" The look of concern darkened Marcus's eyes.

"Your prowess. They have to have heard the screams and moans. You even wake the baby sometimes, or were you not paying attention?"

Paolo said this without an ounce of jealousy, even though his life had been one lonely death after another, with the marriage and death of all three of his mortal wives. Paolo never begrudged his brother's happiness, or his choice to mate with a vampire female. On the contrary. Hope kindled a little bonfire in his soul.

Marcus seemed pleased that the staff had wondered about his stamina. Because he and Anne could go out in the sunlight, their family being the Golden of the vampire lineage, it required they have two sets of staff. One for day. One for night. Though he complained of the infant, Marcus rarely was in bed for sleep.

"Well, I'd say it's time for you to enjoy some of the comforts of the flesh, Paolo. And I believe you have created a most interesting net to catch them in. Rather like bees to honey." Marcus winked and padded back to his room.

On the way to the ball, Paolo allowed his mind to wander over recent changes in his life. He enjoyed staying with Marcus and Anne in California, in the legendary Sonoma County. Living in his native Italy the past year had made him feel morose and brooding. He had often wandered the dark, cobble-stoned streets looking for something to warm his heart. But now there was Lucius to provide warmth. His son.

During one of his brooding walks through Tuscany seven years ago, he'd committed the ultimate sin, creating a debt for which he was now trying to repay. Paolo remembered that night all too vividly, like it was yesterday.

In a cruel twist of fate, Anne killed Maya, a fate punishable by death. His brother had nearly been executed by the High Council, since Marcus attempted to take the blame and was tried and found guilty of it. Paolo managed to save his brother's life by admitting publically he was the boy's father and Maya's fated mate. Marcus was forgiven.

But Paolo still had much to answer for. If there were a god that watched over vampires, would he find it in his heart to grant him peace, forgiveness? Give him a chance to make up for the mistakes he had made all those years ago?

He hoped so.

Like a dark whisper, the limo slid to the sidewalk in front of the grand ballroom. Marcus's driver got out, opening the rear door for Paolo. The night was crisp and without rain. People flocked to the doors looking like actors waiting to go onstage for a performance of *Midsummer Night's Dream*. The grand old hotel, steeped in history from trysts of the San Francisco elite over the past two centuries, sat stoically with its secrets amongst the bevy of faeries, butterflies and princesses. There were stewardesses and nurses so scantily clad they appeared to have costume malfunctions. Several dark vamp women clung to men dressed as pirates or gentlemen, astronauts and, yes, more than a few vampires. A group of blue unisex Smurfs arrived and crowded in behind him, giggling.

Paolo was surprised that tonight, for the first time, he enjoyed appearing as who he really was. Somehow, he was glad he had chosen to become vampire instead of remaining mortal. He'd spent nearly three hundred years regretting the decision to change which was made in haste when he'd seen his mortal parents die.

He didn't really understand why tonight was oddly different. He only knew that his vampire skin felt like his elegant, comfortable cape. Appropriate, dashing and fatally attractive.

Blaring music echoed through the hallway as soon as he stepped out of the metal cage elevator. Warm brown, heavily marbled stone marked his path to the ballroom. His pumps tapped down the stone corridor to the beat of the drums. Music throbbed in rhythms so strong that they tickled and thudded in his chest. His limbs felt the vibration of the beat, and his pulse quickened.

Excitement. It had been centuries since he'd felt this way.

He walked under blue and silver twinkle lights covering two tall tree boughs which framed the ballroom entrance. The photographer's flash blinded him momentarily, but he smiled and nodded his head as he accepted a chit allowing him to purchase the photo later. Perhaps he would. It gave him another thing to smile about.

The heavily gilt walls and ornately carved walnut paneling of the ceiling reminded him of some of the ballrooms in Vienna and Paris he'd seen as a youth, when he and Marcus had danced their way through the lovelies of Europe during the 18th and 19th centuries.

I feel at home.

His instinct was to find a dark table in a secluded corner away from everyone else so he could scope out the crowd. Homing in on the perfect spot, a table with only one shimmering gauze scarf next to a top hat, and the rest of the place settings unoccupied, Paolo selected a chair several spaces over from the party of two, brushed his cape to the side, carefully adjusted his tails, and sat, prepared to enjoy the revelers.

Sparkle dust was in the air, tickling his nose. The amber-colored candle on the table filled the air with the fragrance of blood oranges, Anne's favorite scent. He should know, he chuckled to himself, since Marcus had placed hundreds of them throughout his villa for her.

Paolo watched faeries dance with trolls, and idly ran his gaze over a scantily clad woman in black with huge breasts as she undulated and massaged her body over her partner's. There were werewolves, storm troopers, kings and queens. Some men and women danced with partners of their own sex, some cavorted in groups.

He removed his cape and left it dangling over his chair as he went in search for a good glass of port. He preferred to have the enticing sweetness of port on his breath, should he meet a lady he wanted to speak with. His fangs craved the flesh of a mortal woman tonight.

The scent of jasmine was strong as he edged his way between the dancers and a table filled with donuts of every size, color and confection. The pastries were resting on a bed of candy corn and caramel popcorn. Paolo's teeth ached at the thought of tasting the over-sweet treats.

Lucius would have loved this. Paolo smiled as he mused how sick the boy would have been the next day.

Something soft bumped into his backside. Something that smelled wonderful.

He turned and brushed intimately against a beautiful, auburn-haired woman with green eyes, whose curves made the most of a white Renaissance gown with a plunging neckline . Feathered wings were sewn on the back of the dress, and her long, draping sleeves almost touched the floor when her hands were down. Everything he'd lectured himself about not getting involved with mortal women flew away with the blink of his eye.

Upon seeing Paolo, she raised her palms to her face and hitched her breath, as if startled.

"Oh, my. What have we here?" she said.

To a mortal, the loud music would have made it impossible to hear what her voice. Paolo could hear every breath, every syllable rolling off her pink tongue as clearly as if she'd whispered it in his ear. Something silky slid down his spine as a door within him opened.

"I am a vampire, madam, at your service." Paolo bowed and kissed her extended fingers.

Did I make her offer her hand, or did she volunteer it?

"But your lips are warm. That means you are an imposter." She smiled and the world lit up.

"I assure you, madam, I am no imposter." He felt his groin go rigid. He noted the blue pulsing vein at her neck quicken as her heart fluttered, sending her scent to his waiting nostrils.

She turned and gazed over her shoulder at a young man dancing madly into oblivion. Her partner did not notice his date had been distracted by the charms a new dark visitor. Someone who could be dangerous to her health.

Modern men. So naïve. They let their women wander way too much, allowing them to be gobbled up by straycatchers...

She turned and looked up at him, as though she was expecting Paolo to say something.

"Would you like some refreshment?" he finally asked her. His insides began to flutter in tandem with the beating of her heart.

Her eyes took on a momentary sparkle that thrilled Paolo. She turned and regarded her young dancing partner without much interest. Putting her hands aside her mouth, she shouted to him, "Johnny!"

The blond dancer jerked, then broke out in a toothy grin, raising his palms and undulating his torso in tune with the grinding music. Paolo didn't like the sexual sway and suggestive jest aimed at his new interest

"I'm getting something to drink," the woman mouthed her words silently and followed it by drinking from an imaginary glass in her right hand.

Johnny gave her the thumbs up and started to go back to his wild gyrations, but hesitated as he looked at Paolo. A frown of worry marred his sunny countenance

She shook her head and waved him away from across the dance floor. Paolo heard her say, "No problem. You have fun," but doubted Johnny had heard a thing.

A glittery faerie dancer came up behind Johnny and slid under his knees, pressing into his backside that drew a whoop from him. The young man was instantly distracted by the way the little one rubbed herself all over his trousers.

Paolo's new friend leaned back and laughed, her neck and shoulders sparkling with glitter. He could smell how good she would taste. He saw as well as felt what she liked sexually and knew he could satisfy her—do things, make her feel things, she had never dreamed possible. He stole glances while she was distracted by the bodies writhing on the dance floor and the sparkle of the costumes.

Then she turned. Paolo and his mortal beauty and her red lips faced each other fully at last. Her reddish-brown curls called to his fingers as his mouth anticipated kissing her, tasting her, making her shudder in his arms.

The woman was waiting for him to lead the way. Paolo held his breath. He wanted to be sure she was coming of her own accord. He refrained from glamoring her.

Does it matter?

He decided that tonight it did.

Paolo tucked his arm under hers and led her to the open bar, and away from the loud music. There was a fireplace and a deserted table nearby.

"I'll get us something to drink. Why don't you claim that table over there?"

"Claim?" she asked. Her green eyes reflected tiny fires from the twinkle lights in a canopy of stars overhead. She bit her lower lip, but obviously couldn't keep the ends from upturning into a smile. Her fluttering eyelids danced, flashing fireballs at his heart, allowing himself to be seduced by her mortal charms.

"I figured we'd start on some port. Something deep and red." He waggled his eyebrows, and she giggled, leaning against him. He could feel the firmness of her breasts against his upper torso. He swung his arm around her waist and pulled her even closer with a gentle tug. She arched back and examined his face, while he brushed the laces at the back of her dress, fingering every eyelet and silken strand.

He couldn't resist touching her, and spoke, releasing his dark power as he covered her with glam.

"I'm entranced by your scent. Do you taste as good?"

She was still for a second while she considered his question. Could she feel the threshold they were stepping through like he did? Caught in each other's gaze, he heard a throat being cleared behind him and turned to face the red-haired bartender.

"Something to drink?" the man asked. The bartender's bulbous, deep purple nose seemed to fill his entire face. He held a wet towel in his chubby right hand while he tapped fingers on the bar countertop with his left.

"Two ports. The oldest and rarest you have." Paolo turned and whispered as he stroked the length of his Renaissance angel's cheek and let his finger trail over her red lips, "Rare as the lady at my side." Her eyelids fluttered under the weight of his control. He loved how she was so susceptible to his power, seemed to crave it.

He almost leaned in to kiss her, but couldn't bring himself to take advantage of her vulnerability. He cursed himself for his lack of manners. He held onto her with both hands at her waist, righted her firmly on her feet, separating her warm body from his and waited for her to regain sense of herself.

She shook her head. "Whew, don't know what came over me. I got dizzy there for a second."

"Why don't you sit down, then, and I'll come along with our drinks? Maybe the fire will warm you." He pointed to the corner again.

"Yes. That's a good idea." She shuffled with tiny steps, holding her palm to her forehead and mumbled to herself.

He watched her body move under the silken gown, her hips, her small waist, and the small of her back outlined by a row of lacings that stretched all the way up to her shoulders. He wanted to see her naked. Wanted to rub his hands all over her flesh and kiss every inch of it.

If she'll let me of her own free will.

And if that didn't work—well, he could always use his vampire powers of charm and confusion. He could make her see him for the first time all night long. He could conquer her over and over again.

And no one would be the wiser.

He suddenly didn't want the evening to end.

CHAPTER 2

Cara sat in the corner and thought about how the evening was progressing. Her heart was pounding, a tympanic rhythm she felt all the way to her fingertips. She wasn't here to meet someone. She already had a date—Johnny, the sexy research assistant all her professor girlfriends lusted after. That's why she'd asked him. She wanted to be the talk of the department. What she was doing right now? She was waiting for a handsome, very tall, masculine creature to bring her some refreshment and indulge her senses. It wasn't something she wanted her girlfriends to find out about.

I'll worry about my coworkers and all the rumors tomorrow. Tonight she felt soft, compliant. *Sexy.*

Her friends used to speculate that Johnny must be gay, he was so good looking. When she asked him to accompany her to the ball, he enthusiastically agreed, and then had enticingly curled a strand of her hair around his tanned finger, letting her know non-verbally that he was definitely interested in more. In the past they'd shared dinners, and accompanied each other to University functions, but never to a costume ball.

And then, as soon as he'd accepted her invitation, he blew his bubblegum into a huge, pink bubble, and then grinned mischievously. Johnny was like that. Still a kid at twenty-five.

Cara hadn't been looking for a sexual liaison. At least, not with Johnny. He was five years her junior. Tall and athletic. Well-defined abs she'd seen beneath t-shirts while they studied together at the library. Earlier, she'd watched him show off his dance moves. He was attracting great attention under the strobing lights and heavy beat. Ordinarily, she'd be right there, by his side. They'd have been backup for each other.

But not this time. Cara was being led to a dimly lit corner by a dark gentleman with a whole set of mysterious intentions. Johnny was daytime to this man's night. And right now, she was lingering in his shadowed influence, in a lustful, confused state.

I love the way he makes me feel.

How could that be? She was focused on her career and hadn't found time for a lovelife. Was something else looming on the horizon? A new adventure, perhaps?

God, yes!

She asked herself for permission to follow her hormones several times and came up with the same answer every time: Johnny could take care of himself, and she needed to learn more about this man she'd just—met? *Is that the right word for it?* She felt herself melting into his sphere, somehow being enveloped into his sexy, Continental aura. She felt starved for his affection for some strange reason.

The gentleman was coming back to the corner table she had *claimed.* He made a perfect vampire, tall and brooding, with a devilish smile that made her knees wobble even while sitting. She smiled, enjoying the play-along.

His body had seemed muscular and firm when he drew her close at the bar. He smelled of spice, and something else, an exotic mixture of lemon, nutmeg and cinnamon, like an incense from an ancient land. She remembered reading about exotic fragrances and their pheromone-like effect on the human body.

His breath had been cold, but his lips warm as they'd nibbled on fingers she couldn't help offering up to him, as though she wanted him to taste her. Had she felt the slight touch of his tongue on the knuckle of her third finger? Had he tasted the flesh between her third and fourth fingers? He'd studied her afterward, the clear black eyes searching her face, seeming to search for traces of a reaction, as if he was asking permission. His slow, sexy smile and fluttering of his long lashes, seemed to request approval to advance. To walk through her doorway.

Yes, she felt her heart whisper.

She decided to allow herself to be explored. Her soul tingled with each gentle nod of his head as he looked at her hair, her earlobes, and the soft tissue beneath her jaw, his eyes wandering down to her throat when she couldn't help swallowing. His almost old world charm encouraged her to trust him. A door she usually kept closed and locked had opened.

Normally, she'd be afraid. *But not tonight.*

Tonight she felt positively immortal.

He leaned forward, his shadow falling over her face and shoulders. Their fingers touched as he handed her the little blood-red short-stemmed glass of glittering port.

"To us," he said as he clinked their glasses together and bowed to her.

Please sit with me, she said to herself.

As if he heard her thoughts, he sat, not across the table, but next to her on the burgundy plush cushion, then leaned against her. When he lifted the glass to his lips, she felt compelled to do the same. His eyes drew her to hm. The dark brown edges were tinged with a ring of golden fire at the outsides. His lips tasted the sweet liquid as hers did. He licked his lower lip and she did the same, from right to left. Just as he was doing. If he leaned into her, she knew she would let him...

"Do you like the port?" he asked. Did she see a tiny effort, as though he tried to bridle himself? Tiny creases at the sides of his eyes gave him away.

"Yes. I do." She was rewarded with his smile. She saw the tips of his... *fangs*? Her eyes fluttered again as her pulse quickened. "Your costume is quite realistic."

"Yes?" He raised his eyebrows and hid the fangs.

"Those. Do they come off easily?" She pointed to his mouth.

He smiled, and there were no fangs. "Whatever do you mean?"

"You can make them go up and down like that? I've never seen fangs that can do that."

"Indeed." He smiled again and they were back.

"You must show me how they work."

He leaned into her. The lemon spice flooded her head with erotic images of bonfires and soft music. His lips were close, but not touching. Her flesh craved a caress, and, as if on cue, his fingers wandered to her cheek and stroked her there. "I can show you many things, my dear."

Yes, I want you to—whatever am I doing?

Abruptly, she sat up and pulled away from him. *What is going on?*

She found her glass and took a sip, not wanting to stare into his eyes. An alarm was going off somewhere in the back of her mind. It had broken the moment.

He crossed his legs and moved slightly away from her. The left side of her body noticed the lack of warmth immediately. When she ventured a look back up to his face, he was smiling, his obsidian eyes twinkling in the shadows, as he stared not at her, but into the fire just over her shoulder.

"I'm Carabella Sampson," she said as she extended her hand.

"Paolo Monteleone," he said. His fingers slid into hers, entangling her, making her heart sputter. The touch was intimate.

She withdrew her fingers from his and took another sip of the delicious red port. "I like this. I don't usually drink sweet drinks."

"But you should. Contrary to popular fiction, sweet wine is good for your blood."

She had to chuckle at that one, working not to burst out in a full belly laugh. "You are a method actor. You play the part of a vamp very well."

"Ah. And you are experienced with vamps, no doubt?"

"Very," she said.

At this he started, and his dark sparkly eyes widened. The edges of his full red lips curled up like a thin moustache. "Do tell. I want to hear all about it."

Her face warmed as she looked down at her port. She could tell he was smiling as he watched her. She toyed with him. She wanted to make him wait. She heard something deep and low in his throat. Was there a rumble, a small earthquake?

One of his fingers touched the top of her shoulder and drew a line down her upper arm. "Has another vampire touched your flesh before?"

She shivered, loving the game Her body scooted away from him, yet craved to be chased. He waited. She experienced the distance between them he must have also felt, and she could tell he was having difficulty with that. She was suddenly aware of his heavy breathing.

"I'm an expert on vampire mythology." Cara spoke to her nearly empty glass. "I teach legends and mythology at Sonoma State."

"Really?"

"Yes." She looked back up at him. "Vampire mythology dates back to pre-biblical times. We've had vampires as long as we've had angels. Did you know that?"

"How very interesting." He blinked and she thought he made an effort to keep his smile pasted to his face.

"They are a symbol of something that can never be. Of people's desire to delve into the unknown, the dangerous. Does that make sense?"

"Entirely."

"We want to believe in things that we can't see. Religion is all about believing in things we can't prove, either."

"Like angels, for instance."

"Oh, yes, people have seen angels and lived to tell about it."

"As opposed to vampires."

"Good point. So there you have it. Because they aren't real. Just myth." She threw her head back, downing the rest of her port. Cara loved being in the presence of this man, a man who didn't run away, or scoff, when she told him of her interest in the vampire myths. "I think that's why you find pictures of angels in churches, but not vampires."

"So there's a vampire religion, too?"

Now he *was* toying with her. "Somehow I think not." She smiled at her empty glass.

"You would like more?"

"Yes...no. I—I'm not sure what I want at the present time," she said.

He took her glass in his long fingers and stood. "I know exactly what you want," he said. He was at the bar in seconds.

She sat back and relaxed into the velvet seat cushions, feeling the warmth of the fire on her face, her upper arms and her thighs under the tapestry fabric of her dress. As he stepped onto the brass boot rail of the bar with one long leg, she noticed the shape of his ass and the straightness of his spine. His long, elegant neck and broad shoulders made him a giant specimen of devastating masculinity she'd have noticed anywhere. The fact that he was now coming right towards her, with that crooked smile revealing one fang, thrilled her. Something about their play was natural.

But it defied logic.

He slid in to sit close, one long thigh against hers. He extended his arm over her shoulder in a possessive gesture she didn't fight.

"Let's drink again to us," he said.

"Why not?" She took the first sip, but he did not, seemingly caught in watching her swallow. He looked mesmerized.

POKÉMON

ONLINE
TRADING CARD GAME

UNLOCKS 10 ADDITIONAL CARDS
TO PLAY AND COMPETE ONLINE!

Sun & Moon—Lost Thunder

9LV-2TBN-PY2-WQR

ENSM8BST2

With your parent's permission, log on and use this code within the Pokémon TCG Online to expand your online card collection. This code can be used only once.

www.pokemon.com/redeem

Use this code to unlock your online booster pack. Visit:

"Something wrong?" she asked.

"Not at all." He sipped and then set his glass down on the black tabletop. "So, tell me about your vampires."

"Really?"

"I'm completely serious" he replied.

Cara slipped comfortably into professorial mode. "Vampires throughout history have been used to describe pure evil. To describe things too horrible to consider any other way. Like missing children. Vampires were said to steal them from their beds."

He nodded. "But you don't think they ate children, do you?"

"Of course not." She looked at him. "Vampires aren't real, you know."

"Of course not." His answer triggered a flood of visions of her lying in a huge bed by a raging fireplace as he looked down on her body, with exactly the same expression as now.

She cleared her throat.

"Children were much more likely to become prey to wild animals, or evil members of their own population. But this was a way to blame horrible things on despicable creatures, not members of one's family."

"Despicable?"

"Totally. It's really been in the past few decades that vampires have been thought of as sexy or even desirable, in a crude, repulsive way." She looked at his blank face. His eyes had gone somewhere else.

Had he lost interest? She continued anyway. "Who would want to fall in love with one of the undead? A cold corpse who sucks the life blood from your body? When you think of it, someone who entertains those kinds of thoughts is probably filled with self-loathing. A truly flawed person. Someone whole and sane would never desire it."

"I see." His flat monotone concerned her.

"But we *can* pretend. That's what's so fun about dressing up. For one night of the year we can be anything we want. Halloween is when we dare to be what we would otherwise be repulsed by."

He had truly gone away, mentally. Well, he was probably tired of the subject. She'd done it again. Bored yet another handsome man to distraction. The charming fellow at her side was suddenly interested in anything or anyone but her.

"Are you feeling okay?" she asked.

"Yes. Why?"

"Well, you seem so, well—so different. Have I said something that offended you?"

"I didn't realize you knew so much about—I guess I had a tiny bit of regret at having chosen this costume, now I know how you feel about vampires."

"But we're just play acting. You don't repulse me like the vamps I study do."

It wasn't working. Something was off kilter. His eyes were still dull, like he was forcing himself to smile but didn't want to. She decided perhaps she had picked a scab and didn't want to wait around for the blood and gore. Her common sense returned as she realized she shouldn't have been so trusting.

"You know, I'm sorry—what was your name again?"

"Monteleone. Paolo Monteleone."

"Mr. Monteleone then. I should be returning to my date. I feel like I've ignored him, been impolite." What had she been thinking? She wrinkled up her nose and patted his hand. She felt a faint jolt of electricity at the touch of his flesh. And she heard him hitch his breath.

They both stood. She wasn't sure what was happening, except that she suddenly needed to create distance between them. She needed to think. "Thank you for the port. It was delicious," she said.

"Made even more so by your presence," he said, and bowed.

"Oh, now that was the perfect touch," she said, pointing to him. "You really have it down. You must be an actor. Are you?"

"How did you guess?"

"I can tell. I read people very well. It's a gift."

"Indeed."

"There you are!" Johnny's flushed face appeared before her at the perfect moment. His hairline was dripping with sweat, and he was fanning himself with a cardboard coaster and grinning like the devil. "You've got to come out on the dance floor with me. This band rocks! Please save me, dear, sweet angel, from these women who want to leave their men behind and take me home to have their way with me." His straight white teeth and dimples made him look entirely kissable.

She disliked that she'd been so caught up in conversation with this stranger that she'd let her good friend down. A friend she would normally love to flirt and tease with, perhaps a little more.

But not tonight.

She turned and said a polite goodbye to Paolo, then allowed Johnny to lead her away by the hand. She lost herself in the crush of bodies, the heat, sweat and flashing lights. But just before the crowd filled in behind her, she felt the mysterious dark eyes of the gentleman she'd just met. A gentleman who made her pulse quicken just by being near him.

CHAPTER 3

Paolo was stunned. The blow Cara had delivered had felled him as quickly as a sword. Of course any sane woman would be repulsed by the thought of being with him. The only things in this world that craved him were half-witch vampires who wanted to suck him dry.

I am truly lost.

His glamour had worked on her. She might have been warming to him on her own as well. Things had been going along so beautifully. Then he had to go ask her about what she did and learned that she studied *vampires* and had decided they were *despicable beings.*

Am I despicable? Am I a cold, blood-sucking monster who preys on little children?

With horror, he realized perhaps the answer to his question was…

Yes.

He'd fathered a child. Was he now leading that child to a life of loathing? Could he bear to hear Lucius tell him that some future woman had found him repulsive? How could he be honest with his son, or would he simply not tell Lucius how much he regretted his own decision to become vampire? How could he counsel Lucius when the time came for the boy to make his own irrevocable, permanent, life-altering decision?

What would he say if Lucius asked about how he was created? It hadn't been with love, an act of love. Paolo's cock had lurched, and his balls had constricted and spewed forth the seed that would become Lucius. That's all. It had been a loveless, animal act, a betrayal, he'd believed, of his brother. He'd used Maya, the woman he'd believed was his brother's *fated* mate countless times with abandon over a lost weekend in an animal mating he was powerless to stop.

He'd copulated frantically and repeatedly, despite his revulsion for the object of his animal desire, with the woman who proved to be his—not his brother's—one and only fated female, because only a fated mate could have borne his child. And he still hated the mother of the child he loved so deeply, even now, after her death.

Despicable? Yes. He would shoot his seed into anything. His *fating* had completely owned him, taken over completely during those fateful days. He had been nothing more than a set of balls wanting to heave. Afterwards, when the urge finally released its grip on his soul, he fled back to America and into the arms of his dying mortal wife. He regretted ever having come over to Tuscany for the wedding.

Still mortally shamed by his long-ago decision to turn, there wasn't a day of the centuries that had gone by when he didn't feel the sharp pain of regret. God in Heaven, he wished he'd made the other choice, to remain mortal. He would have died in the 1700's like his parents. He'd be buried right next to them on the plot of land bordered by the family vineyard.

Paolo would be dust and not a danger to anyone else. Not able to feast on the blood of innocents, ruin mortal life.

Lucius would never have existed.

It is what I deserve.

He made his way back to the ballroom. The party was ramping up to full rave Even the windows were foggy with the detritus of frenzied exhalations and hot human sweat. The dull dance beat dispensed like candy from the mobile D.J. made his chest rumble in a not unpleasant way. Paolo felt the pain and anguish pouring out of the partygoers as they danced off their fears, exorcised their demons. Could they feel that death was stalking them? Walking amongst them?

He turned around in the center of the dance floor. Had they made a circle around him? Were they mocking him as they undulated, showed him their flesh, the dark patches usually left in shadow for a lover? Did they wiggle and send their pheromones blasting out to allure him or torture him? Who was master and who was slave here?

Three pixie-like women dressed in butterfly princess costumes flew around him and surrounded his body with the luscious softness of their flesh. They touched him places he never let women touch him in public. His groin tightened and in spite of the debasement he felt, he got rock hard. Two of the ladies sandwiched him and he dry-humped one sweet little faerie, holding her by her tiny glistening waist as she writhed on his hardened member and let him feel the heat of her sex through her flimsy costume. His erection became so strong he feared it would rip through his trousers and take her through the silvery gauze that did little to protect her core from a thrust of his kind.

I could do it. I could show them what I am.

The scent of her body juices made him want to bite the little nymph. He could hold her while she experienced the euphoria of his tongue as he coaxed out her sweet red elixir until it filled the empty spaces inside him. He'd seal off the little holes in her neck, then re-bite her and partake again, then heal her, over and over again, until he was sated.

He could feel what she would taste like, how her sweet scent could fill his nostrils as he explored the penetrations he made, dominating her, and sending his thanks to God that he could immerse himself in the life force of this beautiful creature.

As he readied himself to bite down, he caught sight of Carabella Sampson, watching him from across the room. She stood in partial shadow, but Paolo could see her just as clearly as if she'd been standing in full sun. The dancers almost parted so that he could look upon the wonder of her full, luscious body. It made him stop gyrating his hips. He released the faerie and she tumbled to the floor like a rag doll, glamoured, but otherwise unharmed.

Cara stood to him, unwavering across the expanse of the large room, letting him feast on her beauty, letting his eyes roam in places she should have been shy about revealing to him. She didn't turn, or cover herself up, or fold her arms across her ample chest. Her red lips were moist, and he could hear her breathing across the huge hall. He could smell the tiny beads of sweat condensed on her upper lip, which quivered so very slightly. He drank of her in every way but with his fangs.

The faeries were all over him again, one hugging his thigh between hers, another rubbing her breasts into his chest, raising his shirt, seeking a flesh-to-flesh connection. He continued to stare into the eyes of Carabella. His rod was red hot, but it was Carabella who was touching him, working on the zipper, trying to obtain purchase.

Stop it, he mentally told them. He could not let them do this. He wasn't that far gone yet. He would not subject Carabella to this sort of decadence or the darkness in his lonely heart. He tore his eyes from hers and danced with the nymphs, teasing them, staying just out of reach. He sent glam out to the crowd. More women, and a few men came and joined their circle. He paraded around the perimeter, touching faces and tickling their souls. They were starving. Starving for the passion he could unleash upon them.

He turned and she was still there, watching him. He raised his arms to the ceiling and she did the same. One of the faeries unbuttoned his shirt. Carabella could see his chest, see the muscles that wanted to hold her shuddering body.

Let me love you. There. He'd said it, finally.

Her eyes got wide. Her hands came down over her own chest as she kneaded her breasts together. She searched the floor and then raised her eyes to his. Clear across the room from each other they danced together. Through the space of thin air he kissed her neck and watched as she moaned and rolled her head, exposing the blue vein for him.

Paolo licked his lips. He undulated his lower torso as he barely managed to keep from exploding.

I'm coming into you, lovely Carabella. I will make your flesh sing.

She nodded softly as she lowered her chin and pouted her lips. One hand did what Paolo wished he could do, it laced down from her left breast to the juncture between her legs. Then she grabbed her skirts and raised the hem just enough so he could see a well-developed and tanned thigh. He wanted to bite the soft flesh on the inside, up by her core.

Let me see it.

He fell to his knees. The crowd parted and he was able to again see the lovely angel writhing in tandem with him half way across the room.

I will bring you unspeakable pleasure, Carabella. Use me. I am the instrument of your pleasure. If I cannot be your love, use me—even if you must throw me away.

One of the faeries broke his line of sight, lowering herself onto his lap, dancing on his hardness, driving him crazy by kissing his neck and exposing hers. His natural vampire instincts almost got the better of him. Control was slipping away.

"Take me," the glittery faery whispered. She leaned back and he watched as first one, then the other breast found freedom from her small, restrictive costume as she arched back, planted her palms on the dance floor and bent back.. Ruffles and her scratchy fabric filled his face.

It brought him to his senses. He righted the faerie and whispered an apology with a kiss to her neck.

"I am claimed already, little one."

"Take me anyway," she begged.

"Not tonight."

As he helped get her to her feet, the crowd applauded and the music ended. He searched the room, looking for the angel, but she was gone. He surreptitiously adjusted his pants, took another bow, and then released the faeries to the crowd. As he wandered toward the outer edge of the crowd of dancers, arms and lips grazed him, sought his attention, but his focus was elsewhere.

Where did she go?

Every spark of white caught his eye…and disappointed him when it was not the angel he sought. He searched the bar, hoping to find her tucked in the corner again by the fireplace, revisiting a glass of port, waiting for him. But no luck.

The vision of her lying across his massive bed, all her lovely flesh exposed to the night air, nipples taut and knotted, her heavy breathing as she anticipated his mouth on her sex, his tongue inside her, making her rise and burn. He would take her every way he knew. He would love her until she craved no other. He would work out of her the loathing she felt for his kind, and he would convince her he was alive and everything she needed.

Because he knew he was.

That's when he saw her, over by the table where he had placed his cape. Johnny had grabbed the top hat and she swung the silver scarf around her neck, protecting her lifeblood, demurely covering up what he longed passionately to see, touch and taste.

When she looked up at him, he softened. He would have run to her, but he was unsure.

On a night filled with miracles another one dropped down upon him. The God of vampires touched him when she smiled. It was a sweet smile. No seduction. No play. Just acceptance. He had not sent glamour to her. She smiled of her own free will, so delicious, so innocent.

The world of the possible opened in front of him. It caused him to step softly toward her as she stood straight and tall, awaiting his arrival. One hand fingered her gauzy scarf, the other was tucked into the crook of Johnny's arm as he attempted to draw her away. But she appeared to resist.

She's waiting for me.

When he arrived at her side, she reached into her scarf and pulled out something. It was a business card she held between the tips of two fingers.

"Call me." Her flushed face was moist with a thin layer of her own excitement. Her eyes held his. Unafraid, but needy.

It was all she said. His heart hung on every strand of her bountiful, beautiful hair as he watched her turn her head and follow Johnny from the ballroom.

CHAPTER 4

C ara was silent as Johnny drove her car, taking them both to her house, where he would catch a late bus to his own place across town. They'd only done this twice, gone Dutch and spent the time watching others. Theirs was not the dating relationship they hoped to find in the crowds they scanned. Instead, they worked "cover" for each other.

Cara checked the mirror. Her cheeks were definitely flushed, mirroring the excitement coursing through her veins. She'd never felt so alive, so sexy, and so irresistible. She halfway wished they were on their way to another party. She could dance all night.

She flipped the mirror up and looked across the console at Johnny. He was a *beautiful* man. Even features, smooth tanned skin and white teeth. His vibrantly healthy tanned skin, warm eyes and long lashes made him the perfect cover model or poster man for a milk commercial.

He should be her type, she thought. Though he was younger, he could be a wonderful distraction. But no matter how hard she thought about it, no matter how lusty she felt this evening, to the point that she almost felt immortal, she never could quite see him as a sexual partner. And this made her a little sad.

"I'm sorry I didn't dance with you more." She was feeling melancholy, a little sorry about her lack of attention.

Why? Was she feeling guilty, perhaps?

"That's all right," he flashed her one of his legendary fresh smiles. Johnny could turn on the charm, look just as tempting as any soap opera hunk, but unaffected. He was refreshingly natural, apparently unaffected by his good looks. "I had a good time. But you almost hooked up with that old guy," he said as he winked at her.

"Old guy?" *Was the mystery man old? Hardly!*

"The vampire."

Maybe it was his costume, his makeup. He looked like he was around thirty, not much older than she. However, thinking about him brought a smile to her lips and revved up her engine a couple of notches. She felt in the mood to play with Johnny a bit. "You jealous now?"

"*I'm* the one who's taking you home." He gave her The Bedroom Look. The one that said he meant business.

Cara frowned. Was this getting complicated all of a sudden? Though she was feeling like a free spirit, her affections weren't aimed in Johnny's direction.

He kept his serious tone. "Would you sleep with me some time—one of these evenings?"

Cara was surprised this didn't turn her on. There was absolutely nothing wrong with Johnny or his hunky body. It was something else. "Do you think of me *that* way, Johnny?"

He looked at her as if she had a third eye in the middle of her forehead. "Are you nuts? I'm crazy about you."

"Wouldn't that make me a cougar? Preying on a younger guy?"

"Hardly. You're only five years older. I think you'd have to be ten or twenty years my senior to qualify. Besides," he grabbed her hand and kissed it tenderly, "you're one hot lady. Don't know why, but I saw a different side of you tonight." He dropped her hand after giving her a squeeze. "I kind of like it."

It was true. She was a different person this evening. Some switch had been turned to "on" position, and she was enjoying every minute of it.

She knew he was discreet, so a quick, passionate liaison was possible, and no one need know. But they *worked* together. They had to spend hours in close proximity in her tiny office at the college. They ate Chinese food over research projects and hashing over lecture notes. He was the brother she never had. She needed a true friend. But a lover?

No.

There was only one man on her radar. And for him she'd do just about anything. Even something inappropriate…

"So, what about it?"

"What about what?"

"You gonna make me a lucky man tonight?" He frowned after searching her face, obviously realizing the answer was no. She didn't have to say a word.

"It isn't wise," was all she could think to say as she looked through the windshield at the passing lights . Wet streets and colorful signs twinkled between droplets of rain that diffused and refracted the view. What was she looking for?

"Wasn't asking for wise," Johnny said, his voice deepening. "Was asking for totally hot freaking sex."

She felt the giggle erupt from deep inside her. She loved the way it rippled and fluttered throughout her chest. She was filled with mirth, and it had been years since she'd felt this good.

"You think sex is funny?" he asked. "Or is it just me?" He scowled. "What about you and gramps?"

"Why do you say *gramps*? He doesn't seem old to me," she said. She wasn't going to let anything ruin her evening.

"Because he has something old and sinister on his agenda. Something he's hiding. I don't trust him. It's creepy."

Cara threw her head back onto the headrest and laughed. "Oh, Johnny. I don't get that at all." She scrunched her nose.

"Whatever," he whispered and then sighed.

They remained silent until he pulled into her condo complex. In the underground garage they both got out and he handed her the keys.

"Last chance." His little smile was infectious, but didn't win her over.

"Thanks, but no thanks. I had a really nice time, though."

"Cara, you're a big girl, and a smart one, too. Please, please, for my sake, be careful. I don't like that guy, and it isn't because he's better at mesmerizing the room. There is something really off about him." Johnny hesitated, then stepped closer to Cara, and she moved back to avoid an embrace, in case one was on the way.

"Okay, I get it. But I just don't want to see you get hurt. Aren't you in the least bit concerned?"

Cara had to admit there was some worry there, but it was covered over by something exciting growing inside her soul.

"I can handle myself." She immediately realized she'd hurt him. The flicker of a frown glanced off his face. "But Johnny, it's sweet that you care. Thank you so much for that." Cara moved into his arms and allowed him to encircle her. He was safe.

Am I crazy? What could it hurt?

But the answer was still no. She held him at arm's length. "Thank you. For being my date tonight. For understanding. For being my friend. You don't know how valuable that is to me," she said.

"Me, too," he sighed with a bit of a pout on his brooding face.

He gave her a safe peck on the cheek, backed away, waved, and walked toward the gated door. Carabella headed for the elevator and waved back just as the doors began to close. None of her friends would ever understand how she could just leave him standing there when he'd made himself so totally available to her.

The elevator groaned slowly to the third floor. Inside her condo she turned on her bath and stripped, leaving the angel costume in a heap on the tiled floor. The fuzzy white wings perched in the middle of the pile, stubbornly standing guard over the mounds of white satin. She was grateful to be done with the scratchy protuberances.

Cara swiveled the big screen TV arm so it would angle over her while she soaked. She slipped into the warm, sudsy water and sank up to her neck in lavender-scented bubbles. She flipped on the remote and watched an old Bella Lugosi film. The closeup of his eyes reminded her of the intense way Paolo had looked at her when he whispered, "I can show you many things, my dear." She felt her legs quiver under the warm water.

She sighed and allowed herself to relax against the back of the tub. As her eyes closed, she imagined dancing with him. He spun her around the floor of a grand ballroom filled with candlelight. The hall was empty except for the two of them, but somewhere a string quartet played a waltz as she twirled and leaned back, held by his powerful arms. First they swayed one way, then the other. She wore a golden gown like she'd seen in movies, and felt the taffeta swishing along her hips, the color matching satin dancing slippers encrusted in pearls.

His palm pressed to the small of her back when he stopped her in the middle of the music, as they stood motionless on the polished wooden floor.

His finger traced down the side of her face, rubbing over her lower lip as she opened her mouth to him and she tasted his full lips. She heard his inhale, like he was holding back, trying to be gentle with her.

Then she saw herself on a large bed with cream satin sheets, naked, waiting. He covered her body and watched her face, her body as she moaned her pleasure, as he pumped inside her and made her come again and again, each time leaving her craving more.

The visions continued as she lingered in the state of half dream half erotic trance, surrounded by the foaming bubble bath. Organ music leaked from the TV's low volume control, sounding tinny but somehow fitting. At last she opened her eyes and the visions released her. She was left with the delicious lingering effect of her pulsing orgasm.

Panting, she was still not sated, and she gripped the sides of the tub until her body returned to its relaxed state.

What is this feeling that's come over me? She could almost say she'd been bewitched. The powerful ache she felt for this man defied anything she'd experienced before. It was almost as if he were standing beside her, making her feel what she had felt when he touched her hand, or barely brushed her arm at the party.

It had been a sudden impulse to give him her card tonight. It was his move now, not hers. She was not going to chase him.

She wanted to be pursued. Hunted. She knew she needed to run from him. So he could claim her for his own.

CHAPTER 5

Dag Nielsen, Supreme Dark Vampire Coven Leader hoped that the virgin sex would calm his nerves. His specialty was deflowering young girls with his fangs and then drinking from them until the urge grew so great he had to ram himself deep inside them. Being careful wasn't in his dictionary. He refused to alter his behavior to become acceptable. He rather liked that people ran for the hills or screamed until they passed out when he showed up.

His black Harley was waiting outside. Two members of his coven had parked next to the Harley, trying to look disinterested, but he could tell they had their ears tuned to the little closed window at the cheap motel, listening for the kill bite, after the moans and eventual screams of passion from the blonde waif.

She'd made the mistake of asking him for a little spare change in front of Starbucks. He asked her some questions after putting her into an altered, glamoured state, confirming that she was indeed a virgin, which surprised him. But she told him telepathically she knew how to give good head, which was exciting. Dag offered her a drink and a meal, and glamoured her a bit more so all she could say was, "Please."

"Please," she said again as he licked her nether lips. He could still taste the soap she'd used. He'd required she take a good, hot shower before he would insert his tongue in any of her orifices. He licked her again. She jolted, and then he tasted blood.

Calm down. He was hungry for her, but he needed a meal, not just a snack. And he was pissed off today, so wouldn't be leaving anything around for his bodyguards in the way of sloppy seconds.

He inserted his forefinger in her anus and her eyes flew open.

"Oh, yes, you'll like this. Just relax and feel my finger, Sheila."

"Shirley. My name's—ahhhhhh—Shirley."

He pulled his finger out. "Makes no difference whether your asshole is called Shirley or Shelly. My thumb wants a taste."

He inserted his fat thumb and she gripped the tops of his shoulders, digging her nails into his vampiric flesh.

"Now we're talking, Baby. Go ahead, try to hurt me."

"I don't want to hurt you. I want you to—"

He stretched her enough to insert two fingers into her sweet little ass.

"To what? Fuck you? That what you wanted?" He leaned over her, breathed into her face and saw her eyelids flutter. "Sweet little Susie. You have a lovely pink peach of a twat and a tight little ass. Please, my dear, can I ravage your ass first?"

She was struggling with the answer. He could tell that her real self wanted to say no, but her glamoured self couldn't help but say yes. She bit down on her lip. Hard.

"That's my job," Dag barked. He bent over and bit her lip, drawing just a little blood as his fang moved over her rosy plumpness. His tongue had to work to coax hers out of the black hole that was her upper palate where it was trying to hide. He sucked hard, mumbling, "Mine." She didn't resist him.

They never did.

"Ahh," she moaned. Dag noticed it got one of his guards' attention as the sudden head movement gave him away. The guard licked his lips.

Not today, lover boy. She's all mine.

He tried to send that message telepathically, but Dag was positive the thickheaded dark vampire didn't get it.

He refocused on his meal.

Taking his fingers out of her ass he set himself on her pussy. It was swollen already and bright pink. "Lovely color, my dear Sarah." He said as he admired it.

She opened her eyes and released her grip on his shoulders.

"Did I say to stop that?"

"No, I just, I just like you licking me better than—than—the other—"

Dag inserted his finger back inside her ass. "Than that?" He twisted it.

"Well, okay, but only one, just one, please?"

"Fair enough, my sweet. Fair enough." He kissed her again, leaving her tongue alone. "Only if you scratch me."

She looked at him as if he were crazy. He knew he was, of course.

"Scratch you?" she asked.

"That's right. Grab onto my shoulders and squeeze. Draw blood. I like it rough," he said.

"But—" she couldn't finish because he had laved her clit so hard he tasted her lovely blood again.

"You want it in the butt?"

Her eyes flew open in terror. "No!"

"Then scratch me. Make me hurt. I promise, I won't get angry. I'll get gentler the more you hurt me. It helps me come."

She slowly nodded, disturbing her blonde hair where splayed all over the white pillow, beckoning him like a mermaid under water. He willed her to look deep into his eyes so she could see the danger there. She'd be delicious as she feared for her life.

At first she frowned, but then, as the flames tickled her insides and she appeared to share his passion for the dark side, her eyes became fixed, and she grabbed his right butt cheek and scraped hard enough to actually drag a layer of his skin under her nails.

Dag became hard as granite. He was impressed. He'd figured she didn't have it in her. But this new, sweet gesture on her part to cross the great fiery chasm touched him. Perhaps she was worth saving, like the farmer who ate his fabled pig one limb at a time, as the joke went.

But this was no joke. It was a reveal that someone mortal might be able to share in his pleasure and live to tell the story. And she was virgin. No one else had had her. How wonderful it would be that he would be the only creature to have her. And he could do it again and again and again. Perhaps give her the surgery, make her virgin again so he could rip that from her all over again.

She brought her bloody fingers to her mouth, and, staring hard into his eyes, licked them. Her eyelids fluttered with the new energy his blood gave her.

"Yes, my lovely. That's it. Do you feel the blood on your tongue?"

"Your name."

"Huh?" Dag wasn't sure what she was asking.

"You have a name. I want to speak it to you with your blood on my tongue. I want to kiss you while I moan your name."

He arched back and looked down on her, cocking his head to the side. He quickly surveyed the room, half thinking perhaps she was speaking to someone else. He felt her heartbeat double-tapping his chest in a most unusual rhythm.

Her tongue swiped a pinkish swath across her upper lip. He could see his blood covering her teeth and gums. She did not blink. Her deep blue eyes seemed to go midnight on him. Her lips began to form a word.

"More."

Dag felt his erection falter and then wither completely. She was not afraid of him. Perhaps it had been a mistake to let her taste him.

"More," she whispered again. She scratched across his buttock again. The right side of her lip twitched up in an involuntary reflex. She dug deeper. He found himself sighing into the pain. His dick responded, pressing against her thigh, begging to claim her.

Her fingertips, covered in blood, painted her own lips, then reached up and touched his. She pulled his head down to her and moaned as their flesh touched. Her tongue found one of his fangs and impaled itself. He felt drops of her blood cover his tongue. Her little core arched up against his cock. She whimpered, and he found he loved the sound of her submission. Her total submission.

He was used to the fear, the certainty of death in their eyes just before he took their lives away from them forever. Their violent, terrified thoughts fed his need not only for their blood, but also for the depth of their despair, their fear. This little one was giving herself to him, *willingly*.

He brought his hand up to her face, expecting it to feel plastic, or porcelain, or something not real. She had wispy strands of hair at her temples where the golden curls were unruly. She bowed her forehead into his palm as if she needed the blessing of his touch. She rolled her head to the side and exposed for him her strong jugular vein.

You are virgin. Are you virgin to the bite?

I am yours. He tensed as he heard her reply in his own head. *Take me. Taste me. Master.*

His fingers smoothed over her soft, creamy neck. He licked her on the vein that rose up to the surface. She sighed. *Take me.*

His shaft was thick and pulsing. He had never wanted to be inside anyone this bad during his miserable hundred years of vampiric life. He reached under him and drew her right leg up and over his shoulder. He angled himself at her opening, forcing the head of his cock just inside. She struggled to accept him.

She was so tight he had to force himself deep inside her. He felt the skin protecting her virginity give way. Her eyes glazed over and she rolled her head back, raising her neck to his mouth. He penetrated all the way to the hilt, splitting her insides as he forced his way into her narrow channel. And then he bit down on her neck.

The sweet elixir that was her life's blood covered his tongue and continued down his throat. He brought his fingers up and entangled them in her golden locks, pulling her head up and over. He sucked as he dug himself deeply in her trench.

Dag. Say it. My name is Dag.

"Dag. Fuck me, Dag. Come inside me. Take me."

He had never heard a woman say his name before. He'd been called devil, other names that thrilled him. But never before had he felt pleasure hearing his own name spoken by the bloody lips of his sexual conquest.

She began to shake. He had drained much of her. Her skin was cool. She was at the point where, if he continued, she would be dead to him. Truly dead. Her lifeless body was the vessel he wanted to spew his seed into. His guttural moans shook the windows.

After several minutes, she lay there with her eyes staring off to the side, with practically no pulse or signs of breathing. Her skin was turning a light shade of blue. Bloody saliva dripped from the corner of her mouth.

Her sacrifice had moved him. Suddenly, he didn't want to be done with her. In a totally selfish mood, he used his fang to slit his own wrist and placed it to her lips. She did not respond. Her blue skin was turning purple.

Drink. Drink my blood.

He first felt the tip of her tongue trace the gash he'd made in his wrist. Then her lips puckered and formed a seal around his wound and she sucked. Immediately her color changed. Her breathing started in a rattled rhythm, then dark and deep. She rolled her head back on the pillow and stared into his eyes. Her fingers, still covered in his blood, laced behind his ear. His shaft shuddered inside her and she closed her eyes, then opened them again as she moved against him.

For the first time in his life, he wanted to give a woman pleasure. This woman, who had given herself to him freely. Of her own will.

She was putty for his soul. To do with whatever he wanted.

She suddenly became the most important thing in his world.

CHAPTER 6

Dag told his men the little panhandler was dead and that he'd been interrupted by a cell phone call. It was partly the truth, anyway. He was going
back inside to tidy up, and then they'd go run their errand, he told them.

"You want us to clean up?" The one with the thicker brow and thinner
forehead asked as he drooled over himself. Dag knew the cretin liked fresh kill,
as it would be the closest thing he would ever get to a warm-blooded human
female lover. And the dark vamp was cursed with more than the Neanderthal
forehead; he also exuded the mind-numbing smell. Some said it was like fermented cabbage, or some shit humans liked to eat with their tofu.

On the phone, his watcher had reported a possible lead from a bookseller
in Prague. He had work he needed tonight to prepare for a possible trip.

Dag looked into the bathroom mirror just before he stepped into the
shower for a quick one. The towels were rough and cheap, and he made a
mental note to bring some of his own next time. Cheap motels were great
for anonymity, but not so good for the accommodations. But it had always
been too risky, especially since the purge was nearly upon them, to bring
mortals to his own inner sanctum and his own bed. Maybe it was time to
change that.

He left his phone number for the blonde. He figured that once her head
cleared and she stopped her vomiting—something he didn't like to watch but
which always occurred when he created a new vamp—she'd decide to try out
her new powers. Dag hoped she'd use him as her guinea pig. Was looking

forward to it. If he was right about her, she'd know that no one else would do. She'd find him like a homing beacon on a drone.

The drapes were shuttered tight. The door scraped on the ageing step sill. One last look at the lovely, sleeping lady, who had begun to pink up quite nicely, lying with her legs spread, a sexy little trickle of blood coming from her upper thigh. Her breasts heaved, covered in his blood, or hers, when he'd devoured them, sucked them and covered them with his scent to claim her. He could make her come with just one finger, placed anywhere now. And that electrified him.

He sighed and closed the door behind him. Forcing his fangs back up into his gums, he licked his lips one last time, and felt the lurch in his trousers.

It took a minute before he could look at his two dark cohorts. He didn't want them to see the satisfied lust in his eyes, or that he wasn't nearly done with her. It was God's cruel joke, this miracle that made it so she would regenerate herself, mixing the best of both worlds: her human side, which was retreating in surrender, and her new vamp side, which was commanding her body to change. In this half-changed state, the lady would be an absolutely stunning meal, and the fuck of a lifetime.

In the old days, before the responsibility of Coven Leader had befallen him—well, being totally honest, before he'd murdered his boss and maker—he'd had long evenings of sex and orgies. Now duty called. It was the one thing he regretted and hadn't considered before he took that momentous step.

He thought about *The Book of Spawn*, the "Bat Book," his mentor had called it. There were things in that book that could end his race forever, and give dominance to the Golden Vampires he was hunting down and killing daily. Since he had no intention of giving up his existence without a fight, that book had to be found and eliminated. Much as he wished he could spend time exploring the blonde's beautiful body, scoring it, mutilating it and watching the miracle as she regenerated, the future of his power and dominion over the world for all eternity was at stake.

Even a world-class piece of ass like hers wasn't worth that. If he succeeded, he'd have centuries to enjoy himself later.

After he got rid of all the Goldens and their offspring. After he completed his mission.

CHAPTER 7

Cara awoke to the sound of a car horn blaring. Checking the clock, she realized she had overslept and missed church. Her head ached, as if she'd been drugged. Had someone slipped her something in her drink last night?

She felt as if she was exhausted from staying up all night making love. The feel of a new relationship burned in her belly. As though she'd been intimate with him. As though he'd seen her naked, seen her full of the hot pleasure that was her vivid dreams. And he wanted more.

No. I slept alone. Though she looked around her bedroom, she found no evidence that he had been there last night. She discovered her sex was swollen and sensitive when she stroked herself and discovered she was wet with her own desire. But no man had penetrated her last night. She'd been alone with her naked fantasies.

Cara ripped herself free from the bed and showered. She put her hair in a clip and wore her tightest pair of jeans with a small, pink long-sleeved top. She applied her makeup fast, adding some sparkles to her eyelids and pink cherry lip-gloss.

Just in case, she thought as she smacked her lips together to spread the creamy glitter lip gel.

She was starving and parched for some orange juice and decided to visit a popular bistro she knew was open for Sunday brunch. She found a corner table in the shadows, ordered eggs and French press coffee and settled in to listen to Brazilian love songs and read one of her vampire romance novels.

The hair at the back of her neck and forearms tingled as she read a steamy scene of blood and sex. The vampire hero became the man she met last night. He was the one biting her own neck as she writhed under him.

"Cara?" a female voice interrupted.

Cara had been staring into her coffee, leaning on her book, but not reading, dwelling instead in her own fantasies. She recognized the voice, and looked up with a smile.

"Valerie. Sorry. I was pretty engrossed in this book." Cara held it up to show her friend.

"Hmmm. Let me see that," the redhead demanded as she pulled it out of Cara's hands and began reading where she had left off:

"His thick cock thrust upwards, impaling her with his will to possess every inch of her body. At last she felt the bite on her neck, as he took from her what she had never given before. Her blood. And with it, he took her heart. Completely." Val fanned her face but remained standing in front of Cara's table. "You'll have to lend me this book when you're done."

Cara searched the room, making sure they hadn't attracted the wrong kind of attention, and smiled. "At this rate, that's liable to be tonight. There's sex in every chapter."

"My kind of book," Val answered. "You sure you won't give your friend a little priority claim? I promise to return him in the morning."

Val meant the hero in the book, but Cara felt possessive of the arms and eyes of the man she met last night.

"He's mine," she said and grabbed her book, placing it in her backpack. "Come, sit with me. I'm buying." She motioned to the chair and Val eagerly accepted.

"Thanks." Her friend leaned her chin onto her laced fingers and searched Cara's face. "You have glitter on your forehead. You went to that party last night with Johnny."

"Yes," Cara said as she blushed and searched the tabletop. A waiter took Val's order and afterwards Cara continued. "It was a blast."

"You and Johnny?" Val's face revealed a mock frown as she tilted her head to the side, watching Cara's reaction.

"No. He's all yours, if you want him. We're just friends. You know that, Val."

"I've seen the way he looks at you."

"Not gonna happen." Cara decided not to reveal what Johnny had offered last night. She just couldn't picture the two of them together. With Paolo, she had no problem conjuring up the fantasy of a sexual liaison.

"So what else happened?" Val was her most persistent and, at times, invasive friend. Nothing was off limits, taboo.

"Just beautiful costumes. Great music. My feet are sore from the dancing."

"You wore sparklies. What did you go as, a Fairy Princess?"

Cara remembered the three faeries swarming over Paolo's large frame in sensual abandon. How his face had twisted in lust as she tried to follow him, get his attention and become part of his sexual dance…

"…and they didn't have anything, but—*Cara*, are you listening?"

Cara realized she had gone back to her fantasy evening. She shook her head and rubbed her temples. "Sorry, Val. Sensory overload. Something you said made me think of one of the dances. There was this guy…"

"You thought about a hunky guy when I mentioned the feed store? You're worse off than I thought. How long has it been?"

Cara sipped her coffee, embarrassed. "Hmmm?"

"Since you've been with a man." Val was all military now. No way Cara was going to escape the interrogation.

"A year. Two perhaps."

"Perhaps? Are you insane?"

Am I? Am I filled with need and lust?

The answer deep down in her soul, which felt positively ancient this morning, was…

Yes.

CHAPTER 8

Marcus was up uncharacteristically early. He'd whistled his way past Paolo's door, heading down to the kitchen, his boots thumping on the carpeted staircase.

Paolo thought again that his brother was a happily married man. And very satisfied. He had a child to raise and a beauty in his bed.

Paolo hadn't slept much, and had spent the hours since dawn half hypnotized by the shadow patterns from the old oak tree outside his window, as they danced across his ceiling in the early morning sunlight.

Every fresh, sparkling morning reminded him how grateful he was that his family heritage was Golden vampire and not that of the dark covens. He felt sorry for the dark cousins and friends of his who were destined to go wandering during moonlight hours and could never experience the taste of sunlight he called Heaven. If he had been a dark, he'd have ended his life a couple of centuries ago.

His restless thoughts got him out of bed to dress and head downstairs to catch up with his brother. He could smell pancakes and heard Lucius's voice prattling along, making idle conversation with their sensational cook. The woman was a seventh generation servant to his family. Paolo remembered every one of her ancestors. They were good as gold to the young vampire children they were employed to attend. Part nursemaid, part teacher, they all were excellent cooks and doted on their charges as if they were their own flesh and blood. The Monteleones had been generous with their kind in return.

The relationship between the human and vampire families was cheerfully symbiotic.

"Papa!" Lucius called out. "Look at the mouse ears." He held up his plate as the cook laughed. The pancakes had been made in the face of the famous cartoon mouse, and chocolate chips made eyes, nose and the smiling mouth.

"Perfect," said Paolo. "You spoil the boy," he said to the short, round woman whose salt and pepper braid formed a crown atop her head.

"As is your wish, Signore Monteleone." She nodded to him. "It's been a long time since we've had a child in this house. And now we have two."

"Dad, did you know the baby drinks milk from Anne? She has bottles built right into her chest, right here." He pointed to his own flat chest on the right and then the left. "Do human women do the same?"

Lucius's question reawakened all Paolo's conflicts about the realities of his existence, and his son's. What kind of a boyhood was this for his son, who knew about vampires and humans, and that he was of one kind, for now, and his father belonged to another?

"Of course," he said, as he mussed the top of Lucius's head. "But you must never talk about this in front of non-family, you understand?"

The boy looked up at him. "I know." He was pensive. "But I can talk about it with cook."

"Francesca is like family," Paolo agreed. The little woman quivered with delight at the comment.

Paolo looked outside to find Marcus working on a piece of equipment near an old wooden barn off in the distance. "I'm going to give Marcus a hand, if he'll let me."

"Careful, sir. Your brother has just bought a used tiller. You remember last time he tried to pull it behind his tractor?"

"That's because he forgot to take off the brake on the blasted thing," Paolo said as he made his way out the back.

Stepping out onto the patio overlooking their vineyard revealed one of the most glorious sights of the modern world, he decided. He loved looking at living things. Most the leaves were gone. The grapes were harvested, but the leaves had turned from golden or red to brown with flashes of orange as if they were mourning their loss of fruit, and bled from the wound that took their offspring away to a crusher.

Marcus looked up and wiped his hands on a rag as he addressed his brother.

"I didn't expect you'd be home last night. Rather thought you'd be enjoying the company of a nubile young mortal." Marcus's smile was as wide as the valley before them.

"I enjoyed myself. Nearly had myself a foursome. Lovely little green and silver faeries who worked wonders." He blushed.

"That's a twist, for you."

"Things change," he said as he shrugged his shoulders. "The one I wanted was with another man."

"I imagine you could fix that."

"I have a plan. Going to call her later."

He thought about the card she offered him. She was telling him to find her. She was interested. He adjusted his tight pants.

After they worked in the vineyard and spoke with two winery field hands, the brothers went back up to the house. Before returning to Lucius, they drank stored blood Marcus had delivered to his wine cellar on a regular basis. Anne had joined Lucius and cook in the kitchen. She was holding Ian, their pink baby boy, who had been named after Anne's father. She cooed at the little face, blew into his eyes and held the pink fist that made a handle of her little finger.

"He's so strong," she said as Marcus came to her side and kissed her neck. "I think he will be stubborn, too."

Marcus nodded. "Going to pay you back, my dear." He threw a `
glance to Paolo. "We sure gave our folks hell, didn't we, brother?"

"Absolutely," Paolo agreed. "Ian must learn from his cousin here. Lucius has learned to get his way without being stubborn or petulant."

"Wouldn't go that far," cook muttered.

"Hey, what's petulant?" Lucius asked.

"Means you act like a man inside a boy's body."

"No, it means you're spoiled," Anne amended. "But then, you're supposed to be."

Everyone laughed. Lucius remembered something. "Dad, you taking me trick-or-treating tonight?"

Paolo had started to say no, but then changed his mind. "Yes, sir. We'll go out as soon as the sun sets."

Marcus and Paolo shared a look of concern. One of their nephews in Scotland had recently been abducted and murdered by a black vampire coven leader. The man had demanded ransom, and then as the family was formulating plans for the boy's rescue, his body was discovered. The ransom demand had only been a stalling tactic to allow the killers to get away.

Protecting their mortal children was an all-consuming task. The world was getting more and more dangerous for their kind each day. Fewer children were being born to their lineage. The elders were contracting diseases previously believed impossible, and some began to experience aging for the first time in their history. Tainted blood was showing up in their food supply. And vampire blood began showing up in human blood banks, causing a string of mental cases and near zombie-like creatures that had to be eliminated. The balance of power was shifting, and it was becoming obvious the Goldens were in danger of extinction.

All the more reason to protect Lucius tonight. He didn't want his son to become another statistic.

"Do you mind if I use the Jett boys?" Paolo asked, referring to the four brothers of dark vampire lineage who had sworn allegiance to Marcus and his family, and had protected them for generations. They dedicated their lives, foregoing their own families, to remain single and loyal. In exchange for their sacrifice, the Monteleone family bestowed on them great wealth and property holdings all over the world, which the brothers used to support their other siblings' families and their parents.

Three of the brothers were currently residing in California, now that Marcus had an heir.

"I'll have them drop by. You want them costumed?" Marcus had a twinkle in his eye. "Perhaps dressed up as green faeries?"

Paolo shot him a look and mumbled a curse under his breath. "You'd have to watch your own neck if you asked them to do that."

"And I'd deserve it all." He slapped Paolo on the back. "You going as yourself, like you did last night?"

"No. I'll let the Jett brothers be the scary ones. Tonight I'm just going to play the part of Lucius's father."

CHAPTER 9

Cara went to the college and worked on her lecture for Monday. She scanned her bookshelf filled with novels and books on symbolism and mythology. As she ran her finger along the spines, she stopped at the first edition she'd purchased a month ago and hadn't had time to read

Pulling it out, she flipped open the pages, carefully peeling over an onion-skin that protected a black and white etching of a vampire biting the neck of a buxom young maiden in harem costume. Her expression as she stared back from the page of the old text into Cara's eyes was filled with euphoria. The vampire held her by the waist, two of his long fingers pressing into her right breast. His other arm was entwined with hers as she reached towards heaven.

The book had intrigued her. Printed in 1865, it chronicled the travels of a renowned Scottish theologian who went to India on a pilgrimage to study ancient Hindu texts. Cara had read that this scholar was fascinated with the theory of Divine Coupling he'd discovered through his studies. Before Chapter One of his travels, there was a photograph of the clergyman and scholar. Handsome. Full lips and dark eyes. His curly hair barely submitted to being plastered to his head and brought under control. There was a wild look about him.

Cara turned back to the etching this man had done. The vampire looked just like him.

Self-portrait?

Her fingers idly moved over the leafy parchment-colored page edges. She opened the book to a random spot and began to read.

It was Tuesday when I got to the temple site. Although I had planned on arriving in the morning, I had transportation difficulties and was left stranded for several hours in the heat and morass of the train station. Beggars accosted me everywhere. But with all the filth and death around me in that crowded place, there was a spicy scent to the air, especially as the Sultan's harem literally floated past me as if on a magic carpet. Several sets of dark eyes undressed me from behind veils that covered their entire bodies. One set of blue eyes, heavily lined in black charcoal and accented by three light turquoise stones affixed to her forehead and bridge of her nose, haunted me. I saw those eyes all evening as I lay in my lumpy bed at the hotel, and dreamed of possessing her.

Cara caught her breath.

Possessing her…

That was exactly how she felt. He was possessing her with his eyes, his every action. She wasn't going to go to him. She'd let him come. Willingly, she'd let him come and…

What am I doing?

Angry with herself for wasting her free time, she collected her notes for class, and with the book under her arm, turned out the lights and locked the door to her office.

The evening was beginning to go dusk as she finished her dinner and cleaned up the kitchen, turning on the dishwasher. The neighbor directly below her was having a Halloween party, so Cara resigned herself to the likelihood that she wouldn't be able to turn in early. Only residents and their guests were allowed behind the metal gates of her complex, which meant there would be no trick-or-treaters. Accompanied by the whir of dishwasher water jets, she sat at the kitchen table and opened her old book again.

She'd been thrilled when she received the alert that this text was available. There had been several other first editions that sold for thousands of dollars, and which were, on her salary, totally out of the question. But this one came to her for less than a month's pay. Someone from Prague had sent it, wrapped in green plastic bubble wrap. Parts of the leather cover had flaked off in her hands as she'd eagerly unwrapped and fondled the old tome.

Pieces of that leather cover now lay on her table as she opened the book once more and looked for the passage where the author visited the Shastra Temples.

These temple ruins had pictographs of couples engaging in every kind of sexual liaison possible, and several that were anatomically impossible. Cara's studies had turned up pictures like these for years. In fact, she had been quite stunned that some of the earliest temples erected in this region—which was renowned for its ancient vampire stories—were filled with such erotic and practically pornographic reliefs and statues. It was almost like they were built to honor sex. *All kinds* of sex.

Locals had visited the temples to pray for fertility and long life. Children were conceived here until the government passed decency laws that forbade the sacred coupling that had gone on for generations. It was a portion of Queen Victoria's plan to clean up the heathens of India.

Cara read his words.

As I arrived at the first temple, I was struck with the total lack of sound. All along the way I had heard monkeys screaming and birds calling to one another, yet, when I took the stone steps to stand beneath the twenty-foot statue of Jamal making love to his queen, there wasn't a sound. Not even the chirping insects that had serenaded me on my short hike. It was like the world held its breath in reverence for these sacred sculptures, entwined in each other, pleasure filling the faces of the God and his bride.

The relief was quite good, depicting her sexual cave. Jamal's member was fully embedded in her, but a portion of his shaft was exposed and had been touched by countless pilgrims over the years. The granite was as smooth as a woman's breast.

Cara closed the book at the end of the chapter. She discovered her breathing had become labored. She fingered the spine with the gold letters, *Temples of the Vampire*, by Alasdair Fraser.

She jumped as the phone rang.

The caller ID showed it was a local number, but she didn't recognize it. She picked up the phone anyway. "Hello?"

"Carabella?" The sultry Italian accent was unmistakable.

"Paolo." Her heart was racing. Would he be able to hear it?

Stop this, Cara. You are reading too much into his voice, the sound of his Italian accent and your need for companionship.

"I decided I'd take you up on your offer."

"My offer?"

"Yes. To call you. Invite you to lunch. Isn't that usually what happens when a woman gives a man her telephone number?"

He was right, of course, but she hadn't thought it out that far.

As she dithered, she tapped her fingers on the book, and then picked it up, startled to see a yellowed letter fall out. She was having a hard time reading the flowing script. The red wax seal had been broken, indicating the letter had been previously read.

"Cara, are you still there?" he asked.

She put the letter back inside the book and set it down again, pushing it away.

"Sorry. I just ordered this old book and had been reading some passages. I apologize."

"I could call at another time," he offered.

"No. No, this is fine. Again, I apologize."

"No apology needed, but you can make it up to me by agreeing to have lunch with me tomorrow. Are you free?"

Am I free? Am I able to say no?

"I have class that lets out at noon. I could meet you somewhere near the college. I have office hours in the afternoon, two until five."

"Then I shall have you between noon and two?"

She chuckled. "Yes, I supposed you will."

"Excellent. Shall I meet you at your classroom, then?"

"No." Her radar clicked on. Status: elevated. She didn't want him to know where her office was. Yet. "Meet me at the Chowder Grill on Harrison, okay? That's one of my favorites for lunch."

"The Chowder Grill it shall be. Looking forward to it. Good-bye." He hung up.

CHAPTER 10

"Sidney. Good to hear from you at last. You found the book?" Dag spoke into his black cell phone while waving away the cigar smoke coming from two of the three seats occupied by the hulking dark vampires in front of him. He made an effort not to cough. The squeal of their leathers as they crossed and uncrossed their gangly arms and legs annoyed him. His eyes were irritated but he couldn't let on. That would have shown weakness.

"No, sir. I did not," came the voice on the other end of the line.

Dag sat up and immediately the front row did as well. All three sets of size eighteen shoes slammed onto the concrete floor in unison. It felt like a small earthquake. Dag's eyes were unwillingly drawn to the hole the size of a silver dollar that had been cut from one shoe belonging to the vamp in the middle, revealing a battered big toe with a black curling toenail extending out from the flesh like the horn on a ram.

"So where the hell is it?" Dag demanded.

"He says he sold it."

"Well, ask him again, and this time, make sure he understands he'll lose a body part."

There was silence. Dag knew he wasn't going to like the answer.

"I…I already did that, sir."

"Well then kill his wife, in front of him."

"Did that, too."

"His child then!"

"Yes, and their pet dog before the boy."

"Fuck me." Dag wanted to kill someone. He eyed all three of his comrades, very slowly. They stared back at him, and only the one with the toe problem squirmed, moving back and forth and scratching his ankle. Dag took a deep breath and then let it out. No sense getting upset over a lowly bookstore owner and his family.

"Sir?" Sidney squawked on the line.

"I'm thinking, damn you. This will cost you, Sidney."

Dag could hear water running and realized it was the sound of someone peeing in his pants. No doubt Sidney had been smart enough to call his paramour first, telling her to disappear before he made this call. Dag would find her, if he had to.

"Sir, I think I have a way to find out who bought the book. He uses a book selling service online. I'll have to get the information from the company who actually deposited the funds in his account. Take me, oh, maybe a couple of days, tops." Sidney's words were wavering. Dag heard the heart pounding in the man's mortal chest.

"*One* day. You have only one, then I come and eat you, and everyone you know." Dag flipped his phone shut with a snap of the wrist.

Two of the onlookers stared into the eyes of the third dark vampire. Did they think he was so stupid he didn't know that the third dark vamp was Sidney's halfling son? A vampire/human son of the man he'd just threatened to torture and destroy? They scooted their chairs away from the young vamp, and Dag smiled.

There would be time enough for killing, getting even. He had an errand he wanted them to run first.

CHAPTER 11

Paulo watched Lucius climb the wooden steps to the white gingerbread house on Johnson Street. At least that's what Lucius had called it. Paolo agreed that the ornate Victorian trim did look like frosting on a wedding cake. In San Francisco they called them Painted Ladies. Here in Healdsburg they were sparkling jewels of a bygone era. Summerhouses for the San Francisco elite during the latter part of the 1800's.

A young, beautiful witch with long flaxen curls, about Lucius's age, greeted him at the door with a plastic jack-o-lantern and deposited a healthy handful of candy into the brown shopping bag he had colored at school on Friday. And she gave him a smile that Paolo knew Lucius could not appreciate just yet.

Paolo saw the Jett brothers leaning against a Jeep, whispering to each other. He nodded to them, but didn't get a response. He knew they preferred a racier detail than watching a lone mortal child trick-or-treating with his vampire father. It wasn't personal. It was just boring.

He thought he might release them early to go do whatever it was that they did at night. They weren't celibate, and were known to love women, yet he wondered how much sex, blood, beer and pool they could consume in one evening if they had the night off.

Or, maybe they never had the night off. Paolo had never asked Marcus what the arrangement was.

Lucius had squeezed through an overgrown hedge in front of a dark house next door.

"Hey there, Lucius. Light's not on. That means…"

The front door swung open and a tall, dark female vamp stood in the candlelight of her front room. Heavy blackout curtains were draped over the windows, which had made it appear that no one was home, or that they didn't wish to be disturbed.

Paolo watched the Jett brothers whip to attention and trace right up on the porch to stand guard next to the boy.

She looked them over like they were two enormous pieces of black licorice. Their leather pants showed bulging muscles, and no doubt they had a wild man-scent that charmed her in that dark way. Paolo didn't like the animalistic behavior and hair trigger of the darks. There wasn't anything human or soft or familiar about any of them. It was all force and instinct. It was the part of him as a vamp, although a Golden one, that he despised the most.

"Well, I got me a little boy and his friends. I'll give the boy some candy, but you three can come in for a while, if you'll trust your little charge to the night," She said it as she began to unbutton her black dress.

Lucius was staring at her chest with his mouth open. Lionel Jett grabbed her arm and twisted it behind her, which released her left breast to full visibility. Even Paolo had to admit it was a thing of beauty. But the Jett boys were unmoved.

"Save it, Drucilla. We're correcting the boy's mistake."

"You hear that, young prince?" she said to Lucius, as she wiggled against the Jett bodyguard. "He dares to call you a mistake. I sense a bit of Maya flowing in your veins. Where, pray tell, is your delicious father?"

Lucius started to turn and point to Paolo, but the brothers shoved the vamp inside and picked the boy up, instantly transporting him halfway down the block.

Paolo walked quietly down the sidewalk toward them, but when he looked up, Drucilla stood at the doorjamb and smiled in that way Maya used to, like she had all the secrets and would use them to destroy you. He was relieved to discover his dick did not respond. She toodled with her fingers. He could feel her eyes follow him down the street.

It bothered him for the rest of the evening, how the presence of fearless dark vamps here in California was infringing on the idyllic life they used to have. Encounters like these were more frequent. Everyone in their family had noticed. The darks appeared to be picking a fight, or preparing for war.

He wasn't afraid of war, since it took a lot to cause his death. But war always took its toll on the innocent, as it had claimed the lives of the entire older generation of Monteleones. The mortal women who loved Goldens risked their lives every day by doing so.

And so did Golden children.

Marcus was in the study when Paolo got home with Lucius. The Jett boys took off on their Harleys.

"Straight to your room. Go shower, and I'll come in to read you a story in a bit," he said to his son. With the sound of little footsteps attacking the wooden staircase, Paolo strolled to the open door of the study to consult with his brother. He closed the door behind him.

"Something wrong, brother?" Marcus said as he frowned and looked up from his ledger.

"How well do you know the Jett brothers?"

"Almost as well as you. We spent a lot of time together while you were off in the New World getting yourself serially married."

A flash of anger overtook Paolo and he let his brother see it.

Marcus got up and embraced him. Paolo held his arms straight at his sides. "Those were unkind words, and I apologize. I never understood your decisions, but then, I never spent any time trying to. That's my fault. Not yours."

"It's not anyone's fault . I merely sought a different path." Paolo stepped back and out of the embrace. He twisted the heavy Monteleone ring he wore on his right hand, a ring identical to the one his brother wore. "I should be more used to it. Of course you wouldn't understand."

"Not until I saw Anne that night as a mortal female could I fathom how you could fall for a human woman. But I felt the fating with her that night, even though I didn't smell vampiric blood. Even though I hadn't tasted her, yet."

Paolo nodded at the small acknowledgement from Marcus, and turned to examine the extensive collection of rare books. He thrummed his fingers along the bulging and withering spines. "The woman I met last night studies vampires, can you believe that?"

"Well then, good for you. Although I would warn you to be cautious. She is mortal?"

Paolo nodded. "She thinks they are abominations."

"Ah. I suppose you'll go about changing her opinion, then?"

"I'm thinking I won't tell her anything."

"Well, that's your choice. Probably best. No need to breathe a word to have a pleasurable accommodation, is there?"

Paolo's nostrils flared. Fire burned in his gut. He normally would have been overcome with anger, but the thought of seeing her tomorrow kept him thinking about what she would look like, smell like, taste like. If he had to lie to have that opportunity over and over again, he knew he would.

I am a wretch. Not worthy of this noble family's name.

Marcus came over and stood squarely in front of him. "What in the devil's gotten into you, Paolo? You are not yourself."

Paolo fingered a frayed burgundy book with gold lettering. How many of these books had his mortal father read? How many times had he read them, looking for answers? Looking for a path?

"I feel a swelling in the dark vampire covens. They are everywhere now. We even saw them tonight when Lucius was trick-or-treating. I was most grateful for the Jett brothers."

"Where was this?"

"Johnson Street. You know the house next to the one Lucius calls the Gingerbread House?"

"No. I do not know it."

"There was a dark vamp there who knew Maya, or at least said she did."

"I can see how this would distress you."

"Not sure what would have happened if the brothers hadn't been there. Is the world changing so fast we cannot stroll down a dark street without worrying about them using the opportunity to prey on the most vulnerable of our kind?"

Marcus was deep in thought.

"You obviously trust them—the brothers, I mean," Paolo added. "What if they aren't enough?"

They looked at each other the way they used to when they were reaching their age of decision. Marcus had always been sure he wanted to turn. Paolo waited until the last minute, and had been looking for a sign their other siblings convinced him was never going to come.

In the end, Marcus had waited for Paolo, both brothers taking the step the same day. They spent the sunlight hours watching their skin turn, watching the changes take hold. By nightfall they were completely turned and starved for blood, and for sex. They set out together to satisfy both urges until morning of the next day.

Paolo had spent the next day alone, in bed, in complete despair, sure he would spend eternity in hell.

They heard a soft knock on the door. Marcus opened it to see Lucius standing there in his Batman pajamas with a book under one arm.

"What are you reading, young prince?" Marcus didn't notice Paolo's gasp, but did see Lucius' eyes expand. "Did I say something wrong?" He glanced between Paolo and his son.

"That mean lady called me a prince, too," Lucius blurted. "I could tell she doesn't like children, and she showed me her fangs. Nice ladies don't do that."

"She's the one I was telling you about," Paolo whispered to Marcus.

Marcus knelt in front of the boy. "Well, we have very good security here. You are under my protection. And your father is one of the strongest men I know, Lucius."

The boy nodded and collapsed into Paolo's embrace. Marcus stood and again the brothers shared a look.

It was time for bed and the story Paolo had promised. He set his sights on making sure the rest of the evening went off without a hitch, that Lucius could fall safely asleep in his bed without a care in the world.

He knew he and his brother would be up half the night talking about the dark days and the even darker ones arriving very soon.

CHAPTER 12

C ara pointed to the eastern bulge on the map of India. The overhead pro-jector purred. Heat from the lamp wafted up to her face, making her per-fume bloom. She'd worn a low-cut, fuzzy sweater and had added some cologne between her breasts.

I'm way too young for a hot flash. But that's exactly what it felt like. And the experience was pleasurable, not embarrassing. No mistaking the signs of what she recognized as pure lust, unadulterated animal attraction. She couldn't wait to see the dark man she was meeting today at lunch.

"It was here that Fraser did extensive studies on the temples in the Sind. Being a man, he was fascinated with the harem women there, especially one blue-eyed beauty whose name we do not know." She looked up as her class chuckled. She couldn't see their faces, but noticed the projector light reflecting off the glasses of some of her students.

This was always part of the story classes loved the most. She removed the map of India and replaced it with a cellophane page of text, adjusting the focus so the class could read along with her on the white screen.

"I had heard stories about British officers marrying Indian women and fathering children. Often these daughters came to no good end, as they stood between the thresholds of two cultures. They were dark-skinned beauties with blue eyes. They were not considered British, although they were British subjects without rights. Their mothers could find no place for them in India, and unless they married a Halfling, one of their own caste, they were reduced to becoming

the pleasure things of the Sultans and wealthy families. But Indian society hated them. They were a scourge, a reminder of a failed policy of colonialization, hypocrisy."

The room was silent. Carabella continued. *"I was introduced and allowed access to one harem of the great Sultan scholar, Martam Vishnu, who had been tutored in the classics by a teacher from my birthplace in Scotland.*

I was allowed to study at will. I read scrolls that were nearly 1500 years old. I began reading about the vampires of the Sind for the first time, in documents dating back to some 300 years A.D. The temples at Shastra were conceived at that time. A whole village was planned, and may have flourished there. Very little of that civilization remains, except for some of the precious writings, and the temples.

I found the writings to be fascinating, sensual, and certainly erotic. I was taken aback that they worshiped a blood lord who ruled over their kin. It was rumored that he could raise the dead. He could also cure any number of sexual problems, especially lack of desire on the part of the woman."

Carabella looked up and switched on the lights. There was a groan from the class.

"Have to save something for you to look forward to in Wednesday's class. Until then, write a five- to ten-page essay as though you were this explorer Alasdair Fraser. Go on your own private journey. What would you find? What would you write about?"

"Are we supposed to do research?" a student asked.

"You should probably ask a girl out for the first time, Kevin," someone chimed in and the class burst into laughter.

"Only into your own psyche. That's all the research I want you to do," Cara told her class with a smile.

"That's going to be a scary place, Ms. Sampson," one student shouted out.

"Well, do your best, then. Borrow someone else's fantasy," Cara answered. "Remember, this isn't real. Vampires aren't real. But just pretend, if they were, how would you go about doing your own research. What could you find?"

The class spilled out, one by one. Cara collected her things and slung her computer case over her shoulder, heading to the parking lot.

He was seated at a table near the rear of the restaurant, in a corner. The Monday lunch crowd was never a large one. She'd forgotten how tall he was, so when he rose to his feet when she approached, it startled her. Her shortness of breath made the room seem to spin. He wore a citrus and spice combination cologne she didn't recognize, but instantly loved, almost as though it was laced with pheromones.

"Thank you for coming," he said without touching her. Her hand had started to wander out in front of her, so she diverted it to remove her jacket.

"It's self-service. Everything is very good here," she said trying to calm her nerves.

"What can I get for you, then?" He moved along the wall and brushed past her on his way to the counter. The glancing touch warmed her skin and she felt her cheeks flush.

"Chicken Caesar salad. I'm afraid that's what I order every time."

"And to drink?"

"What are you having?"

"I was having a glass of red wine. They have a very good Merlot."

"Um…too soon for me. I'll have an iced tea."

He motioned to the chair in front of her. "Please. I will be right back."

She felt him looking at her while she heard him ordering her food. Though she was facing the back wall, she had the sensation that his gaze covered her in a thin, sensual veil. It felt like she was protected as well as being held in a golden cage. She closed her eyes and wet her lips. She remembered the moment at the ball when he had run his finger down her cheek and over her lower lip. She could feel it all over again right now.

"Your food, Carabella," he said as he leaned very close and whispered in her ear. The feel of his warm breath on the side of her face brought her gently out of her trance. One hand rested on her shoulder, and the other offered a plate of crisp romaine covered in slices of chicken breast and grated Romano cheese.

He sat across from her and raised his wineglass. She raised her iced tea and sipped, dropping her eyes. But he did not.

"You aren't eating?" she said.

"My schedule's been hectic. I ate something earlier. Sorry."

She shrugged her shoulders and breathed in deeply to gather herself. She picked up her fork and began to dig into the salad. He was leaning back, tipping the wooden chair, and smiling right at her.

"Have we met before?" she asked between bites.

Whatever are you doing? Where did that come from?

"No. I think I would have remembered." After a brief pause, he added, "Why do you ask?"

"It's just the way you…I don't know. You act like you know me. Like there's some joke I'm not privy to."

His face dropped the smile and he adopted a serious tone. "I'm not joking with you. And I'm sorry if I make you feel…uncomfortable."

"No, it's just me. I spook easily."

"No doubt due to the dark creatures you study all the time."

Cara had to agree he was right. "My friends say I find conspiracies behind every corner, mysteries everywhere. Drives them crazy sometimes."

"But it's what you love."

It was a strange thing to say, but again he was right.

He leaned forward, resting his elbow on the table, and continued. "Studying mythology and symbolism makes you seek out and notice the unexpected, and things that can't be explained easily. Like vampires."

"Exactly."

"But you don't believe they exist."

"God, no." Her hunger evaporated. "I'm going to take this home and have it for dinner." She got up and requested a take-home box. After the server left she transferred most of her salad to the cardboard carton. "I'm more thirsty than hungry right now for some reason."

He nodded.

Cara drank some of her iced tea and crunched on the ice chips. Placing the box and her plate to the side, she leaned onto the table and asked him, "So, what did you think of the ball?"

"It was wonderful. The first one I've been to in many years. I've missed them. The costumes were…over the top."

Cara laughed, thinking about some of the outfits. "I'd say you have a fondness for little green faeries."

"I admit to it," he said with his hand to his heart. He leaned toward her. "But my fondness for angels is unequaled."

Cara could feel the blush coming on, and suspected the top of her chest was covered with blotchy red marks. The centers of his eyes took on an iridescent coppery glow, as if small bonfires resided there. He dropped his eyes to her heaving chest and she allowed herself to be admired. When their eyes connected again, something was understood between them.

What is this?

"I'd like to hear about your studies, Cara. May I call you Cara?"

"Please. Well, I became interested in the myth of the vampire because of the symbolism. They represent the ultimate alpha male figure. Strong. All-powerful. Dominant and controlling. Immortal. The ultimate bad boy you wouldn't want to bring home to meet your mother."

"Interesting. Go on."

"Women read romance novels today because they are looking for the hero in their fantasy life they would never find in real life."

"And you think that's wrong?"

"Of course not. I read romance novels all the time, especially paranormal romance, with vampire heroes."

"For pleasure?"

"Yes."

"And so you began studying them?"

"Well, no. I am new to reading romance. Probably a good thing, too, or I would have never made it through college. Hard to tear me away from my favorites."

"You like your alpha males."

"Love them."

"And do you have alpha males in your real life?"

It was a very personal question and it brought her up short. She grabbed for her iced tea, swallowed heavily and averted her eyes. With her forefinger, she traced the beads of vapor on the outside of her glass of tea. He was very still, awaiting an answer.

"I think the answer to that would be no," she said to the top of her glass.

He squirmed in his chair, recrossing his long legs, tilting slightly back again. "Tell me more."

"About my studies or about alpha males?"

"Whatever you want to tell me. Tell me something I wouldn't think to ask you."

Another strange question. His proximity made it so she couldn't respond to the alarm bell sounding somewhere. It was like her body wanted to, but couldn't for some reason.

"I've recently discovered some books by a 19th century Scottish theologian and scholar. He claims to have located the first written recordings of vampire myth. He found evidence of stories of raising the dead, giving life. Sort of like what we read about in novels about a turning."

"Vampires turning humans. Into vampires."

"Yes. Only this clergyman claims there was a group of people who worshiped and studied these myths shortly after the time of Christ. He wrote that there were people who practiced these black arts, but also practiced what he calls the *Divine Coupling.* Like there's some blood mating ritual."

The smile had erased from Paolo's face. Cara knew she'd lost him again.

"I'm sorry. You asked me to tell you something I wouldn't have normally, and I can see this was a mistake."

He was watching her fingers move up and down her iced tea tumbler. "Couldn't these texts be explained away as just a healthy curiosity in sex? It has been something men and women have worshiped and studied for centuries," he finished.

"No. Well, maybe for others, but that's not why I'm interested in it. If it's true, he may have stumbled on the secret to immortality. I don't think it was about the sex. It was about living forever, and dealing with living forever. What does one do when one lives forever?"

"He drinks port?"

She smiled, glad he wasn't taking her seriously. It didn't hurt her feelings in the slightest. "I keep wondering what sex would be like after having a thousand years of it. Maybe the temples were built, the religion of the divine coupling was created, to fill the needs of a bored society. Maybe some of them didn't want to live forever, and that was a problem for them."

"Why do you say that?"

"Because I think they lost their immortality. On purpose. Chose to be mortal. That's why they and most of the evidence of their civilization disappeared."

CHAPTER 13

Paolo had never been curious about the origins of his species, which was odd, since he loved mysteries. Perhaps he was unsure what he'd find if he dug too deeply. He assumed vampires, both dark and golden, had always co-existed with the human population. But many of his kin had lived centuries, longer than his three hundred years, and could see changes occurring in their vampiric DNA. New children were born with special powers. Certainly there were breeding oddities forming when a dark and a golden vampire mated. Exceptions were occurring at an alarming rate.

He searched what he had been taught. He'd been a gentleman scholar, in the classical sense, almost three hundred years ago, growing up in Tuscany. But what fascinated him for most of his life was *human* nature. Paolo knew he wanted to be mortal—be and live life as a human—even with its brevity. It was these mortals he befriended, drawn like a moth to the flame. Once he had accepted the turning, he never could really *be* human again, even though he walked amongst them as much as was possible.

To idle the time away, he focused on amassing wealth, something he did very successfully, and tried to live as "normal" a life as possible. He guarded the secret of his vampire genes, and was a dedicated husband to his mortal wives. In the end, though he tried very hard, he failed miserably.

Could someone have discovered the apex? When their immortality began? He also wondered if these early vampires were dark or golden.

Or was there a difference at the beginning?

He was fascinated.

"Where have you gone?" she asked him, and he realized he'd been daydreaming.

"I'm enchanted with your story, Cara. I've never heard it before." It was the truth.

"Well, at this point that is all it is, a good story. But I just feel like there's something to it. My classes are the way I pay my bills. But what I'd rather do is research full time. I haunt libraries like some haunt bars."

They both laughed. It felt good to see her smile. It seemed to bring out the sun in the room.

"So this is what you do with your free time?" he asked.

"Pretty much. I have to force myself to get out and do something decadent, like going to that costume ball."

"Where you meet a mysterious gentlemen dressed as the creature you study."

"Exactly. Like it was fated."

She was smiling, shaking her head from side to side and looking down at the table. Paolo wanted to take her in his arms and cover her body with kisses. He consciously toned down the glamour, releasing her reluctantly. But then he couldn't help it. His soul needed warming.

Come to me, Carabella. Show me you have interest and I will fulfill your wildest fantasies.

She was making figure eights with her forefinger in the water spot from her iced tea. The design was flowing, sensual. Curved, and that point she seemed to linger on where the two rings touched and crossed over one another. Unexpectedly, she looked up into his face and he felt her need. It wasn't a glamoured attraction. It was coming purely from her.

"Tell me about yourself, Paolo."

He sat up straight and laid his forearms on the wooden table, sliding them over so that his palms rested on her fingers. "Gladly," he said as he gently squeezed her hands. He waited to feel any hesitation on her part. There was none.

"I'm from an old family in Tuscany. Generations of Monteleones have lived all over the Mediterranean, but mostly in Italy." He searched the warmth of her cheeks, down her neck, examining the length of it, and the curve as it connected to her shoulders.

"And?" she asked.

"You must forgive me, but I find you so beautiful, it is distracting."

That brought a flush of blood to her face. She jerked her fingers slightly, but did not remove them from under his large hands. He rubbed the side of her palm with his thumb. Slowly, he brought her hand to his mouth and kissed the delicate flesh of the backs of her fingers, which smelled of jasmine and lavender. He felt her pulse quicken.

"Thank you," he whispered.

"For what?" She smiled through a sudden realization that she'd been blushing, embarrassed.

"For not running away."

She slipped her hands free and dropped them in her lap. He resisted the temptation to glam her as she straightened her spine and averted her eyes. But then she came back to him, her lips slightly open, moist. And she looked at his mouth.

You come to me of your own free will, Carabella. I will not hurt you.

"I, too, am a bit of a loner," he began. "I like dark corners in large rooms, stay to the outside. Don't like to attract attention. I don't have any alpha females in my life, either."

Her face lit up at that.

"You certainly looked like you enjoyed being the center of attention at the ball," she said.

"Faeries. Faeries are always beta. Angels are alpha." He tilted his head to see how these words affected her. She leaned in, putting her chin in her palm, not seeming to notice that she'd planted her elbow in the small puddle of condensation on the table. She finally shrugged, as if unable to give him a comment, her eyes wandering all over his face, down the front of his chest.

"Sometimes I get carried away." He said as he looked directly at her and was rewarded when he saw the blue vein at her neck pop up, as if greeting his hungry fangs. He was filled with desire to taste her, and to mate with this charming mortal woman.

"So tell me something about you I wouldn't ask," she whispered.

"I am staying with my brother and his wife in Healdsburg. They have a small winery there. But I have a home in Tuscany."

"That wasn't a very daring reveal. Surely you can do better than that." Her eyes sparkled with the taunt.

He hesitated, and then answered, "I have never found the love of my life. I am the only one of my brothers who has not found that special someone."

She raised her eyebrows, and waited for more.

"I have tasted wines from all over the world. You might call me a professional taster, but I have no degrees."

"A professional taster of women, too, it seems. Never been close to taking the plunge?"

"Close, yes. Several times. I do enjoy mortal women." His slip-up earned him a frown from across the table. He quickly recovered with a smile, indicating it was a joke, "I identify playing the part of your vampires. The dark loner, brooding type, occasionally bored with my life. I don't attract women who last very long."

It was the truth, and seemed to satisfy her.

"What do you do to them to send them away?"

That was a good question. "Every good fantasy has an untimely death, right? You believed in Santa Claus and the Tooth Fairy..."

"You really believe a fantasy love can't last forever?" she asked, dismissing the childhood references.

"As in immortal?" he asked. He was coming closer to the dangerous edge of a reveal, and he knew she'd rein herself in very soon.

"I mean a love that can last a lifetime," she spoke the innocent words which captured him. He could see this was important to her.

"With all my heart. Yes." He placed one palm on his chest as his other hand wanted to hold hers. But Cara was primly sitting, hiding her hands under the table. He could feel her resolve, a combination of control and desire.

Let me unleash your inner fantasies, Carabella. Let me teach you the pleasures of...

Cara's cell phone blurted out the sound of a car horn. She fished for it from her computer case and answered, "Hello Johnny. What's up?"

Paolo listened to the squawking on the other end of the line. He looked out the window as he heard her assistant's tinny words. "You wanted me to go down to Berkeley to speak to that researcher. Can I bail on the office time if I promise to do it for you this afternoon?"

"Anyone signed up?" Cara asked.

"Well, I'd blocked out the afternoon for our discussion time, so I don't think anyone will be here. I can't go to Berkeley tomorrow, so thought I'd take advantage of the time today. You okay with that?"

Cara looked at Paolo, who was pretending he had no idea the lovely woman in front of him was now free for the entire afternoon.

"I'm fine with that. Leave it marked off. I'll see you Wednesday. Thanks for calling." She ended the call and placed her phone on the table.

Cara's screen saver was a picture of Frank Langella dressed as Dracula.

"Good news?" he asked. He tried not to stare at the actor's picture.

"It seems my office hours have been cancelled."

Paolo took her hands in his. "I've got some excellent thoughts on how we might spend the afternoon. If you're willing."

She stared at their entwined fingers as she allowed her forefinger to rub along his flesh. Her touch sent him into a trance of desire.

"I think I might like that."

And that was all she had to say.

CHAPTER 14

T he driver took them the back way, up through vineyards in Alexander Valley. Paolo leaned back into the leather seat so he could get a side view of Cara, who was fascinated with the dark limo's interior and sparkling lights. She looked like she was on her first chauffeur-driven ride for her high school prom. She turned and caught him staring at her, but he didn't care. If it concerned her, she didn't show it.

"I like all the colors this time of year," she said, looking out the window at the richness of vineyards bursting with gold and burgundy.

It was true, but the color he liked best was the red of her lips, and her flushed cheeks, and her light pink fingernail polish. He wanted to feel those pink fingers on his flesh, feel the sharpness of her nails digging into his back as he plundered her deeply, claimed her for his own over and over again.

Even though he didn't use glamour, she leaned into him, as he pulled an arm around her shoulder. She sighed and seemed to melt into his frame. Her hot flesh sent warmth to every cell of his body. "I feel absolutely decadent," she whispered. "Have never done this in the middle of a school day."

"Ah. And here I thought it was perhaps the company you're keeping."

She grinned. "That, too."

"Come. We shall celebrate." He leaned forward and opened a glass of port, pouring one for each of them.

"You come prepared."

"Always." He did not tell her he traveled with a case at all times.

"So you had a feeling this would happen?"

"Eventually, yes." It was difficult not to give her the gloating grin he knew would turn her off.

"Eventually? What's that supposed to mean?"

"Like you, I'm a fairly good judge of people."

"People, or women?"

"Women too." *Like I can tell what you are feeling.* He didn't think he would have the gift of mindspeech with Cara, but perhaps could develop it in time. If he was given the time, that is. Paolo could sense her emotions.

He felt her pulse quicken slightly. Her eyes widened and he could hear the little breath she sucked in and tried to hide.

"Bella—may I call you Bella?"

"Yes."

"Bella, you are safe with me. And," he pointed to the chauffer, "we have a witness."

"Behind glass," she said.

"Absolutely, so even your words are safe with me." She was lovely the way her eyes danced in the afternoon sunlight. *For my eyes only. Words for my ears only.*

"This rather reminds me of one of those novels I read. The vampire seducing a mortal woman."

"Hmmm…I thought I was being subtle," he whispered to the top of her head. He was going to say more, but the giggle she gave him as she squeezed herself against his chest sent a spark traveling straight down to his groin.

Was it always going to be like this around her? Her lightness of spirit thrilled him. His fondness for mortal women was driving his delight higher than it ever had been before. So uncomplicated, simple, and with a lack of the darkness he found in vamp women, who liked to dominate and push their power. Sex with them was a tug of war and a near fight to the death. When he was younger, he used to love it. But especially since Maya, he'd lost all desire to bed women with fangs. In between his wives, he'd usually sought the arms of mortal women.

With Bella, he *wanted* to be gentle. He liked the feeling of being bridled.

"Is there anything you want?" he asked as he played with curls falling at the base of her neck. He lightly touched her skin with the tips of his fingers. She jumped like this gesture scared her at first.

Relax.

"Did you just ask me to relax?" She leaned forward and looked back at him with a frown.

Incredible. She'd heard his thoughts.

"As a matter of fact, *I did*. That's very strange. We must have an extra connection." He was barely able to hold back his desire to ravish her with kisses.

"And why did you say that?"

"I felt you were nervous, perhaps." He laughed at how trusting she was. "No, Bella, I'm just making it all up. I had no idea."

That seemed to settle her.

He knocked on the glass as they pulled up to the popular Jim Town Store, a Healdsburg icon. The chauffer opened their door, Paolo helped her alight, and she held his hand as they climbed the old wooden steps of the roadside café and eclectic general store.

"Coffee?" he asked. "You want a cappuccino?"

"Sure."

Overlooking the two-lane highway with the occasional car driving past, she sipped her cappuccino, her gaze far away. He tried not to look, but it was hard keeping his eyes off her face, the soft lips leaving a pink semicircle on the edge of the white paper cup. He wanted everything about her, even the paper cup she would eventually discard.

Enchanting. She is enchanting.

"So tell me," she said.

He didn't know what she meant. "Tell you what?"

"Where are we going? Didn't you expect me to ask you?"

"My brother has a home in Healdsburg. I thought I would show it to you. He and his wife have recently had a baby."

"You're visiting from Italy. For how long?"

"Haven't decided." He fingered the back of her hand as it clutched the cup. "When I'm ready."

She nodded. "What are you here for?"

Very good question. Perhaps to fall in love. To forget. To learn to be a father. To start to live again. "I came here so my son could spend some time in California with my brother and his wife."

"He has been raised in Italy, then?"

"Actually, no. But we do travel a lot.

"I see," she said.

Do you see, my Bella? Do you feel the urgency between us? As if she could feel what he said, she sat up straight. She smiled. Did she hear him?

"So what do you do for a living?" she asked.

"I study human nature."

"A psychologist?"

"No."

"A psychiatrist, a doctor?"

"No. I read. I live. I have the luxury of being a gentleman of means, free to do what I wish, to pursue my interests as I will."

"You sound positively ancient. Johnny warned me about you." Her eyes twinkled as she tilted her head.

He stopped smiling. Some of his mirth was bottled. The pause was pregnant, on purpose. He wanted to see how she would answer herself.

She had blushed. "I don't mean to suggest you're way older than I am. Perhaps a couple of years…"

I like that guess, Bella.

"But I haven't heard anyone calling themselves a gentleman other than in a movie, or in one of my romance novels." She took another sip of her cappuccino. "You have a funny way of speaking sometimes. Like you've traveled here from another time."

He was nailed by her warm brown eyes, caught, as if staked through the heart. He willingly allowed himself to squirm, if it meant she was looking at him. Anything to have her look at him.

"It is my family, my old family roots you are sensing." *That and the way my fangs ache to taste you, to throw up your skirts and take the blood from your upper thigh, to satisfy myself by plunging in and looking at the rapture of your sweet, peach-colored face. I could bring you to heaven and back, if you will allow me…allow me in…*

The glamour had taken hold. Her eyes slightly crossed and she became stiff, motionless and staring straight at him, as if tethered. He was sorry for this lapse, but couldn't help himself. He slipped to a chair next to her, placed his palm under her chin, turned her face toward his as she fell against him. Without knowing if it was right or wrong, he covered her mouth with his. Her soft lips welcomed him.

She turned her body into his chest, her right arm coming up over his shoulder to play with the hair at the back of his neck. She drew her fingers under his ear and along the bone of his jaw, and touched his lips, as if needing to feel the kisses between them.

He whispered words he used to hear in his dreams as a young man. Words of love passed down to him from others who spoke a tongue that was long dead. The incantation sent her pulse soaring. His followed along right behind.

"Bella I need..."

"Yes. I need this, too," she said. Her eyes told him he could have his way with her right here on the table in the Jim Town Store, if he wanted. But he wanted her all to himself.

"I know a place," he said.

"Your brother's home?"

"No. Some place we can be alone."

"Yes." She held his head in her palms and kissed him of her own free will. He could hear the pulsing of the veins underneath the delicate white flesh at her wrists, which were positioned right over his ears. His mouth went to one wrist as he kissed her there, and felt the lifeblood inside her rise up to meet his tongue.

He held back. This would have to be just sex. He couldn't bite her. Not yet. Perhaps not ever. But God in Heaven, the sex would be glorious, and that would have to be enough for now.

Almost lifting her out of the chair, he took her back to the waiting limo. The driver had been asleep in the front, and came round to open the door for them.

"Is she all right, sir?" he asked as he frowned at Cara's flushed face and half-opened eyes.

"She's tired. I'm going to take her to the Stone Creek Inn. You know it?"

"Sure. You need me to call ahead?"

"Please."

"No problem," the driver said as he closed the door. In the privacy of the darkened limo interior, he had her all to himself, for a few seconds.

"Bella, are you okay going with me some place where we can..."

"Yes," she said breathlessly. "Please. I would like that."

He covered her mouth again, his hand finding the thrill of the feel of her nipples budding through her bra. He couldn't wait to have her naked.

The car purred along the curved country road and up a noisy crushed granite driveway to a stone structure with a water wheel turning slowly to the side.

"I will call for you when she feels more like traveling," he said to the driver, who grinned back at him in response.

"Of course, sir. I'll return to Marcus' home, then."

"Perfect."

Inside the reception area he secured a room on the upper floor, one with a view of the vineyards below. Cara was leaning against him, her hands untucking his shirt, her palms finding his chest as she slid them up and rubbed herself against his back.

The clerk was efficient, seeming to take no notice.

"Would you have a bottle of your best port delivered to our room?"

By the time they were at the top of the stairs and had passed the water wheel, Cara had his shirt completely unbuttoned. He was glad there wasn't much of a crowd on a Monday afternoon. They didn't pass a soul.

He unlocked the heavy carved door and stepped inside an oversized room with a roaring fireplace and huge four-poster bed covered in silk pillows. He turned to see her expression, and was hit with her flying body as she slammed into him and they toppled to the bed.

CHAPTER 15

Cara was beyond shame. The need she had for this man—he had called it *urgency* and that certainly was a great way to put it—consumed her like she was a piece of tissue paper that had hit water. She was melting, floating into his rock hard body as he laughed and allowed her to overcome him, not because she was in any way stronger than he, but because he seemed to love watching her have her way with him.

Him.

Who was this man? She knew practically nothing about him, yet she was going to let him see her naked, let him kiss her in places where she ached to be kissed. Like her life depended on it to feed her soul.

She had read about animal attraction between a man and a woman, like an ancient hormonal rule of nature passed down through generations, but she hadn't been close to feeling it. This was...

What? She heard him say something in a language she didn't understand. Some internal memory. She saw torches, and a campfire. She saw the stars over a village lit by candlelight. Not a trace of an incandescent bulb or neon sign anywhere.

"Amore," he was saying over and over again in his mind. He was thinking of that word over and over again.

She loved the feel of his hands as they slid under her skirt, as they smoothed over her bottom. She raised her fuzzy shirt so the tops of her breasts could brush against his hard chest. She held the back of his neck and leaned in to his ear and whispered, "Amore."

He flinched as he heard her speak it. With eyes wide open and full of wonder, he held her face between his long fingers.

"Amore," he said. "Love me, Carabella."

But she heard something else, too.

"Heal me. Make me believe."

He was saying other things as well, but she didn't understand. His thumbs were rubbing against her lips as he held her just an inch from his face. He studied her, with his dark eyes and rich brown hair. Her fingers sifted through the hair at his temples, smooth as silk. She saw the delicious movement of his Adam's apple as it bobbed when he swallowed. She kissed him there, under his chin. Then along his neck, under his ear. Again, she whispered to him,

"Yes, amore."

His groin arched up and she felt his erection—so large she was certain it hurt as she ground herself down on him, rubbing the length of him against her pubic bone.

She removed her fuzzy top and bra in one smooth move, and drank in the look on his face. He was hungry for her. Her breasts overflowed in his hands as he squeezed them. As she gave her flesh to him.

She peeled his shirt over his massive shoulders and stared down at the wonder of his well-defined chest and trim waist. Beautiful. A sculpture of Adonis himself couldn't have appeared more masculine, more luscious. He watched as she partook of the vision that was this man's wonderful body.

She reached for his belt buckle and found he had none. He was wearing old-fashioned pants with filigreed silver hooks and eyes. One by one, she undid them, and slid her cool hands into the darkness to find his sex. She removed his pants and his arousal sprang forth. She could hardly close her hand around it, as its girth was nearly as large as her own wrist.

"Too large, Bella?" she heard him think.

She shook her head from side to side and slowly climbed down his torso, and, while looking up at his face, put her red lips on the tip of his cock. His head fell back into the pillow as he arched to her touch, as the stiffness of his sex grew even further, as she sheathed him with her lips, her tongue, and tasted him.

A flash of golden light blinded her, as if his precum had a psychedelic quality to it. Her body shuddered, convulsed with need. She moaned as he sunk himself deep into her mouth.

"Carabella, mi amore. Carabella, mi amore," he rasped repeatedly as his hands played in her hair, as he pulled her to him, pulled her up so he could plunge his tongue deep down her throat. The musty, spicy taste of his arousal, the warm heat arising from his chest and from the moist warm places in his hair drove her to new heights with every inhaled breath. His taste, his scent—everything was an elixir. The lips of her sex were quivering with desire.

In one smooth move he had flipped her over onto the bed.

"Your turn," he thought.

She smiled her complete compliance. "Yes," she whispered as she followed the arc of her fingers as they traced the shape of his ear. They listened to each other's breathing. She watched his eyes grow darker to almost black.

He lifted her skirt very slowly, slid his long fingers up her thighs to her panties covering her swollen sex. He took forever to slip down the lacy black underwear she'd had the good fortune to wear today. He let it trail along her thighs until he bent one of her knees, slipped the panty over it, extricating her leg. Then he drew the panties down the other leg, watching her face as she waited, her heart pounding in her chest with lust for him.

He deftly slid a hand under her and unzipped her skirt, removing it. She was naked to him now as he watched her breathing, watched the juncture between her thighs and watched the rise and fall of her breasts. Gently he parted her knees and gazed upon her, and sighed.

Let me see your desire, Carabella, he said to her in thought.

She guided his long fingers to her opening, and pressed two of them inside her, arching her back up, bracing herself up so he could penetrate fully. He manipulated his hand, pressing in and out. She heard how wet and hot and swollen she was. He tasted his forefinger, closing his eyes, and when he opened them again, his eyes were jet black, with small flames in the center. His nostrils flared as she saw him press his teeth with his tongue, pushing against his own canines.

He had pressed so hard, a small drop of blood formed at his mouth on one side, as if his teeth had been so sharp he had cut himself. She licked her lips, and looked at the blood. She wanted…

What am I doing? She felt her arms pull him down to her mouth, and she sucked the blood from his cut tongue. Another golden flash overtook her. Every cell in her body sparked with need for the taste of this man.

His eyes were wide. He looked surprised. Had she gone too far? Was this something he didn't like?

But then she was rewarded with a red, closed-lip smile. He kissed her under her right ear and she pressed her neck into him. Just like the mortal women did with their vampire lovers. She wanted him to taste her, bite her neck.

What would it feel like, if?

But then he was down on her chest, kissing first one, and then the other nipple, sucking them, making noises as he played with them and flicked them about with his agile tongue. That tongue that left the promise of things to come.

No man had tasted her sex before. She wanted him to be the first. He kissed her belly button, nipping a sharp pinch that made her jump. He followed this with the laving of his tongue that stimulated her as well as took away the pain of the sting. Inch by inch, he kissed from her belly button to the top of her hairless mound.

"I love hairless women," she heard his thought. She felt her mound swell.

She was grateful she had thought to shave closely this morning. His lip crinkled as he kissed the top of her slit, as he slid his tongue into the cavern there, over her nub on its way to her opening. She was shuddering with pleasure. The room was spinning. He made noise, slurping her sweet moisture, drinking from her, letting her feel his eagerness feeding her own.

She was beginning a slow orgasm that was sure to explode soon. His slow and steady ministrations played her body like an instrument, demanded she feel the intensity of his desire for her.

She didn't want him to stop. She could have spent the afternoon with his mouth on her sex, but at last she felt the cooler room air on her and felt him climb atop her. She noticed he had sheathed himself in a light pink condom, but the burgundy red from his blood-bulging cock still shone through. It looked like he would burst it if he got any bigger. He settled himself between her legs and pressed just the head of his cock into her opening and stopped.

She took in a breath. He was already stretching her. She drew her hands to his buttocks and pressed his groin into her. He resisted, making her pull hard to get him firmly planted all the way to his root, watching her struggle to accept his full girth.

And then he began a gentle, rhythmic in and out movement. He looked down upon her. His face faded and came back into focus as she moaned, closing and opening her eyes. Those dark eyes spoke to her.

"Need this."

Yes. She needed it too. She hoped it would be the first of many, as he pumped her deeply. In between he would stop, she would feel the thrill of how he filled her. He'd kiss her tenderly, licking and sucking at her neck, arching back to watch her face. Just holding him inside her was delicious. Her core began to vibrate as if the flesh of his member gave her flashes of passion. The crescendo of their mating was intensely increasing. She'd never felt so sated, and left so vacant between his powerful thrusts. His voice, deep and low inside his chest, rumbled, making her nipples taught. He was whispering things in a foreign tongue she understood as ancient, a sad litany of need and desire, something overcoming him and consuming him.

She arched back and groaned, and felt him seek her mouth, cover it possessively and take her breath, holding her chest underneath with his huge hands, pressing her breasts into him while pressing his thumbs into her waist at her hips. He rooted deep again and again, setting up a rhythmic tantra as he adjusted his hips to angle with his thrusts, sending her new scitters of pleasure, making her shudder with delight. Their skin made slapping sounds as his movements picked up, as she was sent into higher and higher orbit with every deep stroke into her. She was on the edge of something…

The orgasm hit her hard as he pressed against her cervix, almost causing her pain. The soft folds of her pussy separated and violated as he trembled, whispering her name in raspy tones. She recognized the jerking movements as he was spending into the condom, but it went on for long luscious minutes. The low satisfying rumble in his chest as he spent his last drop made her want him all over again.

At last he collapsed on top of her. She stroked his back, his backside and explored the nape of his neck with her fingers. His scent was like oranges. His skin was sweet and salty on her tongue. She could still taste the remnants of his small tongue injury in her mouth, giving her another little spark as she licked her lips.

What is this? Who is this man?

Most of her sexual partners had not lived up to her expectations, and she found herself actually grateful when the sexual act was over. She cared more about the closeness than the flesh on flesh experience.

But with this man, she wondered if she would ever be able to get enough. She hoped he would recover soon, because she could hardly wait to be penetrated again.

And then maybe again.

In fact, she hoped they could stay naked and stay in this room all night.

No one had ever made her feel this way before. She knew she wouldn't be able to say no to him.

Ever.

CHAPTER 16

In the lazy afternoon sun she awoke to the sound of the door to the room opening. She smelled the fresh pine logs in the fireplace, and heard them sputter and crack. Paolo walked back to the bed, naked, holding a tray with a bottle of Port and two glasses.

"Time for fortification." He set it down on the bedside table and sat next to her. "Are you hungry, Carabella?" he asked as he stroked the side of her face, and then down her neck to her breast.

His touch ignited the flame that had been burning inside her, pulsing in the erotic dreams over the past few minutes she had slept. Or was it a lifetime she slept?

"Yes and no," she answered as she scanned his massive shoulders, his flat abdomen and powerful thighs dusted with light brown hair. She rubbed her palm over him, seeking the spot between his legs.

She would gladly burn in the look he gave her in return. The longing he held for her almost made her levitate.

"What is this?" she asked.

"This?" he raised one eyebrow.

"This...attraction. I've always thought authors who wrote about this feeling were making it up. I feel wonderful. Alive for the first time in my life. And I don't even know you." She frowned, but continued rubbing over the muscles in his forearm, up his elbow to his biceps. "It's like the more I touch you the more I want you."

He broke eye contact and looked to the side, outside the room to the orange glow of the late afternoon vineyard view. She followed his line of sight.

"Oh, my God," she giggled, putting a hand over her mouth.

He turned, clearly alarmed.

They hadn't closed the drapes. The person delivering the Port had surely seen them.

"Hotel workers learn to be discreet," he said with a smile. He leaned down and with his soft lips barely touching hers, he whispered, "And I wouldn't care anyway. I'd make love to you at a baseball stadium if I had to."

His long, penetrating kiss put her into a dreamy trance. She saw torches again, roaring fireplaces and stone floors. Her breasts needed his hands, and he obliged. Her thighs needed to be kissed by his, and he obliged, sliding his long body into the warm bed.

His hands were everywhere. He kissed her neck, her breasts. He pressed himself against her as he held the small of her back, stroking down her back-side along the cleft between her buttocks. In gentle movements he felt her warm sex and, peering into her eyes, he inserted his fingers.

"I love feeling, touching your arousal. Seeing how you come to me so willingly," he said.

It was an odd thing to say, but she found herself liking it. As if he had the power to *make* her want him, but wasn't exercising it.

"It's where I belong," she said in return. "In your bed, your hands on me, your cock deep inside me."

"Yes," he said as he angled his head, slid his knees between her legs, opening them, replacing his fingers with his shaft, rubbing against her swollen lips. He stopped until she quit looking at the headboard. She had arched back to accept him. With their eyes locked in a dream-like gaze she never wanted to awaken from, he entered her.

She could hear her own heart beating in time with his slow, persistent pushing, rubbing against the sides of her sex, filling her, melting her. She raised her knees and placed them over his shoulders, allowing him to fill her deeper. He moaned and pumped her fully, back and forth, like rocking a cradle, closing and then opening his eyes.

"*Need this.*"

"Yes, I need this too," she said. "Mi amore," she said between his strokes, noticing that his eyes had started to water. "I do belong here, with you."

He crossed one of her knees in front of him and stroked her from the side. She continued to roll over to her stomach while he continued his rhythmic movements, pulling her hips up to elevate her bottom, holding and fondling her nub with the hand he held underneath her. He pressed her there. She brought her hands to his and entwined his fingers, felt the root of his powerful cock as it stretched and then buried deep within her peach. She squeezed the veined surface of his shaft when he withdrew, and cupped his balls as he dove in to the hilt.

Deep inside her she began the spasms that took her breath away. She raised herself up on her knees, pressing against him, her head buried in the soft down pillows. She moaned into the cotton fabric, tore with her fingers the soft feathers beneath. Her chest was on fire, her breasts had become engorged. Her peach sucked at him, begging for more.

"Yes. Please. Oh yes, *please*," she shouted to the pillow.

He leaned in and something sharp nicked her neck, which gave her a start. But then his tongue and his lips were there, heightening the delicious feel, turning the stinging pain into something she craved. His lips were sucking her neck, drinking from her.

Like a vampire.

CHAPTER 17

S he looked into the mirror in the bathroom, alone at last. Raising the glitter-ing glass of port to her lips, she stared hard into her own eyes. She wasn't sure if she wanted to know what was real and what wasn't. Or if it was impor-tant. Her imagination had been working overtime.

She angled her neck to dare look at the place where she had felt his lips on her, the sharp stinging sensation, but, other than a reddened area from a deep kiss, there was no wound there. Her forefinger laced up and down the smooth surface of her skin, feeling for a bump, a callus, a...

Bite?

But there wasn't one. Nothing marred the cool surface of her skin. Her cheeks hadn't stopped their flush; her lips were swollen from the claiming kisses he gave and from her pressing against him almost to the point of pain. She pulled up the hair at the nape of her neck and looked at herself again. Her curls fell about her face as she pouted her lips. She felt positively ancient, wicked, and desired as never before.

A gentle knock on the door stopped her daydream.

"Cara, are you okay?" he murmured through the painted wooden door.

"Of course. You can come in," she answered.

He leaned into the doorframe, his dark curls shiny and tousled. His dark eyes wandered from her face, to the pink mounds of her breasts, and down to the juncture between her legs. Just the way he looked at her made her feel like molten chocolate.

He watched as she let go of her curls and they fell about her shoulders.

"Your hair. I love your hair," he said as he stepped in, standing behind her. He kissed her neck as she watched him through the mirror, as she felt him linger on her neck, breathe into her ear and whisper something to her that made her shiver.

"What is it you are saying to me? You put me under some spell with your incantations?"

He raised his face and placed his chin at the top of her head, with the Cheshire cat smile she'd already gotten used to. But not really.

"Guilty," he sighed.

She tilted her head. "Is your brother going to feed us? I am starved."

"We have two choices." He busied himself kissing the back of her neck, and each vertebra down her back. "We can stay here tonight and order room service, or, go to Healdsburg and visit with the family."

The choice was so unfair. She wasn't sure any other afternoon for the rest of her life would ever equal this one. She was hesitant to give it up, or end it with polite conversation of a non-sexual kind.

"I will do whatever you ask of me. Especially if you continue doing that," she whispered as he squeezed her breasts and rubbed his erection up and down the cleft in her behind.

"So willing. So beautiful."

"Can we do both?"

He leaned back and laughed. She turned and faced him, her thighs against his, her mound pressing into his lower belly.

"My dear Carabella. You have school tomorrow, yes?"

"Yes. And I don't require much sleep. I promise."

They showered, sharing her glass of port. She enjoyed the kisses he scattered all over her, the way his tongue probed her, the way his fingers played in her hair, between her legs, massaged her neck and shoulders. He carefully dried her off like a marble statue of Venus. He would say, "I like this," and kiss her there. He made no mystery of his favorite places on her body.

The driver arrived just at sunset and whisked them by moonlight up the narrow winding road until they arrived at a large house built at the side of a hill overlooking rows of vines.

"All this belongs to Marcus," he said as he spread his hand, illustrating the wide expanse without another house in sight. The stone manor house at the top of the hill was lit with torches that crackled and sputtered up into the night sky.

"Torches. I've been seeing them all afternoon," she said.

"Interesting. I love a big fire."

"It was like I could read your mind. I saw old cobblestones and torches in darkened curved hallways."

"I might have been dreaming of Italy," he said absent-mindedly as he stroked her upper arm. "But you are thinking about our family. I told you we have a very old family, although none of the older ones are alive today."

"Must be what I was dreaming. In any case, I don't want it to end, if it is a dream."

He adjusted her against him again and gave her upper body a squeeze.

At the front door, a young boy waited. Warm yellow light spilled out onto him and the stoop as he stood, holding a very tall man's hand.

The man was a darker version of Paolo, but perhaps a little taller.

"Welcome to Villa Monteleone, Cara," Paolo whispered to the top of her head. The driver opened the door and she allowed him to get out first, then allowed him to pull her hand and present her to the man and the boy.

"Carabella Sampson, this is my brother Marcus Monteleone and my son, Lucius."

The boy was as handsome as his father. He stepped forward with a stiff bow and extended his hand. "Lucius Monteleone," he said, as if there might be some question.

"Nice to meet you, Lucius," she said as she grasped his little hand in both of hers. "Please call me Cara." She stepped toward Marcus and extended her hand, which he quickly took and kissed, just as his brother had done two nights ago at the ball. The way they behaved was identical. She felt herself blush, as if Paolo had touched her himself. "Wonderful to meet you as well, Mr. Monteleone."

"Marcus."

She saw the darker brother give a tiny wink to Paolo and show them the way inside.

The foyer was done in deep red tones. Old tattered and faded flags and oil paintings of long-ago ancestors graced all four of the wallpapered surfaces in the entryway. Paintings depicting hunting trips, exotic animals and castles were scattered here and there. "These are some of your ancestors. No one current, I see?"

"They've been gone a long time."

In the doorway to the kitchen, a beautiful auburn-haired woman carrying a blanket-wrapped baby suddenly appeared. "Welcome to our home. I'm Anne," she said as she reached out and shook Cara's hand firmly.

Cara had never seen such a strikingly handsome family. She was at a loss for words.

"Thank you for allowing us to just pop in on you without notice," Cara said.

"Oh no, the driver told us you would be coming as soon as you were done at the Inn." Lucius piped up. This surprised a chuckle from Marcus, though he worked to stifle it. Cara saw he'd earned a reproachful look from his wife.

Cara felt her cheeks flush. Paolo placed his arm around her waist and squeezed her. The nearness and electricity of his body touching hers was intoxicating and her knees wobbled. She heard a low rumble inside Paolo's chest.

"Lucius was anxious to see his father, and when the driver returned, he naturally ran out to greet him, and was told you two had decided to stay in town *for a while*," Anne's quick explanation was adequate, but Cara felt there was something else she wasn't privy to. "Are you hungry, Cara?" Anne asked as she handed the baby to her husband.

"Yes. Starved," Cara said and stepped closer to the baby. "What a beautiful little girl."

Lucius laughed out loud. Marcus spoke up first, "I'm not going to tell him you said that" He smiled down on her with the same commanding presence Paolo had. "His name is Ian."

She needed to change the subject. "Anne, may I help with anything?"

"Oh, I'm not fussing. We're going very casual and simple tonight" She looked at Paolo, "Paolo, are you hungry this evening?"

"Of course. Haven't eaten in hours." His words were stiff, but he winked at Cara.

"I know, silly question." She motioned for Cara to follow her into the kitchen.

Cara had never seen such a beautiful, grand room. Ornately carved crown molding hovered in the tall shadows above the kitchen cabinets. The ceiling was at least twelve feet above them. Old Italian tile covered the countertops, but the floor was a light hardwood. One end of the kitchen was open to an intimate room with leather couch and a floor-to-ceiling brick fireplace. A two-foot tree trunk was burning on ornate iron grates with dragon's heads on them. Fire flickered in the cut out eyes of the fierce beasts of burden.

Anne was setting out some hand-painted square plates. With the crackling sounds and smoky scent of the fireplace as background, she started to ask the questions Cara knew were coming.

"How long have you and Paolo known each other?" Her nimble fingers were adjusting light green lettuce leaves on the plates, placing one leaf on the small plate Cara knew must be for Lucius. She didn't look up, but when Cara didn't answer right away, she stopped and waited.

"Well, let's see, since day before yesterday."

Anne's face beamed with a warm smile.

"I completely understand," she said.

How could you? "He is rather handsome. I find he has quite an effect on me," Cara answered.

"Yes…" Anne drifted off into a reverie all her own. "The brothers are like that. Women falling all over them, yet, they are discreet, and they choose wisely." She smiled again, and licked her lips.

"How long have you and Marcus been married?"

"About a year, a little longer."

"Was it sudden. Did you—"

"Yes." The look Anne gave her said she was done talking about it. Some divide had opened up a chasm, and nothing Cara knew would be able to bridge it.

Anne took a hot casserole out of the oven with red oven mitts. Smells of bubbling cheeses warmed Cara's spirits. She bent over to look at it carefully, her eyebrows coming to a point on her forehead.

"Macaroni and cheese?"

"Yes. It's Lucius' favorite. He asks for it every night. We humor him when we have guests. Keeps him at the table a little longer." With a spatula, she scooped a square onto each plate. She then added tomatoes and sliced peppers to the lettuce, poured a hand-shaken dressing mix over the top and garnished them with crumbled blue cheese.

"You guys eat a lot of cheese, I see."

"We always have tons of it around. Goes with the wine. And actually, I think it is our biggest source of protein."

Cara looked at Anne's beautiful figure and wondered how she could stay so slim on a diet of cheese. "No fish, other meats?"

"Very little. We're practically vegetarians, although we love fresh eggs and our cheeses. We make many of our own here at the winery."

"I'd have a hard time not devouring a good steak now and then. Don't think I could ever be a vegetarian."

Anne gave her a thoughtful look. "I had an unfortunate experience with some beef liver, got very ill. Ever since then, I cannot stomach meat from animal flesh."

"Ah." It was certainly an odd thing, Cara thought.

"Although, sometimes the boys do enjoy a good barbeque, maybe a couple of times a year, and usually when we're entertaining."

Anne handed Cara two plates. "This one is for you and this is for Paolo. If you would serve them and take your seat, I'd be so grateful. I'm going to check on Ian first, and then I'll join you."

"No problem."

Cara presented Paolo with his plate, and just after she seated herself, he leaned over and gave her a sweet kiss on her cheek that tingled all the way to her sex.

Anne returned to the table. "He's sleeping like a log, which means he will keep us up all night."

Marcus looked brightly at his wife as she seated herself and motioned for everyone to begin.

"No worries, pet. I'll take one shift so you can sleep," Marcus told her.

"He has an appetite like his father," Anne said, and then blushed. "We'll figure it out."

Paolo leaned an arm over the back of Cara's chair, letting his fingers make little circles in the top of her arm. She'd remembered those circles he'd made this afternoon around her nipples, those same fingers.

Her panties were sopping wet already. She thought perhaps she could even smell her own arousal. Turning to face Paolo, with his beautiful tanned face framed with dark curly hair, with his high cheekbones and full lips, his stormy dark eyes, his nostrils flaring—she saw that he understood. He leaned into her as his warm breath drifted over her ear, making her shiver. Then her body began to hum to some frequency. It was something she'd never felt before.

"I feel the same way every time I look at you, Bella," he said.

Again the hair at the back of her neck prickled. Paolo's warm hand clamped down on it and he massaged the top of her spine with his long fingers.

Those fingers that have been all over my body.

She closed her eyes and fell into his rhythm. When she opened her eyes, both Marcus and Anne diverted their gazes quickly. But they had been watching.

Marcus made a grand gesture of opening up one of his favorite red wines and pouring them each a handsome goblet. A coat of arms was etched into the crystal of each glass, along with a design around the letter M.

Monteleone.

The four grownups listened to Lucius tell them about school and his day. Cara helped Anne clear the table, but as she leaned over Paolo, she felt his hand slip along her backside, felt the heat through the fabric of her pants. She gave him a nudge with her hip.

"Not at the table," she whispered in his ear.

He grabbed her onto his lap as she glanced at Marcus with embarrassment, and then he whispered in her ear, "On the table, under the table, anywhere. Anytime."

She stood up and lurched away, cheeks flushed. "You have an impossible brother, Mr. Monteleone."

"Not impossible. A very healthy alpha male vamp—" Concern flashed all over Marcus' face as he corrected himself. "A very healthy alpha male vagabond from Tuscany—a land legendary for men who mess with women before they have a right to."

She wondered if he was going to say vampire. No doubt, Paolo had told him of her studies.

"I do study vampires, Mr. Monteleone. In fact, I gave my favorite lecture today."

"Yes, Paolo has told me."

Cara had removed all the dishes. "To be continued," she said as she exited to the kitchen.

Anne had dished up a piece of berry pie and a scoop of ice cream for each of them. She handed two to Cara. "Give the big one to Lucius. The other one is for Paolo. I'll bring the rest."

Lucius inhaled the berry pie and didn't say a word. He politely asked to be excused, and Paolo gave him permission, instructing him to go upstairs to study.

First, the boy came around the table and shook Cara's hand again.

"Nice to meet you. I'd like to show you my room some time, if you come back again. I have a big collection of vampire books as well."

"You do?" Cara was momentarily distracted from the tension she'd caused. "I used to read about them too, when I was your age, until I discovered romance novels. Somehow romance and vampires didn't mix very well for a young girl." She smiled, expecting a smile on the faces of her hosts, but not one of them did so.

Lucius withdrew his hand and turned, giving his father a hug, burying his face in his father's neck.

Paolo said something to Lucius in a foreign tongue and the young boy nodded, leaving the room without looking back.

The pie was delicious, but neither of the brothers touched theirs. She saw Marcus lift his fork and then stop before cutting himself a bite, as if he was trying to decide whether he wanted it. Anne nibbled on the tip of her slice, and after having only a few bites, lay her fork down beside the unfinished piece, and sighed.

Cara decided to bring up the verbal slip from Marcus' earlier in the conversation. "So, I got the impression you were going to say male alpha vampire, were you not?"

"You reading my mind now?" Marcus asked with a mock frown. Ann sat up, wary.

"I'm afraid I may have told him too much of our encounter at the ball, Bella. Forgive me." It looked like an honest apology.

"But I want to know why he said it. Was it because of the costume? You guys play vampire around here or something?"

No one said a word, which Cara thought was extremely strange. She felt like she'd just said the seven forbidden words on a live radio program.

Paolo took her left hand in his and squeezed it on top of the table. "Bella, dear. Our family comes from Italy, where they have a healthy respect for the legends of the past. You probably know about the little superstitions in the Black Sea countries about vampires. We trace some of our roots to that ancient land."

"So, you grew up hearing the old stories."

"Exactly," Marcus said.

She looked at Anne.

"Don't look at me. My upbringing was totally Northern California. No vamps in my past, except for some of the guys I used to date. And my ex-hus— my almost husband." Anne said, holding her palms out to the group. Marcus looked pained.

"So, sometime could I interview the both of you, ask you some questions, for my research? I've recently discovered some really interesting things."

"Certainly. We can arrange that," Marcus said as he eyed his brother carefully and winked at his wife. "Start with Paolo, though. He knows everything I know."

"Fair enough." Cara squeezed Paolo's hand. Her gaze traveled to his lips. "Let me ask you both one thing first. Have you ever heard of a historian named Alasdair Fraser?"

Marcus dropped his wine glass onto his pie plate.

CHAPTER 18

Cara felt like she'd committed a sin in front of the pope. In the dangerous silence that ticked past like the mechanisms of several ornately carved clocks in the living room, she looked up at Paolo, asking him in her mind what was wrong.

"*Nothing, mi amore,*" came the non-verbal reply.

"*These dark stories, Paolo? Did I do wrong to bring them up?*"

Paolo picked up her hand, turned it palm side up and kissed her there with more tenderness than she'd ever felt. He seemed to devour her in his lingering kiss, inhaling every bit, as if his life depended on it.

"Our family has secrets, Cara," Marcus began. "These things must remain secrets until such time as, as—" he looked over at Paolo before completing his sentence. Anne had a frown line between her lovely brows. Marcus continued, "When Paolo selects a life mate, there are things that must be discussed."

"Don't you think someone would want to know about the family secrets beforehand? How would they know they wanted to join the family?" Cara's back was erect as she reacted to the fact that she wasn't going to be told any of those secrets. And yet she desperately wanted to know.

She searched Paolo's eyes, which had grown dark and dangerous.

"*You fucked me, Paolo. You kissed parts of my body no man has ever touched—*"

Paolo nodded. His huge body rose. He threw the damask napkin down on top of the pie and stomped off into the hallway.

"What did you say to him?" Marcus asked as he stood to go after his brother.

Cara was alarmed that Marcus knew they had telepathic communication. "How did you know that?"

"Because I told him," Paolo said. He had silently arrived and was leaning into the doorframe at the other end of the dining hall. She'd not heard him take a single step. "Sit, Marcus. Since I made a muck of this, I'll straighten it out. If I can. I'm going to need help explaining a few things to Bella."

Anne began to rise, but Cara stopped her. "No. Stay, Anne. Please." Anne assumed her position at the other head of the table and leaned over, placing her elbows on the tablecloth and weaving her fingers together.

Cara tried to pick up a faint conversation in a foreign tongue between the two brothers. Paolo nodded and began to speak.

"I've told you we are an old family. Unfortunately, not all of our family history is pleasant. We have some family members who have done things—" he glanced up to Marcus, who added,

"Been outlaws. There are some family members who engaged in activities that got them and the family into trouble."

"Okay. Every family has these people."

"It is perhaps difficult to understand here in the States, where families can be traced back maybe a hundred years, and of course, some longer. But in Europe, family dynasties can last for centuries. Wars fought. Kingdoms claimed." Marcus began to pace back and forth.

The way he gestured, the way he turned and took those long strides, reminded Cara of Paolo. She remembered his naked frame coming towards her as she lay on the bed full of ripe anticipation. She blushed and looked at her lap, ashamed that her lover might be able to discern her transference onto his brother.

"No shame, mi amore. You are mine, and it is me you are thinking about."

Cara began to well up inside. At last, the floodgates opened and she burst into tears. In a flash, Paolo was next to her, on his knees, his long arm wrapped around her shoulder.

"I'm sorry, but this is beginning to get to me. I've just—" The sexual glow had worn off, and she was staring down into the dark cavern of what she'd just done. She'd met a strange man who made her feel excited sexually as never before in her life, a man she had made love to half a dozen times. And she knew nothing about him. He could be a serial axe murderer, for all she knew.

And now, sitting here, with his family around her, she felt literally *sucked* in to their stories, like she was beginning to lose control over her own life's course. There was something dangerous and predatory about them all, even Paolo.

As if he felt her change of heart, he rose, and stood a healthy few feet from her. Her mind cleared. She was grateful for the space.

What is this power?

She could feel that he stood inside her mind, ready with an answer. But she didn't have the nerve to ask the question. She felt his unease. Out of the corner of her eye saw him grip his hands and squeeze his fists down by his sides.

"I think it would be best if you took her home, Paolo," Marcus said with finality.

"Of course," Paolo's reply was barely audible. He didn't tell her anything telepathically, but she could feel something hurting him.

It's your secret, Paolo. Cara sent him the message but was dying to ask him more. Then she realized with certainty that his secret was going to be something she didn't want to know.

And that was what was causing him the pain.

CHAPTER 19

Cara was grateful Paolo allowed her to be driven home alone. She knew he'd be monitoring her thoughts, and that drove her deeper into despair. On the one hand, this man had awakened something inside her soul that gave her more happiness and pure pleasure than she'd ever experienced.

And on the other hand, she wasn't ready to give up her own free will. She'd never before felt tempted to sink into some dark abyss, do risky things with someone she barely knew, someone who demanded everything from her.

She decided it wasn't good for her, no matter how wonderful she felt when he kissed her, when he whispered incantations that heightened her sexual arousal, even when he just stood next to her. It wouldn't be long before she'd need him too much. She just couldn't allow that to happen.

The leather seats of his brother's limo felt like the cool flesh of a giant serpent against her warm skin. She leaned back and closed her eyes. She recalled him standing by the front door to the villa, his white shirt billowing out from his trim black, old-fashioned pants with the silver clasps. He was such an odd combination of sensual softness and almost a predator's thirst. As the prey, she longed to be captured again and again. She knew she would be safe. Somehow she knew this.

But that didn't make it wise.

Mi amore. She heard him say this as the driver drove down the crushed granite driveway, away to the safety of her own apartment. Paolo hadn't been afraid to let her feel his pain at their separation. She refused to reassure him. She needed space and time.

When they arrived in Santa Rosa, Cara thanked the driver, who waited until she was inside her gated entrance before driving off. She wondered what Marcus' servant thought about taking his master's brother and his new lover to a bed and breakfast for the obvious purpose of having an afternoon of sex. Was this a common occurrence? Did their wealth allow them almost unlimited freedom to explore their sexual appetites with abandon, without drawing attention to the activity? Anne had said that the brothers were discreet. Just what did that mean?

She thought about Marcus' wife, the beautiful Anne, and the little one. She was a California girl, not from an ancient lineage like the rest of the Monteleones she'd married into. Cara thought perhaps someday she could have a frank discussion with Anne, if—

If what? If I let him touch me again?

Cara wondered how she would ever be able to feel another man's touch on her flesh and not remember Paolo. Somehow, he'd claimed her.

"You are mine," he'd told her. The thrill of those words sent a shiver down her spine again as she dropped her purse and keys on the kitchen counter. She thought about them as she pulled off her clothes and left them in a heap in the bathroom. She started the shower but was hit with the warm cloud of Paolo's scent that ricocheted off her own moist skin. She closed her eyes and felt her sex clench. The obvious truth was, she ached for him.

Cara decided against the shower at the last minute. Picking up her clothing, she walked back to her bedroom, hung up her things and slipped naked into the huge bed she'd tossed and turned in last night. The cool sheets warmed quickly. His scent was all over her. As she began to drift off to sleep, she wondered if he could hear her dreams, too.

Paolo held the little glass of port up, looking through it to the flames of the fire as he sat in a winged back chair next to his brother. He was working to push his emotions back. He'd felt her distance growing, like blood draining from his veins, as he'd watched the limo escort his love home to where she thought she was safe. She would be safe from his thoughts, at least, since she was mortal. If she were vampire, she'd be able to feel him across the ocean.

He forced himself to find solace in the ruby color of the port, which was stunning. The sharp sweetness bit down on his palate and filled his nostrils with a heady bouquet. He was grateful for the distraction.

"This is outstanding port, Marcus."

"Yes. Can you imagine how it will be ten or twenty years from now? This is barely two years bottled."

"You must save some for Ian's wedding day."

"That I must. Won't that be a day?" Marcus was admiring the color in his glass just the same way his brother did. Without looking at him, he added, "The girl is lovely, Paolo."

"Carabella. Her name is Carabella."

"Yes. You speak of her in a haunted, almost fated manner. Is there some evidence you could be fated?"

"I feel something like it, yes." Paolo didn't want to think about the brief few days of savage sex he spent with his son's mother, the way he couldn't stay away from her. Maya hadn't loved Paolo any more than he loved her. But their species instincts pulled them together in a tangle of arms and legs, resulting in her bearing him a son.

With Cara, it was an animal attraction, but not without reason. If they were truly fated, he never would have been able to send her home in the limo by herself. He'd have fucked her several times, with or without the audience of the driver in the front seat.

He had been a good husband to his three mortal wives, who, one by one, died in his arms. He hated himself for the fating that had taken over his body, forcing him to break his marriage vows.

Being married to mortal women was pleasant, but they were childless years as he watched them age, watched as each of them grew to realize he wasn't aging like they were. He never minded the wrinkles and sags of older flesh. He loved and was devoted to his wives. His love wasn't about the flesh, it was about the heart.

Cara, even if he could convince her to be with him, would someday want a family and children of her own. A marriage or long-term relationship with her would therefore be out of the question. He might even be prohibited by the Vampire Council from contacting her further, based on tonight's events. Perhaps the God of vampires had been kind to him by removing the distraction of her scent, her body, before he became too involved. The lady was going to talk herself out of anything that could have happened, and if he resisted the urge to glamour her, she could successfully escape his influence.

Pain was a constant companion to Paolo, who had learned to hold it inside, tuck it away in a satin drawer inside his heart and move on. Three hundred years of practice made him good at it. He knew some day he'd become brittle, perhaps sarcastic, as he watched others of his clan raise their children, love their wives forever and live an eternity wrapped in love and family. This would not be his fate.

As bad as this was, it would have been worse had the half witch-half Golden vampire Maya survived the war she'd started. Paolo would have forever been tethered to a loveless bed of obligation, doing so only to protect his son.

What kind of a father would he be to Lucius, who would have to make the choice some day to either remain mortal or become a Golden vampire? Paolo felt he was a bad role model for the young boy. It might have been better had Marcus married Maya, as she demanded, and raised the boy as his own. Marcus was a better man, Paolo thought. He doubted he could have done it himself.

And then beautiful Anne, so sweet and lovely, Anne, with the force of all the goddesses his ancestors had worshiped centuries ago, herself a new vampire, brought to life by Marcus' blood, sacrificed herself by committing an act punishable by death.

Paolo felt weak when compared to his other family members. His turmoil about becoming vampire at first, added to his pain that the decision could not be undone. He longed for the simple human emotions of loving with a full heart, free of glamour and manipulation, in a measured lifespan of some eighty to one hundred years and no more. It wasn't the living forever that bothered him. It was the feeling that he wanted to love and be loved as a mortal.

He finished his port and pretended to be settled inside. He would be grateful to be alone tonight. Cara would have certainly sensed his scathing pain. Marcus would have to guess.

"Your plans for her?" Marcus asked.

"Why, brother? You doubting my prowess?"

"You know what I mean. Don't joke about that. There is an attraction there. No denying that. You continue seeing her and she will find out things on her own that I'd rather she learned from us."

"Us? Or you? Can't you trust I will do the right thing?"

"That's just it, Paolo, I don't know what that is anymore. Do you?"

The two brothers fixed gazes on each other without moving a muscle. They used to do this when they were boys in a stare-down contest to see who could show emotion first. It was the same now.

Paolo flinched and looked at the fire.

"I am lost, brother. I want what I cannot have. What I could have I didn't want."

"And your son will pay the price," Marcus whispered. Paolo could tell he was a bit angry.

"Without my son, I wouldn't be here." Paolo looked back at Marcus. "I'd be gone."

"Don't say such things. You are a member of this family. Just because you will never have a fated female doesn't mean your life is over, without meaning. You have a legacy to pass on to Lucius. You know this should be your prime directive."

Paolo nodded.

"And with this war coming on, you owe your best efforts to defeat the dark forces descending upon us. In short, we need you. Too many of our kind are disappearing. Something evil is happening."

"The apex." Paolo whispered into the fire.

"Yes, I feel it, brother. Something has shifted. I feel like this is the last stand of our species. We are under open attack."

"I pledge to protect the family. Protect my flesh and blood." He extended his hand to Marcus. "You have my solemn vow, brother. No harm will come to you or your family, *our* family, as long as I'm alive."

CHAPTER 20

Dag transported himself to his flat in San Francisco so he could pick up his Harley Road King. He liked to scare the mortals as he fired up the beast and drove at midnight over to the little coven library his uncle ran in the heart of the Tenderloin. His black leather spiked saddlebags were full of mayhem, but he also kept a spare change of clothes in case his encounters got messy.

The storefront said *Mystical Books*, but everyone in the coven knew it was just a ploy to bring in young unsuspecting college-age coeds who wanted to dabble in the black arts. It was a storefront even the homeless didn't dare sleep under.

They'd had séances in the library. But after the séances, there were some mighty fine orgies, which usually left half the attendees dead. For those who survived, unless they were special, and it was getting difficult to find special ones, their memories would be wiped and they'd never return.

No one ever commented about the fact that the store was only open at night. Daylight hours were spent recovering from the roaming nights of sex and death. Although most the dark vampire hordes didn't sleep in coffins as the old myths described, they did have to stay out of the sunlight. Even a pin-hole in a shade or drape could cause burning and pain.

It was another reason Dag never brought any mortal to his own bed. And he detested other dark vampire women, mostly because they were not easily scared. Therefore, he would be heirless, since darks could only successfully breed with other dark vampires. And unlike Goldens, darks became blood-sucking babies and toddlers prone to feasting on their nannies and housekeepers.

So be it. Dag didn't want the little shits running around his household causing chaos, anyway. Besides, it could be something someone could hold over on him. He made a point of not having anyone around him he couldn't do without. The little blonde was already becoming a problem, messing up his focus as his anticipation heightened for their next encounter, but he knew it was way too early to tell how that would turn out.

Colin was sorting a box of books that had come in the mail. He was "made" later in life, so he looked more than twice Dag's age, more like Dag's grandfather than uncle, despite the fact that they would both live forever. The older vamp had been despondent over the theft of his younger wife's life. She'd been turned by a warring coven that used her as a pleasure doll for nearly a year before she was found. The fact that she had strange desires and needs after the turning made their reunion pure hell, so Colin begged the Supreme Leader to be allowed to join her in vampiric form, and was granted the request. It was Dag's last turning before he himself became Supreme.

And then Dag and his cohorts took care of the coven, eliminating its members one by one in a slow and excruciatingly painful death, as an example to other covens. No one ever questioned their power again, until the Supreme Leader began to make nice with Golden vamps, which was something Dag and his family could not tolerate, so they eliminated him as well.

And now there would be a satisfying, blood-spewing purge to take the final solution to its last stages. It had been foretold in the book. The book Dag needed to find in order to complete his plans.

"Uncle Colin, what have you found for me today?" Dag knew his uncle didn't necessarily like him, but he respected his power and authority. Colin had no taste for the vampire wars or politics.

"'Fraid nothing, Dag. Everyone's into eBooks these days, and we haven't had any large scale invasions lately, so no looted libraries, sorry to say."

"What have you got here?" Dag pawed through the opened brown box with the Priority Mail sticker on it.

"Not much you'd like." Colin took a leather-bound book from Dag's fingers, "*King Arthur's Witch*—somehow I think that wouldn't interest you."

"Pictures?" Dag smiled. "Even black and white ones? Naked mortals?"

Colin flipped through the gold edged tome and shook his head. "Not a one. Sorry."

"You know we've heard the Bat Book has surfaced?"

This got Colin's attention. "Yes, I know. Where is it?" Dag wondered if Colin was keeping something from him.

"A bookseller in Prague has sold it to someone. We're trying to locate it now. Can't believe it was there practically under our noses all this time."

"Was beginning to think it was another urban legend. You really think this book exists? Sure it's not a hoax?" Colin asked.

"Not many mortal men can withstand the kind of pain we dispensed to find out."

Colin frowned and mumbled something to the armful of books he took back to his desk. It didn't bother Dag in the slightest that Uncle Colin was afraid of him. He liked it that way.

"So you will let me know if you hear of this book, or anything about it, won't you, Colin?"

"Of course," Colin said to the desk.

"How's dark Vicky?" Dag was referring to Colin's young vampire wife, who had been spared death by the competing coven because of what she could do in the bedroom. Whispers still surrounded her whenever there was a gathering.

"She's shopping."

"At midnight?" Dag noticed Colin's expression was pained and suspected that his aunt, who had expressed an interest in her own nephew, was not exactly faithful to her dumpy librarian of a husband.

The front door opened with a tinkling bell. Two very thin male vamps in their twenties with spikes in their ears and lips entered. Dag regarded them carefully. There was something a bit off about their appearance, and he didn't recognize them. They also had the smell of Vicky on them.

"Hey pops, we found a couple books at a garage sale and thought perhaps they might be worth something," the slightly taller one of the two said. He nodded to Dag, obviously not realizing he was the Coven Supreme Leader.

Dag considered a punishment, but decided to table it. If these two were Vicky's new playthings, then perhaps Colin might enjoy the sport at a later time. He doubted it, but stored it away in his memory just in case.

"Boys, first I'd like you to meet the Supreme Leader, Dag Nielsen," Colin blurted out before the young vamp could hand him the book. "You'd be wise to address him with respect," he continued. To Dag, he added, "They're Vicky's progeny." His uncle's bloodshot eyes shifted from side to side. Dag could tell Colin was nervous as hell. "Just babes, really."

Colin shrugged and started to examine the first of two large books he'd been handed.

The young vamps bowed and left their heads cowed, avoiding eye contact. *That's way more like it.*

"Sir, we mean you no disrespect," the other vamp whispered. "New to this fiefdom."

Dag inhaled briskly, like he'd been slapped. The younglings darted quick glances at him. "That smacks of attitude." Dag pounced in front of the taller boy. "You like fucking Vicky? What's she like?"

"S-s-sir. I'm sure I don't know." The boy was trying to get Colin's attention and help.

"Liar." Dag grabbed him by the collar and shook him until the boy's head rocked back, exposing bite marks under his jaw line and purple hickeys like a collar of blueberry jam around his neck. "She's a mean bitch, isn't she?"

Dag heard the sound of water running and realized the youngling had peed his pants, and all over Dag's shoes. The boy's friend stepped away, out of Dag's reach and separating himself from the whimpering vamp. Dag took a bite from the boy's neck and only drew a mouthful before he released him and spit the blood out.

"You filthy, dope-smoking, pieces of shit. What'd she do, offer you free sex for the rest of your miserable lives? Tell you to bring her husband books to keep him happy and occupied while you fucked her brains out?"

"Dag—" the librarian pleaded.

"Why do you let her humiliate you so, uncle? Wouldn't you love to watch your wife's lover have his dick torn off?"

Colin looked horrified. Dag wasn't sure if it was the retribution Vicky would bring down upon him if the boy were harmed, or whether he was really averse to the violence. In an uncharacteristic act of mercy, Dag released the young vamp, sending him to the floor. The two scrambled out the door.

"This is getting out of control, Colin. You have to teach your woman how to respect you."

"I know. I am just not her type. Ever since—"

"First you begged us to turn her so she wouldn't die. Then you begged the Supreme, which really pissed him off, to turn you so you weren't such a disappointment to her, with her new appetites. Now what? I can't undo what is already done. You're gonna have to man up, Colin. Or, do you want me to show you how it's done?"

"Dag, she's your *aunt!*"

"By marriage only. But believe me, I'd have to hold my nose if I fucked her. No telling where that twat's been. Most men, especially vamps, would love a woman who wants to have sex 24/7. And you're complaining?"

"Not when she's—"

"You think I'm stupid, Uncle Colin? I know she doesn't fuck when she sleeps. But I've done it. Left my cock inside them while we slept and resumed screwing at sunset when we awoke at night again" Dag picked up one of the books and fingered the spine. "Of course, now I only fuck mortals. I have no taste for vamp whores. You should try young human flesh again. Perhaps give you good practice for Queen Vicky."

"Dag, it's no use. She doesn't fancy me."

"Then glamour her."

"I don't have the gift."

"Then get a potion."

"Where?"

"Damn it, man. You've got books all over the place here. Do a little research."

"I suppose—"

"Tie her up, make her submit to you. I think she'd actually like that. You're too easy with her. She liked it rough before, am I right?"

"Yes. A little."

"And that's what you liked, too."

"She got rough with *me*. I didn't—"

"She was trying to egg you on, get you to be a man. Don't you get it?"

"I just want to love her. I don't want to cause her pain. I don't care if she hurts me. If that's what she likes, I can take it, especially now that I am vampire. I heal within 24 hours. I just don't want her to leave me."

Dag spat on the wooden floor. "I can't believe we are even blood related. You are a fuckin' disgrace."

For the second time today he took pity on someone. Dag hoped it wasn't going to be an annoying trend. Looking at the shaking form of his uncle, his hair disheveled, shirt barely tucked into his banana slug yellow-brown corduroy pants, his jiggling pot belly taking up all the extra slack and making it impossible for him to wear a belt, Dag felt sorry for him. He knew Colin to be a gentle soul. Not many vamps had any real family, so they would have eternity to work out their relationship.

He gripped Colin's shoulder and stared back at him across the length of his outstretched arm. "Let's talk about books, shall we? That's a more pleasant topic."

Colin's eyes lit up. "Yes."

"How can I get a track on that book? Where it got shipped to?" Dag asked.

"If it was a credit card order, they would have the record. If you get me that detail, I can perhaps have an answer within a few hours. Will the bookseller cooperate?"

"Not now." Dag said with a scowl.

Colin backed up just a hair. "I see. Well, then, perhaps someone else who manages the shop can find it. He has a family?"

Dag cleared his throat. "That's a problem, too."

"Ah. Well then, take his computer. It would all be done online. He have an Amazon account? It would be easier if it were through eBay or Craigslist. But the credit card company would be best."

"I'll get the computer and see what we find and have it emailed to you."

"No problem. I'll drop everything and devote my day to it. I promise, Dag."

"Thank you, Colin. You've been a great help already." Dag slapped his uncle on the back. "We'll work on that other problem, too. I think I can help you there in exchange."

"No. Not necessary, but thanks anyway." Colin was in visible distress again.

"No? Well then, I want you to promise me one thing."

Colin hung his head, clearly afraid to hear what kind of an order Dag was going to deliver.

"I want you to try tying up your wife when she's asleep. Bind her hands and feet to the bedpost. Let her squirm. Use silver if you have to. You have some silver chain?"

"I do. I know Vicky has some in her underwear drawer."

"Your wife's a fuckin' freak, Colin."

"I know this, but I love her."

"Well, tie her up with the silver—her own silver for fuck's sake—and make it really secure. Don't worry yourself about the wounds; you know she'll heal. But she'll think twice before hurting your heart again, believe me. Let her stay there for a day. Careful not to let any light in while you are taking your sleep. Ask her first to be more docile and tell her you'll let her go if she can act convincingly. She's going to be mad as hell, but she'll like the game I think. See if she's interested in playing along. Can you do that for me and report to me in a day?"

Colin appeared to hesitate.

"Colin. You know you are required to master her. Otherwise, she's a loose cannon. I cannot afford to have someone out of control so close to me. You understand how it would look?"

"Yes."

"Try it. You might discover a part of yourself you never knew existed."

Dag chuckled as he rode his Harley back to his rented flat. There was going to be one of two outcomes in the next twenty-four hours. Either the problem of wild Vicky would be solved, or Colin would wind up with a hatchet between his eyes.

Either solution worked for Dag. Now that he was close to finding the book, the need for a coven librarian was soon going to be redundant.

CHAPTER 21

Lionel Jett searched the sparkling lights of the City of Healdsburg from his loft apartment overlooking the square. A trio of young men laughed sharply, and it drew his attention to the sidewalk below, where fall tourists had descended upon the little wine country town to feast at one of the two hundred wineries nearby. There weren't many days he wished he was mortal. He didn't often wish he was Golden vampire, instead of the dark vamp of his ancestors. But today, he definitely wished he possessed the powers the Goldens enjoyed.

His weariness was beginning to creep into his everyday consciousness, almost like a kind of aging process. Of course, he would never age. He'd seen changes in the world, especially with the explosion of the mortal population over the past four hundred years since his birth. The Golden population had remained about the same, or perhaps decreased slightly recently. But that was just something he sensed, rather than knew. He wasn't privy to all the inner workings of the Golden society, which was as it should be.

He'd been hired on roughly four hundred years ago to help Marcus and Paolo's father establish his little estate in Tuscany and raise his eight children, and sadly, watched both Sr. Monteleone, a lion of a mortal man, as was his namesake, and his beautiful wife, who was Lionel's contemporary in school, die as mortals, without taking the change. He wondered if the brothers he now served understood the depth of his feeling for their mother. His service was the least he could do for a kind lady who took pity on him as a young, struggling waif trying to raise two orphaned brothers after the death of their parents.

Serving the Monteleones had given his life purpose, and the routine hadn't bothered him one bit. He served at night, unless he was given an unusual night off, like tonight. During the day, he was dead to the mortal world, locked in a special bedroom that might be impenetrable to anything but a direct RPG attack. It would withstand a 9.0 earthquake.

No, the vulnerabilities were happening within. Something was brewing inside him. A sense of loneliness and perhaps a little despair. He'd scented down dark coven lords who wanted to do injury to the Monteleones, and "liquidated" their blood, as he was fond of saying.

Sending them back to the source.

That part of his life wasn't what was causing the problem. It was the living forever, alone, that began to eat a small hole, like a pinhole in a curtain during daylight.

This war felt different from all the other attacks he'd survived and protected the Goldens from. More than about power, this war almost seemed like a planned annihilation of the Goldens and their progeny. And for what purpose? He didn't like fighting a mission he knew nothing about.

So, though it was his night off, he decided to do a little R&R, check out some haunts some of his dark brethren frequented on the fringes of mortal society, where it was dangerous, but sometimes delicious. He was in need of information, but a sexual liaison wouldn't be half bad, either. It might even release the tension dwelling in his loins.

He decided to connect with his brothers, Jeb and Hugh. He picked up his black cell phone and pushed number two. Jeb's voice came on the line immediately.

"Hola."

"Hello, brother. You available?" Lionel asked.

"You need me tonight? Thought we had the night off." Jeb's husky voice was somehow reassuring to him.

"Yes. But I'm going to go mingle, see if I can pick up some information on the currents I'm feeling."

"You too, huh?"

"Yes."

"You talk with Marcus and Paolo tonight?" Jeb asked.

"You mean, do they feel it?" Lionel wished he'd brought it up when Marcus called him at dusk to tell him he could have the evening off. "I'm sure they do. But no, I haven't discussed it with them. He's been pretty focused on Paolo and the girl."

"She's a stunner. Mortal, though, isn't that right?"

"Very much so."

"Paolo's playing with fire. That one will get the whole family in trouble if he doesn't decide which side of the gene pool he belongs to."

It was true. It could get more than the Monteleone family in trouble. It could cost him on a more personal basis. Lionel was not only protector to the Goldens, he would do anything to keep his two brothers safe, being the elder of the three.

Though they'd never discussed it, Lionel knew Marcus was worried about his brother, and the little one Paolo was learning to raise. That was the hard part, he thought. The innocents who were in danger. The Goldens didn't worry about defending themselves, but it was their children who were vulnerable. Hard to live forever with the loss of a mortal child, and he knew that was part of the strategy of the dark covens encroaching upon the Golden vamps and their community.

"I wonder how smart it is for Marcus to be set up here in California. Much safer, I would think, back in Tuscany, where there is a certain safety in numbers," Lionel said.

"But I kind of dig it here. From what I can see of it."

Both the brothers laughed. They lived in one of the most picturesque places in the whole world, except they couldn't enjoy it because they only came out at dark.

"You want to go out?" Lionel asked at last.

"If you need me. Sure. But I had plans."

"That would be that little red-headed witch you fancy, brother?"

"The very same. She's been experimenting with some herbs, and I rather like the effect, if you know what I mean."

"Be careful."

"Always. You going to call Huge?"

The nickname was an apt description of the youngest of the three Jett brothers. Hugh Jett was the tallest by nearly five inches, and stood a whopping

6'7," a tad taller than his employer, Marcus Monteleone. His size also made him a favorite of women of all species. It was with some regret that Lionel watched his youngest brother's life roll out before him. The vamp would have made a good family man. But that wasn't their fate.

No sense arguing with the gods.

"Right after you tell me you'll not do something foolish. Like fall asleep in the sun. Remember, Jeb, to indulge in a little play, but keep your wits about you."

"Most definitely. "

"In service, then," Lionel said.

"In service, brother," Jeb echoed.

Lionel pushed number three on his cell. He heard dead air space at first, then a lot of static as it sounded like the phone had been dropped right after it had been answered.

"Hugh here."

"You all right, brother?" Lionel asked. Huge's heavy breathing was a little disconcerting.

"Working out before they close. Why do they call it 24 Hour Abs when they close at nine o'clock?" Hugh exhaled and Lionel could hear the sound of a barbell either being dropped or thrown onto a rubber mat.

"You up for a little downtown time?" Lionel asked.

"Sure. I need a few to get cleaned up. Almost done. Got one more rep. Then I'll shower."

"Why do you go to all that work? You're going to return to your natural state tomorrow, you know."

"But what a glorious twelve hours I get, and it makes me feel double-immortal, if you can wrap your head around that. Totally awesome."

"Okay, meet me at PRESS in half an hour?"

"Sure. This official, or recreational?"

"Kinda little bit of both. Just doing some digging around, but who knows, perhaps we could share a little sweet thing, if the right one comes along?"

"Hell yes. Didn't get pumped up for nothing. I'm going to infect the whole square with my pheromones."

"So I'll have to keep careful watch over you. You feel the dark forces?" Lionel asked.

"Like a rash. All over the place. Wish they'd just come out and meet us directly. If it's going to be a fuckin' war, wish they'd just get on with it."

"Could be part of the plan," Lionel added.

"Or calm before the storm. Maybe they don't have their ducks in line yet."

Lionel laughed, thinking he heard it wrong. "You say dicks?"

"Those, too."

They shared another throaty laugh.

"That's why I gotta go rooting around, investigate. Things just aren't adding up, Huge. Something major is brewing."

"You know they have a new dark coven leader, this Dag fellow?" Hugh said.

"I've met him a time or two. Newcomer."

"Like one of their dark toddlers. Hosted off the hands that created him. Not a good dude. Definitely someone to watch, if we can catch him."

"Okay, well laters, and Huge—"

"Yeah?"

"Go light on the cologne, 'kay? I was sneezing blood last time we made the rounds."

Hugh's chuckle was deep and rich like chocolate. Like what he'd tasted of chocolate, anyhow.

"Au naturel, but fresh soap. They won't be able to keep their hands off me."

"Let's be discreet, though."

"Always."

"In service."

"In service."

CHAPTER 22

Downtown Healdsburg was balmy at night this time of year, though it was tickling winter on this particular late fall evening. Scores of tourists came too late for crush, when the newly picked fruit was placed in it's first fermentation. But they were just in time for some early barrel tasting. Outsiders liked to demonstrate their ignorance, he thought. While they were imbibing wine and getting high, the dark coven hordes were feasting off the lifeblood of the tourist population, then glamouring them to forget their night of wild decadence The result was that the strangers would go back home and say they had a great time, but would remember little of it.

It was the same anywhere in the world where the innocent would gather and the dark creatures would come to host off them in their altered and unsuspecting state. Lionel had never before asked a man if he could sleep with his new young wife, but his brother had on numerous occasions. Hugh said he liked to watch the anger of the husband for a few seconds before he sent out the glam and put him in a most agreeable state.

"Sure, show her a good time," they would say. Hugh would promise to do his best. He would promise the husband he'd send his wife back well trained to be a most avid sexual partner. And that is usually what happened. So, Hugh never thought he was doing anything wrong. He was, in fact, enhancing the human sexual experience, in his opinion.

But it gave Lionel problems. "Just because they don't remember doesn't mean it's right," he'd argued with his brother. It was the old tree-in-the-forest-with-no-one-to-hear-it-fall-argument. In Lionel's mind, the tree fell whether or not anyone was around to hear it. If a woman was violated and forced to go outside of her marriage vows, it mattered little that she didn't remember it afterwards. It was never right. Lionel would never take a woman who didn't fully consent and wasn't free to choose.

Young Maria Monteleone, Marcus and Paolo's mother, had gotten dangerously close to Lionel on several occasions in their young adult years, after he'd been recently turned. He used to watch her close the drapes and ask him if he was comfortable on the few occasions he'd had to be alone with her, as her security detail. She knew he had to sleep during long sunny days, and had tried to make him feel at ease with her. But there was a dark side that had wanted to reach up and take hold of this woman and claim her for himself.

Thoughts. Just thoughts. He hoped his actions never revealed his inner feelings, but somehow he knew she did suspect his loyalty was more than just duty and honor. It was as close to a love as he'd ever experienced, though one-sided. That was more than three hundred years ago, and nothing had tarnished the bright memory of that lady since, even as he watched her age and wither, as he tended to her physical needs in the end, after the death of her husband, carrying her to the garden pools at midnight or pushing her around in the wheelchair by starlight. They'd watch the moon set together. She used to love the stars, and it was on one starry night that she died of natural causes, as a human. He'd made a solemn vow to protect her children throughout eternity. He intended to keep that promise.

Unlike the Goldens, dark vampires had no Council that ruled on disputes. Dark covens were created by leaders who risked their immortal lives to grow in power and stature, and their culture became, in a strange Darwinian fashion, a survivor of the fittest society, ruled by the darkest covens and the wars they could generate. Outside of a coven supreme leader, there wasn't anyone in authority, unlike the Golden vampire community with its Council.

So where, exactly, did that leave him and his brothers?

Employed. They had nearly unlimited funds, but nowhere to spend it. Sexual powers and desires that would rival the Goldens, but no time to use them. They existed to protect the families of what Lionel had begun to believe was the master race of vampires. He'd never thought about whether or not it was a fair tradeoff. He'd never considered any other line of work.

Lionel was relaxed but wary as he strode down the wet streets of the little winery town. The heels of his scuffed Doc Martens pounded along the sidewalk, causing storefront glass to wobble. He made a point to go lighter, so as not to draw attention to his preternatural powers. He wanted to spend the evening without drawing undue attention, if he could.

His standard uniform was black leather jacket with the myriad of zippered pockets, his tight black Levis with more pockets, and the lace-up boots with the steel toes he wore everywhere except for a tuxedo affair. Since those only came along a couple of times a century, he still had a pair of pumps he'd bought back in the 1800's made from pressed alligator—an illegal substance in today's world—which were perfect and drew little attention.

PRESS was full of people tonight. The first thing that struck him was the giddy laughter coming from the bar and dark corners of the place, even though the lighting was darker than usual. It wasn't the romantic quiet he usually found at a hook-up place. There were groups of people everywhere. Things were being said indiscreetly. Boundaries were being pushed. He was hit with glamour from all directions, indicating the dark forces were very present.

Perfect. Just what you wanted, right?

He felt his brother's words coming from his right and he turned to find Hugh toasting him with a dark red glass of what was probably Meritage, his favorite blend of three wines, which matched his sexual tastes to a T.

That it is, brother. "You are eager tonight, Huge," Lionel said as he took his seat in front of him and watched his brother's features by light of the little votive candle on the shiny laminate tabletop.

"As ever." Hugh nodded to a couple of new lovelies who had just walked into the den of sins, eyes as wide and blue-green as the ocean. Lionel knew they had no idea what was in store for them. They were expensively dressed, and obviously not aware of what a rough crowd they'd walked in on.

Hugh apologized to him, and stood, then walked over to the two mortal girls and invited them to their table. They had to crane their necks to look up into their host's face, and then pulled a look around him to see Lionel sitting at the table. He nodded to them, and the redhead smiled and started walking right toward him. That left Hugh with the brunette, and Lionel knew that would be just fine.

The redhead's light pink skin and fresh scent pounded a flush to Lionel's groin area and his pants became unbearably tight. Then she touched his shoulder, balancing herself on him while she tried to sit down gracefully in spite of an impossibly short skirt and four-inch heels with laces that came to her knees. The dark shadow between her thighs made Lionel's fangs ache, but he pressed them back up and swallowed. He'd surely bite himself if he couldn't have her, and very soon.

But then he remembered himself and his mission. He needed to gather information about the dark hordes lounging here this evening, looking for recreation and perhaps willing to slip their guard a bit. He chuckled as the redhead removed her jacket to reveal an exquisite set of breasts that all but shouted his name, and this time his fangs dropped properly low and would not behave.

Did she see?

He send a little glam her way just as Hugh and the other girl slid past her shoulders and took a place next to each other on the bench seat across from him.

Hugh was having great fun watching him, Lionel could tell. Not that his brother hadn't taken the time to adequately appreciate the redhead's mammary glands.

Would be a shame to have a dark toddler suck those beautiful orbs and deform them, brother. Not that you were thinking along those lines, Hugh sent out to him.

Not possible, Huge. You know that.

No? With the powerful cum you're going to lay inside her, who knows what could happen? I know you can see what she'd look like.

Keep your eyes on your own plate, brother, Lionel answered.

You suggested sharing…

Lionel squinted a dark glare at Hugh, who sat back, and draped his arm around the brunette. Her impossibly red lips parted and a whole new set of visions flooded Lionel's head.

Hugh chuckled, raised his glass to his brother, and then motioned for a cocktail waitress. The redhead touched her bare thigh against Lionel's, and through the jeans he felt the intentional caress of a mortal woman who had come to the bar to find sex. Well, he'd have to oblige, but not until his need for information was satisfied. Then he could satisfy himself with the knowledge of what she had barely covered up so with her panties. The knowledge of what it would feel like to slip in and out of her, what the taste of her blood would be as she moaned his name. He didn't need to drink wine to get high. He'd get it from her.

The cocktail waitress went off in search of a very expensive bottle of Ravenswood Meritage, mumbling something about having to go downstairs to the cave storage to look for it. Lionel could tell Hugh had glamoured her too. Hugh had a fondness for taking his mortal conquests in wine caves and cool refrigerated private collections.

Lionel adjusted his jacket and the blue-green-eyed beauty on his right smiled as she appraised the leather and what lay underneath. "Can I help you with your jacket? You look hot."

Her scent came to him like a blast furnace, along with the double meaning. It was good to be coveted, he thought. Nice that it happened without him having to expend an ounce of glam on her, too. Totally willing.

"Sure," he said, adjusting his fangs before breaking a smile. She'd probably think he was trying not to smile, but he didn't want to scare her, until it was time to do so. Just a little scare before the bite. Before the rapture of what it would feel like as he breathed into her ear, whispered incantations and took her. "But mind your hands. I have vera vera sensitive skin," he added in a mock accent.

"Oh, I hope so," she gushed. Her tiny pink fingers traveled quickly over his pecs, and tugged at the thick collar of the jacket, pulling it off his shoulders. He leaned forward, his face close to hers, allowing his dark hair to brush against her cheek, and felt her body shudder in response. She finished removing the heavy jacket and let it drape behind him on the chair. "Sorry, it's very heavy, and a little too heavy for me. I'm afraid I've made a bit of a mess."

You have no idea. He had practically come in his pants, but willed himself some control. He nodded, slowly perusing her chest while she watched him do it. "I don't mind. I'm enjoying whatever your hands can do, and I can see you are skilled."

The girl blushed. Had he glammed her? If she caught a little breath from him, it wasn't intentional. He loved that his proximity made her tingle, blush, feel self-conscious. It's what he loved most about mortal women. He never liked women that threw themselves at him. Her combination of subtlety and grace charmed him, and he allowed it to be so. Even fantasized she could glamour him.

Lionel broke the tension by looking over at his brother. Hugh had his tongue down the brunette's throat and had already a hand under the table, snaking up her red knit dress. He would be no use tonight, Lionel thought. He could feel his brother sending sexual fantasies into the lady's consciousness, and could hear her slight moan in response.

So far so good. Lionel scanned the room just before the waitress returned with the bottle of wine Hugh had selected. She frowned when Hugh didn't acknowledge it, being otherwise occupied.

"Thank you," Lionel said to the waitress as he pressed a one hundred dollar bill into her palm. This got her attention.

"Oh, thank you so much. Let me know if you need anything else?" Her smile was brave, but Lionel could see she fancied his brother, as most mortal women did.

Lionel removed the cork and slowly poured the wine while tipping the glass, so that the deep burgundy substance rolled back in a wave that resembled thick blood. The aroma was excellent, but he put the glass to his nose anyway the way humans did when savoring a nice bouquet. He closed his eyes as he swirled the liquid over his palate, wishing it were the feel and taste of the redhead's lovely life force.

There will be time enough for that.

"You like?" He said to her. She had been watching his Adam's apple, almost like a vamp female. But her scent told him she clearly wasn't.

"Yes, I like." She looked him straight in the eyes. He could feel her saying words, although unclear, like there was a filter between them, but part of the telepathy was working. *Take me,* she was saying.

"Good." He tipped the glass to her lips. She closed her eyes and mirrored his tasting actions, swirling the liquid over her tongue. She licked her lips and coated them with the fermented elixir.

It was totally spontaneous. With her eyes still closed, he covered her mouth with his and she parted quickly and allowed him access. She sucked at his lips as he did the same. She was lovely, and just what he needed. He brought his hand to the back of her head and sifted through her long locks. She was intoxicating to him.

"More wine?" he asked as they parted and stared into each other's eyes.

"Please." It meant more than the wine.

"Your wish is my command." They both smiled.

He was suddenly aware of motion coming from his left. The room had taken on an agitated air. He heard a chair crash and something very large hit the floor.

Lionel saw that his brother had surfaced from his erotic reverie and had noticed the same thing. A large enforcer for one of the dark coven lords had been thrown on the floor. He was the lord's executioner, and Lionel had always thought the man had been brought to modern times from the sixteen hundreds, where he no doubt worked as an executioner in a dungeon before turning. He was legendary for his torture methods. The fact that he was in obvious pain concerned Lionel.

Both brothers stood, as did most the non-mortal males in the bar. Several couples made it discreetly out the entrance into the night air. A wall of males began to form in a circle around the two fighting vamps.

The challenging vamp was Rory Monteleone, Marcus and Paolo's young nephew, who had just undergone the change. The struggle on the floor was between a Golden and dark vamp. Last Lionel knew, Rory was attending school in France, but his family lived in Tuscany. He wasn't sure Marcus or Paolo even knew he was in California.

Lionel was in a quandary. Hugh was ready to jump in, though it might cost him his night of sex.

Hold it, brother. Not now. Observe first. Lionel was satisfied to see that although Hugh had made fists with his hands, his giant brother inhaled and slumped his shoulders in resignation. He knew it was hard for his brother to control his urge for a good, hot fight.

The large dark vamp hit the back wall this time. Rory appeared to have gotten the better of him, having used some new moves he must have learned recently. He acted without hesitation, and anticipated the large giant's moves. No doubt the Executioner wasn't used to working out, nor felt any need to.

Both girls had scooted their chairs together and were clearly distressed. Lionel let his fingers lace through the redhead's hair and patted her head to reassure her.

Lionel watched the two sparring vamps who were making the whole block rumble, until the dark one suddenly straightened up to attention and turned at the arrival of another dark vamp, dressed all in black. Lionel remembered hearing a motorcycle revving up outside when the door had opened, and he knew this was probably Dag Nielsen, the new Coven Supreme Leader, though he couldn't see his face.

He wanted to ask Hugh mentally what Dag was doing here, but he didn't want to risk the uncloaking that could create. If he focused on it, Dag would realize who he was.

"Rory, my friend," Dag said as he grabbed the young Golden's shoulder and wrenched him around and back into the crowd of his friends. "You'd do well to leave California to our kind. We don't need you stirring up trouble."

Rory spat out blood and glared back at Dag. He looked from face to face, and Lionel could tell the Golden vamp was assessing who would be for him and who would be against him. The executioner was clearly taking directions from Dag. Hugh hung a worried look back as Lionel sought to ask a question without raising it mentally. What in the hell was happening? Had Dag been consolidating his ranks by eliminating another coven leader and adopting his Executioner?

The two brothers were careful, but Lionel could see Hugh gently nodding, biting his lip.

Rory took a swig of beer, straightening himself to address Dag. "I hold him personally responsible for the death of my little brother," he said.

This was news to Lionel. Had Morgan, Rory's ten-year-old mortal brother, been killed at the hands of this dark vamp? It made his stomach seethe, and he could feel Hugh wanting to step closer and get right in the middle of the fray. Loyalty and honor made Hugh spread his chest and take a deep breath.

Not now, Lionel quickly blurted out with mental energy. Dag immediately turned and looked over the faces in the crowd. The Jett brothers focused on Rory and turned off their minds. Their training was to go into focus on some detail of someone or something they hadn't noticed before, and that would mask them.

Through their peripheral vision, they saw that Dag appeared to stop searching for the thought source and returned to the two enemies before him.

"Rory, that has yet to be proven. But I think you need to understand you are way outnumbered here in California. And it's getting more so. You run home to mama, and tell her I send my love," Dag snickered in triumph.

Rory started to bolt toward the dark coven leader at the insult to his beautiful mother, Daria, but was held back by a cadre of dark security forces, who hauled him out of the bar.

Dag breathed in the agitation and smiled. It was like he got energy from the strife and Lionel could feel the power surging in the other man's veins. But that masked a probe he could feel like barbs in a wire fence. He wasn't going to fall for it. He resisted nothing, allowed the barbs to mentally scrape his flesh and did not flinch. He hoped his brother did the same, as they both sat down.

The one thing he would not do was look directly at Dag; otherwise the safety of their anonymity would be shattered. He pulled the redhead to his lap and laid down a kiss so intense she nearly fainted. Her arms were wrapped around his neck, her fingers making luscious circles through the dark curls of his scalp. He wished she would pull his hair a little, and she did.

He drew his head back and looked at the dizzy expression she wore. The woman was a walking, talking sex doll, and he planned to take his time learning every inch of her. He felt the dark coven leader swish by him on his way outside. The executioner was on his heels.

A few stilted minutes later the room returned to its party atmosphere. The music resumed, but the laughter was careful. The reckless abandon of the last hour was clearly altered. Lionel felt a grip on his upper arm.

"Let's get out of here, brother," Hugh said.

"Brothers? You two are brothers?" the redhead said.

Lionel smiled and nodded, focused on her lips. He'd caused a tiny cut and there was a drop of blood near the corner of her mouth he wanted to suck dry.

"We're sisters!" she said, her breasts giggling like they were bursting to break out in song.

"Perfect."

It was all he could think to say.

CHAPTER 23

Cara was anxious to return to poring over the old book she'd recently acquired from the bookseller in Prague. As she pried open the thick green leather, the letter she'd seen before but never read fell from the interior. The cream-colored envelope had a distinctive letter "M" embossed on the upper left corner. As she noted before, it did appear to be addressed to an A. Fraser of Edinburgh.

Her fingers smoothed over the ripped surface of the flap on the back where a red seal had been broken. The relief pattern in the fragile sealing wax was that of a Medusa-like face with lips that drew together as if mouthing the letter "O." Cara held it closer to her and detected a faint lemony-camphor wax scent as she examined the puffy checks of the image, and realized the face was caught in the act of blowing something in the reader's direction.

Strange.

Her fingers shook with anticipation as she removed the single sheet from the envelope and began reading the old black script.

Dear Brother Ignatius,

I fear I must warn you of something that has come to light recently. I believe you have purchased a book, specifically The Book of Spawn, as it is known. This book has been illegally sold from our family library, and is of great personal value to us, and is the final book of a series of volumes. My wife and I are worried sick about it, fearing it might have fallen into black hands.

My dear Brother, your calling to God on high has no doubt acquainted you with the black arts and those who practice them. They would use these sacred texts which have been handed down from generation to generation amongst clergy trained to contain and dampen the effects of these black arts. In the wrong hands, the book could prove to be lethal, not only to the possessor, but to those who would cause our society harm.

I must implore you to return the tome to my estate in Tuscany immediately. You will be compensated handsomely, and will be free from prosecution, I assure you.

As a further warning, I need to inform you that the person who sold you the book has met a most disagreeable end, and not by my hand, or that of any of my family. I believe there are other dark forces at work who will stop at nothing to make sure they have full possession of this book.

You will be doing your race and the future of mankind a great service by returning the book to me as soon as humanly possible I would be happy to entertain you at my estate as well as make a sizeable donation to the church, or to any one person or organization you choose.

Again, this is not a matter of money. It is a matter of life and death. And you, my dear Brother, are in grave danger until you divest yourself of this book.

Ever yours,
The—

Cara couldn't make out the signature, except for the fact that it was heavily inscribed in an artistic scrawl. The black letters bounced across the page in front of her, appearing to be breathing. Under the signature line was scripted the date *14 February 1710.*

She closed the letter in half again and slipped it inside the envelope. She was going to put it back into the book, but thought better of it. She added the book to the false bottom compartment of the old desk in her living room. The letter she slipped under the floral drawer liner of the underwear compartment in her bedroom dresser.

She was distressed by this new bit of information, and had a twinge of regret that she'd been so preoccupied with the party and meeting the mysterious Paolo that she hadn't taken time to study the Fraser book. She would have found the letter much sooner, in time to reconsider Johnny's field trip to

Berkeley on her behalf. She became concerned for his safety and decided she needed to hear from him. She called his cell phone.

"And here I thought you'd perhaps had second thoughts about spending the night with me," Johnny said with a chuckle.

"You're persistent. I'll give you that."

"Well, I'll take whatever I can get." He turned down his radio and continued. "I was given the name of an occult bookstore owner in San Francisco, although it was too late to call. Will do so tomorrow."

"What did the research assistant say about the book?" Cara asked.

"Said the book you're looking for is called *The Book of Spawn*, but he doubted it really exists. Like pieces of the true cross. Urban legend."

"Ah." Cara hesitated to tell Johnny about the letter she'd found. "When did this book last appear, or did the assistant know?"

"There is some notation of it being recovered in the charred remains of an abbey that burned to the ground in early 1700's in a little village in Tuscany. The brothers there poured over it, tried to restore it, and spend some time cataloguing it. In the end, it seemed to have disappeared until your friend Alasdair Fraser started digging around. Cara, he may have found it."

"Interesting. Is that what the assistant said?"

"He said Fraser was known for his braggadocio. Lots of exaggeration, and who knows what. Up until his death. It was pegged a suicide, but we know the guy just disappeared, along with much of his research."

"Yes, and we know there was a big book burning after he was declared legally dead."

"True."

"Anything else?"

"The assistant seemed to think the bookseller in Prague would be your link, unless the San Francisco bookstore owner, who he says specializes in witchcraft and vampire books, and has one of the most extensive collection of rare books in the world, knows where it is. He thought it even possible the bookstore owner himself might have it, or know where it is."

"Good. That's a great lead, Johnny. Maybe you and I will have to go there sometime soon."

"It would be fun. I'd like that."

"Good. Well, we'll plan it, then."

"Can I ask you something?" Johnny's voice had lowered an octave.

"Sure."

"You talk to your mystery man?"

Cara quivered at the thought of *her* mystery man, and what they had done this afternoon. The way his kisses scorched her flesh. The way his tongue had its way with her private parts...

"Cara? You still there?"

She wondered what she should say. What was wise? Paolo Monteleone was her own private dream, a fantasy she wasn't sure she should even be having. He was dangerous, but his presence demanded consort with her psyche.

She sighed and resigned herself to the fact that she would never be able to keep the secret she hoped she could. Just containing the ripeness of the facts would send her into frenzy. "I had lunch with him today. Right when you called, as a matter of fact."

"I see. I thought about you. For some reason, I was worried. Are you all right? Are you with him now?" The last question he whispered as if he'd been seated next to her, instead of on the other end of the phone. As if Paolo could hear him ask the words.

That was a good question. She somehow felt *with* Paolo Monteleone, even though she had requested, and been granted, her leave. She did not expect to see him again. Not if she could help herself.

"We had lunch. He showed me a little of his family estate in Healdsburg. I had supper with his brother and sister-in-law and his son."

"Son? He's married?"

"No. His wife has passed."

"Ah, dark widower, then. Mysterious. Did he kill her?"

"Johnny, I'm going to stop talking about this if you don't behave."

"Couldn't help it."

"Yes, you can. You can do a lot better. We had a nice supper and then he returned me quite safely to my home, where I am right now, Johnny. No worries. I'm quite safe, and alone."

"And in need of company?"

She paused long enough to briefly think about what she would have con-sidered just a couple of days ago. But not now.

"No. I'm sorry, Johnny. We are not going to have that kind of relationship. We work together. And right now, my work comes first."

She was so close to uncovering the mystery and the myth of the sacred joining, she felt as excited as she had on her first day of school when she was five. She knew her theory of the union between the God of Love, Jamal, and his queen consort had something to do with sexual liaisons, and the mixture of bloodlines.

"I get it. But if I find you the book, you will be sufficiently grateful, right?" he asked.

Cara let a tiny laugh bubble up "Very. But don't pin your hopes on it meaning a night of sex. The book might turn out to be the directions for collecting data on birth control in the third century instead of some divine coupling treatise."

"Yes, boss. I will be your lackey. Your yard dog. But I'm going to exact a price if I find it."

"I'm sure you will. But let's not worry until we find it, okay, Johnny?"

"Yes, ma'am. I'm nearly home. See you in the morning, teach?"

"Most definitely." She was about to sign off when she had another thought. "Johnny, why don't you leave a message for the bookstore owner tonight? Then perhaps he'll call you tomorrow while we're in class, or early before he opens."

"Good idea."

Johnny hung up.

It had been an exhausting day. Cara wanted another hot bath, but hesi-tated. She'd been enjoying the faint scent of his flesh on her skin. Even the backs of her hands where he had kissed her smelled of him. The side of her neck, where she could swear he had bitten her, was sensitive to touch. Laying her fingers there, she could feel her pulse flow strong and steady. The vein in her neck seemed to press against the fingers she held lightly in place.

She felt something cold at her neck and turned around. No one was there. She walked to the bathroom and tuned on the bath water, sprinkling lavender salts and bubble bath generously into the swirling hot water. With steam ris-ing beside her, she examined her face in the mirror. She closed her eyes and removed her top. She removed her bra and felt her hardened nipples under the tips of her fingers as they squeezed and kneaded the soft skin of her breasts. She thought perhaps there was a second set of hands helping her along in the process, helping her slip down her skirt and panties until she stood naked.

Something warm between her legs seemed to vibrate, a gentle sensation and she began to orgasm, imagining him tasting her there, lapping and nibbling on the lips of her labia. But when she opened her eyes, there was no one near her, no one appeared behind her in the mirror. Swinging her arms out, she turned and could neither feel nor see anyone standing in her bathroom.

The water continued to pour into the lavender scented bubbles, calling her.

She stepped into the tub and then sat, keeping her knees to her chest until she got used to the heat. She shut off the water and relaxed, leaning back into the tub and closing her eyes.

That's when she heard his words faintly caressing her face as if he was suspended above her.

"Mi amore."

Her eyes flashed open, but no one was there. Cutting across the light purple bubbles and pungent floral scent was the smell of fresh-picked lemons.

The same scent she'd found on the sealing wax.

Paolo had been surprised his whisper traveled to her. Although he was clear across the valley from Cara's home, he could see her in his mind. He saw the beautiful flesh he had tasted, the tapered ends of her fingers as he felt what she felt, those rich pillows of flesh that were her ample bosom. He knew what it tasted like to be between her legs, and his mouth watered as his fangs dropped. He'd been heartbroken when she slipped into the water where her scent would be buried in the lavender.

He'd conjured her, rubbing her vision all over the erection he felt in his pants and he'd said it—"Mi amore,"—more as a need than a prayer. And he saw her react in his dream. She'd *heard* him. He could see it on her face.

"Can you love me, Carabella?" he whispered. He watched as she turned around in the tub and checked the wall behind her. She was looking for him. She rose to her knees. The delicious shape of her shoulders, narrowing at her waist, and the soap bubbles slipping down her back to the upper reaches of her bottom. He was tantalized. With her hair up atop her head she turned again and looked right at him, except he knew she really didn't see him. But she felt him spying on her.

And the lovely object of his desire wasn't afraid.

Thank the God of vampires.

Still on her knees, she inserted a finger between her legs, arching backwards.

"Give me your pleasure, Carabella," he whispered, as he stroked himself. His cock had gotten rock hard and was seeking freedom. He felt her shudder just as if he was deep inside her. "You feel me? You feel my hardness? You feel my seed wanting to find solace in your folds?

He heard her moan, "Yes. Mi amore."

Could it be? Could she hear him, feel him when he wasn't there? What was this connection?

"Deeper, I want you deeper," she said.

Paolo grasped the arms of the chair in his bedroom, then hastily unfastened his pants, peeling them off his thighs and letting his penis leap out unbridled. "Need to be inside you, Bella. Invite me in, please let me come inside you," he whispered.

And then he heard it.

"Yes. Come to me."

The summons took only a second and he had traced to her bedroom. He was in the tub with her, his shirt wet and clinging to his skin, but his cock had found her opening and he raised her knees up over his shoulders and, pulling her buttocks toward him with both his hands, forced her over him, sending him deep inside her.

She opened her eyes wide and saw him. Really saw him.

In a flash of energy, water was splashing everywhere as Cara struggled to get herself out of the tub, knocking bottles of bubble bath and crystals all around the granite ledge, some breaking on the floor. She then stepped on the broken glass and cried out as she began to hop, holding one bloody foot behind her as she ran for a pile of clothes on her bed.

Paolo stood up, at first unaware of how ridiculous he must look, with a wet white cotton shirt and nothing else, his cock drooping, his limbs covered in bubbles.

"Bella, please, love. Let me explain."

"Don't you fucking get near me you animal!" she screamed. She held a knitting needle in her right hand like a dagger.

"I can explain this to you. Please, let me do so."

"I don't want to hear anything from your mouth except the apology you'll give me after I've had you arrested."

"Don't you want to know what happened? Don't you want to know how I got here?"

She looked at him for a second, and he thought perhaps there was a chance she would allow herself a glimpse of the truth. But sadly, she was full of anger and fear. Her naked body shivered, but she seemed not to notice. There was no place where logic could take hold, he realized.

"You get out of my house this instant. I'm still calling the cops. I'll let you explain yourself to them."

"Cara, it isn't what you think. Honestly. Please."

"No? You sneak in and fuck me when I'm taking a bath. Violate me when I'm daydreaming. Did you slip something into my wine or something? I'll bet your creepy brother is on his way over here, too, and you'll both do me and laugh about it all the way home. That the way you rich playboys operate? Can't get girls the right way, so you have to drug them to get your jollies. Well, not with me, you cretin."

"Bel—"

"Get the hell out of here."

"Bella, you called me."

"I did nothing of the sort."

"Yes, you called me. I *traced* here. But you called me. I couldn't help but come."

"You lying son of a bitch. Get out!" she screamed. Paolo was worried someone would come inquiring, she was so loud. Soon her phone began to ring.

"I hope this is the cops that someone in my building called. If I had a gun I'd shoot out both your kneecaps."

"I'll go. But you need to know one thing."

"Just go."

"You need to know I am vampire."

"Just—what? What did you say?"

"I am a Golden vampire. An old race. Yes, Carabella, vampires do exist. There are many of us—"

The phone stopped ringing abruptly, like someone had ripped it out of the wall. Paolo wondered if his powers had done this.

"Shut up with your lies," she said.

"It's the truth. Think about it. One moment you were daydreaming, then you called my name, asked me to come, and I did. You wanted me inside you. I obliged, I am sorry to say." Paolo noticed his member had begun to arch up again at the talk about coming and obliging. In a horrible twist of fate, Cara glanced back at his groin. Her frown and look of utter disgust broke his heart.

"Who do you think I am, some bimbo you have to give some fantastical explanation to so you can get laid? I'm not falling for it. Or, are you one of those who get off on violence. Well, if you want violence—"

She stepped towards him, holding the knitting needle high above her head, ready to strike. He traced to her side so fast she looked everywhere in front but didn't suspect he'd made it all the way around her. He grabbed the knitting needle and tossed it out of the bedroom and down the hallway. His arms encircled hers as he held her in place, covering her back with his chest, making her immobile. He whispered into her ear, with a trace of glamour.

"I love you. I would never hurt you, mi amore."

He could feel the softness of her limbs, the warmth in her heart he had touched, but then her natural human instincts kicked in and she went rigid with fear again. It was no use, he realized.

"You are an animal. Get your filthy hands off me or I'll scream and alert the whole building."

Paolo traced back in front of her, standing now longer than an arm's length away. "Enough," he said. "In time, you will have questions. When you do, I would be happy to answer them."

Cara started to shake. Paolo reached for a large bath towel and threw it toward her so she could cover up, which she quickly did. He found another towel for himself and wrapped it around his waist. He felt completely ridiculous in his sopping shirt, wrapped in a light yellow-colored bath sheet, dripping wet, naked and barefoot.

"I'll return the towel tomorrow," he mumbled, staring at the wet bedroom floor.

"Keep it. I never want to see you again."

Paolo loved the stern fixture of her jaw, lips slammed shut together, the determined stare as she tried to be brave. He knew she'd have a problem with this next part, but he couldn't help himself. He broke a wide grin, and before she could react, he traced home.

CHAPTER 24

No way this happened in my bedroom. No fucking way.
Cara was still shaking as she looked at the bamboo floor where he'd just been standing. A puddle of bubbly water quivered and began to fill in two small dry patches where his feet had been. Just five seconds ago. He'd been standing there, wrapped in her bath sheet with that smirk, that satisfied smile on his face.

Is it evil that I am still attracted to this—man?

But he wasn't a man, was he? She walked over to the puddles he'd left behind, as if they held some clue. She dropped to her knees and hesitated before she wiped it up with her towel. His towel's mate. The towel he said he'd return and she said, "don't bother." She didn't care about the damned thing. She cared about the male she'd spent the afternoon and early evening with, shared a bubble bath with. The male she allowed to violate her again.

'I am vampire,' he'd said. *'Vampires exist. There are lots of them.'*

He was completely delusional. Or was she? It didn't make any sense. None of it. She lassoed her mind to focus on him, searching to see if the connection was still intact.

Are you there? No! Don't answer that. Don't contact me unless I call you.

A tiny flame inside her belly made her insides glow, and she had her answer. Yes, he was still there, and he could hear her.

Now what do I do? Don't answer that, she said to him across time and space. *It's a question I have to answer for myself.*

She waited. No answer. This was a good sign. She told herself it was a good sign.

Thank you, she told him mentally.

Always, mi amore, came the reply.

"No!" she screamed. "You can't do this to me," she said out loud to the room. She checked the ceiling, behind furniture, and in the closet. She let out the water in her tub and checked under the bed.

I am right here. At Marcus and Anne's home. In the guest bedroom.

Stop it, she answered. *Get out of my head. Go away and don't come back unless I call you. No exceptions. My rules. We go by my rules.*

There was no response.

Reassured he wouldn't interfere unless called, Cara began to focus on her own body. The shaking began again, like she was going through some kind of withdrawal. The stress and roller coaster of her emotions had made her very tired. She knew she needed sleep.

Cara put on a white satin nightie with a fuzzy lining to take the chill off her skin. She did have the fleeting thought about one way she could instantly warm up; she could have him in her bed and immediately the shaking would stop. But the craving would continue. Her memory of his hot kisses, the feel of his limbs against hers, his chest pressing against hers, the incantations he liked to whisper to her belly were becoming hard to ignore.

She turned off all the lights, but lit a lemony votive candle beside her bed.

Why?

Well, she knew why. She slipped between the smooth cotton sheets, lay back watching the fluttering circle of light from the candle as it projected onto the ceiling, and began to smell its scent filling the room. With heavy eyes, she drifted off to sleep, but not before she saw bonfires, old stone buildings, some of them ruined. Wet cobblestoned streets glowed in the moonlight. She could hear the clop clop of horses. She heard weeping; she saw the tear-streaked faces of beautiful women. Some were modern women, some in older dress, like a parade of characters throughout time. She saw Lucius picking apples on the top of a ladder in a sunny orchard, being steadied by strong masculine hands around the little boy's waist. Paolo's hands. She felt the trembling body of the boy as if she'd hugged him herself.

She sank into oblivion, grateful for her life.

And feeling oddly protected.

Paolo gazed out the opened window in his bedroom and watched over the nearly bare, leafless vineyard by moonlight. A spitting, raging fire in the fireplace had not sufficiently warmed him. His bones were cold, as if they'd been made of iron. He felt brooding, heavy.

He was both delighted and annoyed that she could still communicate with him. His emotions balanced on the edge of a sabre's blade. While it meant she wasn't dead to him, psychically, he also knew that there was no way he could predict her choice in outcome. If she chose to stay away—and she was strong-willed for a human woman, stronger than his wives had been—perhaps she could physically will herself to stay away from him forever. In time, perhaps she could learn this. They were not fated, after all. That horrible fact felt like the stake in his chest that the dark vamps dreaded.

He was losing her. He'd shown her his horrible, animal side when she summoned him and he had no choice but to obey that summons. Fuck her in a bathtub when all she wanted to do was have an erotic fantasy about him. He had no control. He felt despicable, like a dark vampire animal. Like his enemies. Was he becoming his enemy?

When Cara's natural human psyche took over, she would be dead to him, just as his three wives were. Perhaps that's what had made him think of them, and the pain of watching them age, and their eventual passing. He did not want to bury a fourth. Cara had a human life to live and Paolo refused to take that away from her.

He had been just as addicted to Maya and the fates of their kind as Cara was feeling about him. But Cara had a chance at freedom, whereas Paolo had none. He'd be forever caught between the mortal world he missed and the Golden vampire world he couldn't fully embrace. Which meant no happy household filled with lots of brothers and sisters for Lucius.

Lucius. The little boy would need a father who could wisely counsel him.

He'd made his wives comfortable, showering them with riches, with travel, with things to make them forget their empty wombs. But the emptiness, the grief was still there, after all the gifts and fantastic excursions to all the corners of the earth. And while he could heal many of their physical ailments, but he could not cheat death. All passed into the afterlife mortals go while he held them. While he prayed for their souls. While he grieved, again and again.

Paolo had begun to think it was his purpose in life to grieve. The God of vampires had put him on the planet to demonstrate to Golden vamps everywhere what not to do with their lives. Should he have tried to make a life with that half-witch mother of Lucius? Could that have been the right action he'd missed along the way?

The answer he came up with was always the same.

No.

With the coming war brewing, romantic love, at least for now, would have to take a back seat to the safety of his son, his brother's family, and the future of the Golden vampire race.

He sighed and hoped Cara would find restoration from her much-needed sleep. Sleep that would not come to him tonight. Though he tried to hold the tears back, he found himself weeping silently, looking at the stars exploding in the night sky, wishing for something he could never have. He wondered if the God of man was capable of taking pity on him as well.

He said his prayer for healing Cara's confusion and hurt. He said his prayer for the safety of his son. He asked for courage to do the right thing, and for peace to come flooding into his soul as he prepared for battle and for the uncertain future that awaited them all.

CHAPTER 25

Dag returned to his rented two-story flat, and found the little blonde waif waiting for him just the way he'd dreamt he would. She was naked, spread-eagled, and handcuffed by wrists and ankles to his iron bed frame. He had a burning desire to hurt and maim something, and it was the first time he was sorry he was about to fuck his brains out and perhaps kill the mortal woman. This, and this time only, it would have been nice to screw a female vamp so that she could heal and he could do it again later on. Fuck her to death again and again. After all, his needs came first, before that of any other living being, human, Golden or dark.

"Who did this to you?" he asked. Her eyes were dark, and he realized she had taken some drug.

"You did, master." Her throaty voice made him want to shove his cock into her mouth and make her choke on it. He traced next to her and felt the delicious ripple of fear that went like a lightning rod through her tender pink flesh. He liked surprising, scaring her.

"You altered yourself." He sniffed her, then licked one armpit, feeling the elixir of her sweat turn his dick hard as steel. It hung cold and heavy between his legs. He wanted her to feel how ripe he was for her.

"I asked permission of your houseboy."

"Houseboy? I don't have a houseboy."

"The one who opens your front door? I assumed he was your male plea-sure partner."

"Can it," He barked and took another lick, this time running his tongue down and over her left breast, over the knot of her nipple that went purple and welted under the sandpaper of his tongue. He could eat that breast, but the pain would distract her from coming, and he so much wanted her to come for him. "I don't fuck boys."

She smiled in that sweet innocent way that had hooked him the first time he'd seen her panhandling in front of Starbuck's.

"Not even their—"

"So you decided you liked it in the ass after all? Is that why you're back?"

"No. I'm back for your cock. I need to be filled with your will." Her eyes were having trouble focusing. She moved her head back on the pillow, jutted out her chin, which arched her back and put her breasts very close.

"Take me, if I am worthy, master."

"Did the 'houseboy' fuck you?"

"What if he did?"

"I would have to wash you. Or kill you. And then I'd kill him."

"If you wish me cleaner than I would otherwise make myself for you, you may wash me. But I have not had another man's cock inside me since the last time you gave me your blessing. I have fingered myself, though. Many times. Remembering—"She groaned into the pillow, exposing her lovely long neck. He could smell her arousal since her legs were wide apart for him.

He wanted to ram himself inside her so bad he felt like shredding his clothes and getting to it. But his phone rang. He swore and looked at the display.

Uncle Colin.

He stood, adjusting himself. She had focused on his package, which pulsed and ached inside his leather pants.

"Uncle?"

"I have good news about the book."

Hope began to grow in Dag's black heart and he momentarily forgot about the girl, until he began to smell her again. "I'm all ears," he said as he watched her struggle against the handcuffs. The pink folds of her labia made his fangs drop and his mouth water. His tongue slid across one sharp point and he tasted his own blood, sending him an erotic jolt.

"The bookseller's transaction records just came through. I told American Express I was his only surviving relative, explained the tragedy of his whole family, you know." Colin's voice trailed off. He continued, after taking a deep gulp of air. "The transaction paperwork and his seller ID you gave me helped."

"Let's not fuck with each other Uncle Colin. Tell me what you know."

"Well, the book was shipped to a post office box in Sonoma County, just north of here." Colin sounded pleased with himself.

"Ah. Very good. And to whom was it shipped?"

"Ah, let me see," Dag could hear the rustle of the slips of notes Colin had pasted all over the wall behind his desk. "Here it is. Carabella Sampson in Santa Rosa."

"They shipped a rare book to a post office box?"

"I suppose so. That way it requires a signature, I believe. Here is the box number. Perhaps you can get more information from the postal authorities."

Dag smirked at the thought. "Not likely. But I think a night visit is in order, and their customer service desk will be closed."

"Well, I wish you luck. Let me know if you need anything else."

"I appreciate that, Colin."

"If that is all, then—"

"Wait a minute. Did you tie up dark Vicky?"

Dag felt the pregnant pause on the other end of the phone. He could barely hear the response. "No."

"You're a lamb playing with a coyote. She'll scratch your eyes out and leave you for dead if you don't control her." Dag glanced at the blonde and gave her a wolfish grin, showing his fangs. Her eyes momentarily got huge and he felt his cock lurch. God, he wanted to fuck her till dawn, but now the book was calling to him.

"Please, Dag, she hasn't been home in a day. Over a day now. I had no opportunity."

Dag knew it was a lie. "Then I suppose I'll have to do it and show you how. You will bring her to me in a few nights, understood?"

"Dag, I don't think that is necessary—"

"Of course it's necessary. I'm going to show you how to control a woman. Make her come until she wishes for death." His upper lip twitched, as the blonde understood the meaning of his words. Tears began to stream down her cheeks as she gave him that soft, pitiful, waif-like look. It tore a hole in his heart, for some reason. And it made him damned mad at the same time. He didn't like anyone to show weakness. He wanted her to defy him so he could break her. So he could scare her to death. Then he'd decide if she could live. Her life was putty in his hands, and he wanted her to know it. Wait for it. Not know what the outcome would be.

"Uncle Colin?" he asked as he licked his lips and crawled onto the bed. "Yes?"

"Bring her by Friday night around eight. This will be a life-changing event. For both of you." Dag flipped the phone closed and tossed it onto the bear rug on the floor. "Where were we?"

She said nothing. Her tears did not stop in defiance. She bore her fear and pain like a mantle of gold. Her pride made her breasts swell. He sniffed the air, filled with the scent of her. "Shall I ravish you now? Or later?"

"You are going to kill me. What difference does it make?" Her tears had stopped. Her lower lip quivered as her moist lips framed the words.

Dag bent down and kissed her hard, forcing his tongue down her throat until she gagged. "Would you swallow my cock this way?"

"Please."

Dag was filled with the power of his dark passions. His phone rang again. "Fuck!" he shouted and was going to throw it against the wall until he noticed the display. His first lieutenant was trying to reach him.

"Rhys? This had better be important or I'm going to cut off your left big toe, which I understand might not seem like much of a punishment, considering the state of your toenail."

Rhys had a chuckle, and Dag found himself suddenly lighthearted as well. The delay in sexual satisfaction had become pleasurable all of a sudden.

"Supreme, we wanted to be sure we did the right thing by letting the girl into your chambers. She is no longer mortal. But she insisted you'd made her for your own pleasure, and had summoned her."

"Yes, I thought you rather would. You didn't mind sneaking a little something while you cuffed her to my bed?"

"We thought it best she be restrained so she wouldn't get into things. And we figured you wouldn't want us to wait by her side, watching her."

"You did well. Except for the drugs."

"Not my idea. It was hers."

Dag swiveled around and stared at her eyes looking back at him innocently. *She is such a liar. I'm going to be extra rough until she tells me more lies.*

Rhys chuckled again. The blonde raised her sex as high as she could. Her buttocks hung beneath her and quivered. He could hear the slick moisture between her legs.

"Hurry it up or I'm going to come in my pants. Anything else?"

"You sending us out on a mission tonight? I can get Rubin and we can go back and do Rory. Thought you might like that."

"Rory's mine. But you can get the executioner and call on the Librarian. He has a name and a post office box to look up in Santa Rosa. You could go do that. See if you can find the person who has the book. Colin will give you all the details."

"The Post Office will be closed, sir."

"Then open it. You do know how to do that, don't you?"

"Yessir. Will do."

"And Rhys, what did she take?"

"Don't know, sir. She brought it with her."

Dag signed off and turned off his phone. The next person to interrupt him would pay for it with his life. He'd come out when he was good and ready. He hoped to get drunk with lust, and the girl's blood. If she was lucky, and very good, he'd let her live.

CHAPTER 26

Cara awoke with a start and then realized she'd slept so soundly, probably in the same position all night long, that her body ached. Daylight had produced a pink blush on the blue-grey sky. Checking the time, she decided to get up early and prepare for a long day of classes and meeting with Johnny.

She smiled as she thought about her research assistant and his proposal the night before. Could she consider him a welcome distraction? Someone she could pass some pleasurable time with as she tried to rid herself of the vision of Paolo? And how awkward would it be if she experienced a wonderful evening of sex with someone else, knowing Paolo would also feel every ripple, shudder and her body's inner explosion?

Would she be able to let herself go, feel the joy of sex with any other man? Ever? Could she beg that he stay away, stay out of her head?

"I am vampire," he'd said. Incredible as that idea was, she could not trust herself right now to believe him. Even though all the evidence pointed to that undeniable fact. Maybe he could be some kind of psychic who could control her thoughts. Maybe he'd convinced himself he was a vampire and she was falling under his mental spell. That she might be able to wrap her mind around and believe.

She lathered herself with shower gel, enjoying the silky feeling of her own skin, letting her fingers slide over areas he'd kissed. Her nipples were taught and tender, her pulse boomed throughout her body as she remembered him beside her, inside her. He was, after all, the man of her dreams, but a vampire? *No way.*

Cara pushed the visions of him in the shower with her out of her head and concentrated on getting clean.

She hardly thought Paolo could be the sort to suck the lifeblood from unsuspecting females in the night, she decided as she toweled off. Besides, she'd been with him in the day, in the sunny afternoon. There were no ill effects, other than the craving she felt for him and his lovemaking, how he satisfied every sexual desire she'd ever had and a lot she'd never imagined by herself. Something just yesterday she'd have thought was heaven-sent.

She hung up her damp towel and looked at herself in the mirror.

I've had sex with a vampire? No. It wasn't true. There must be some other explanation for the things happening around her.

But how could she explain the sudden disappearance, right before her eyes, she wondered as she slipped on her black lace panties and matching bra. She brushed her hair, staring again into the mirror. Would he like the way she looked right now?

Stop this, she scolded herself. Cara tried to focus on the facts, the details of his disappearance. There had to be something she was missing.

Must be some trick. Some sleight of hand. But, she'd checked her room last night, and he simply hadn't been there. And yet she still heard him respond to her, telling her where he was after she questioned it. She knew if she asked him right now, he'd answer her. Should she try it again?

This is crazy.

Cara finished dressing. She had chosen a little black dress and patterned stockings with black pumps. She scrunched her hair up with a crystal-embedded black clip, and wore bright red lipstick.

My version of Elvira, she thought. Yes. He would love the way she looked. Only things missing were red fingernails, and she wouldn't go that far.

Paolo had watched the sun rise, sitting at the kitchen table by himself. He was filled with loneliness and regret. She hadn't called to him, although he'd stayed awake most of the night. He wished she had needed him in her bed. Maybe she *was* going to be able to live without him. He knew he was going to have to prepare himself to live without her. Question was, who would be stronger?

But then he felt her hands smooth down the black wool dress, over her breasts, her hips and her flat tummy. He closed his eyes and could feel the heat of her body as he imagined her standing in front of him, as he bent to kiss her lovely neck so nicely exposed for him. He imagined his palm sliding up under the black fabric to feel—no—to need to feel the softness of her flesh encased in black panties. She wore black for him today. His groin became granite.

Would he be able to concentrate on anything today except the thought of her? He decided he'd better learn to.

Marcus entered the kitchen in his boxers, bare-chested.

"Morning, brother," he said to Paolo.

"It is a beautiful morning. I watched it being born." Paolo tried to sound cheerful.

Marcus went to the coffee maker and poured himself a fresh cup Paolo had brewed. The smells of the Mocha Java blend swirled around the room as Paolo sensed his brother was hesitating to speak of something. Marcus joined him at the table and sipped the hot, black liquid.

"Got a disturbing call from Lionel Jett last night."

Paolo felt alarm spread up and down his spine as he sat up straight and focused on the handsome face of his older brother and the worry lines between his eyebrows.

"Oh? How so?"

"You know Rubin, the executioner?"

"I can hardly say I know him, but, yes, I've seen his despicable work. Don't tell me Lionel had to experience one of Rubin's trophies."

"Rubin was emasculated in front of a whole crowd of onlookers at Press. Not physically emasculated, mind you, but it appears he has a new master," Marcus' dark eyes focused on Paolo's coffee cup, avoiding his brother's questioning gaze.

"Who might that be?" Paolo knew it before his brother answered.

"Dag Nielsen."

Paolo looked out the kitchen window to the garden and bare-limbed orchard that spread down the hill. This was definitely not a good sign.

"Rory Monteleone confronted him about the death of young Thomas. Dag stopped the fight."

"What happened to his protection team?" Paolo wanted to know.

"They were there, but outnumbered by Rubin's men and some new dark vamps Lionel had never seen before. I think they were hoping the fight would just die on its own, but when Dag showed up, Lionel decided to stand down. He was with his brother, Huge."

Paolo nodded. "You sent him out?"

"Not exactly. Took it on his own."

"Where are they now?"

"I'm assuming they're sleeping, hopefully alone."

Paolo found light amusement in the fact that the Jett brothers were extremely attractive to human females and had never had trouble finding fleeting companionship without strings over the decades. Something he was unable to do.

Good for them.

"I have to tell you Lionel is worried. Very worried," Marcus continued. "It appears the numbers of darks are increasing at an alarming rate, almost like an army is being assembled here in California."

"Why here?" Paolo asked.

"Good question."

"So the executioner is now Dag's man. Hard to imagine Trevor Farnsworth would relinquish him," Paolo said.

"Which means Trevor Farnsworth is dead. As is Dag's former Coven Supreme Leader."

Paolo wondered how the other dark coven leaders were handling this turn of events. He suspected there could be an ally or two amongst them, but wasn't sure who he could trust.

"In case you're thinking of getting further involved, I forbid it, brother," Marcus said over the top of his coffee cup.

"I already am, Marcus. As long as I'm in your household here in California, if you are a target, I am certainly the secondary."

"Not true."

"Excuse me?" Paolo knew he wouldn't like what Marcus was going to say next.

"Brother, search your heart. Look at what they have been doing, picking a fight, luring out the younger Goldens. You know as well as I do that the real target is Lucius."

Paolo didn't want to agree, but he had to.

"Leave the research and covert stuff to us. I think Lionel was born for this kind of caper. Your primary responsibility is to your son, to see to it that nothing happens to him. Mine is to Anne and little Ian. I've asked Lionel to find us some human ex-special forces guards he can trust. We may need the protection both day and night now."

"So living in idyllic Sonoma County with heavily armed guards—will this be the kind of lifestyle you wanted, brother?" Paolo asked.

"I have no choice. Not until they come out in the open. I think this will become an all-out assault soon. Don't think we have much time. I've already notified the Council, and they are sending an ambassador.

Paolo knew this had not happened in more than a hundred years. Their species had enjoyed a relative peace with the mortal as well as the dark vampire world, allowing the Goldens to blend into human society and amass great wealth and power. But he knew nothing human could stop the dark forces looming in the distance.

Best keep my wits about me. Humans have gods they can pray to. Right now I can't be bothered with such drivel.

Cara parked her car in the employee lot. She was a half hour early for class, so decided to stop by her office to see if Johnny had thought to do the same. Oddly, she felt happy to get back into the routine of teaching, being of service to her students. It would give her delicious moments away from thoughts of—

The moment she opened the glass door to Montgomery Hall, she noticed that a small group of people had formed a semicircle outside her office door. Her pumps clacked down the shiny vinyl tiles of the otherwise deserted, wide hallway.

The circle parted and left just enough room for Cara to insert herself. She looked down at the floor, where everyone's eyes were focused. Seeping from under the locked door to her personal office was a puddle of thick, red blood. It was getting larger.

She dug in her coat pocket for her keys, setting down her computer. As she reached for the door handle, ready to insert a brass key into the lock she heard a shout from the opposite entrance to the hallway.

"Stop! Wait. Don't touch anything." Two uniformed policemen were running down the vinyl hallway, their equipment jangling on their leather utility belts. "I must ask you to step away—all of you," the heavyset older officer said, scanning the crowd and finally landing on Cara with a scowl. "You have the key to this office?" he said to her.

"Yes. It's my office."

"Any idea what's gone on in there? Who I might find on the other side of this door?" the officer said.

"The only other person who has a key, other than someone in Admin, is my research assistant, Johnny Davis." Cara stared at the blood and for a brief moment, thought she would lose her breakfast all over the policeman's shoes. She inhaled sharply and added, "I was to meet him here, or in the classroom this morning."

"He acting funny or out of sorts?" the officer asked.

"No. I talked to him last night. He seemed fine."

"Let's see your key," the other officer held out his hand. It was clad in a plastic glove. Cara deposited the keys in his palm, isolating the office key. The officer stepped wide to avoid the puddle of blood and knocked on the door while the other officer dispersed the crowd. Sirens were shrieking in the background. When there was no answer, he tried the handle and found it locked.

Cara felt strangely disconnected, and numb as the officer inserted the key into the lock and turned the handle. She watched the other officer with his gun drawn, holding it with both hands with mild detachment. As the door creaked open, the limp body of Johnny fell out into the hallway. His face was caught in a grimace, lips beginning to turn blue, his face ghastly white and not the tanned, healthy look Cara was used to. His head rolled at a weird angle, barely connected to his neck.

Someone had practically ripped Johnny's head from his torso. Cara's blood went ice cold. She couldn't stop herself from staring into the glassy blue-grey eyes of her once fun-loving assistant. It was as if she expected him to sit up and tell her he was playing a prank.

But this was no prank. Death stared back at her and for the first time in her life she was terrified, frozen in place, unable to do a thing about it.

A woman onlooker fainted and another started to scream. People began retching and racing through the hallway doors to the outside. More uniformed officers arrived and took control of the crowd. Cara remained transfixed. She slowly began to wonder if the person who had laid in wait for Johnny had intended her to be the target. She wondered how someone managed to get out of the office without leaving the door unlocked, since the door could only be locked from the inside without a key, almost as if someone could walk through walls.

Or transport.

"That's—that's Johnny, my assistant…" Cara heard her voice waver. Tears had started to collect in her eyes. The sickly smell of fresh blood singed her nostrils. She turned her face to the side and examined the inside of her office door.

"What is it?" one of the officers asked her.

"Someone must have a key. You can't walk out and have it lock behind you automatically. I had the locks changed because I was locking myself out all the time."

"Found a key here," one of the officers said as he searched Johnny's pockets.

"So I gotta ask you one more time, who else has a key?"

"The admin staff, and probably the college janitorial service. They have a whole crew."

The second officer stepped aside and spoke quietly into his shoulder microphone. Cara looked into the office after the light was turned on. Papers and books were scattered everywhere, some with their edges soaking up Johnny's lifeblood. Every drawer in her desk had been upended. All her shelves were wiped clean, the books nearly covering the entire floor of her tiny office. The telephone receiver was left off the hook. Even her trash appeared to have been searched and dumped on the desktop.

"Can you tell if anything obvious is missing?" one of the uniforms asked Cara.

She shook her head. "Impossible to tell. Who would do this?"

"Not a robbery, because it doesn't look like his wallet has been removed," one of the officers said from his kneeling position next to the body.

"I'd say, from the looks of it, someone was looking for something stored in a book or file somewhere. You got anything, a valuable document maybe, that someone would want?"

CHAPTER 27

Paolo felt the terror in Cara's heart. He saw the body in front of her just as if he was standing there. He had to work on himself not to trace to her side for protection. But he had given his word.

He'd gone back to the guest wing and was planning to take Lucius to school personally when he received the vision of Cara's office. The to-do list he had created was crumpled in his right hand.

"Father, I'm ready." Lucius ran into the room and gave him a hug. The boy's fresh mortal scent always made him feel lucky, and incredibly happy. But today, knowing there was probably a dark vamp on a killing spree, his need to protect his son weighed on him. It was suddenly urgent he talk with the Jett boys to make sure the daytime detail was in place. He wanted to personally interview every one of them.

"You've had your breakfast?" he said to Lucius' dark brown eyes. The boy's freckled nose scrunched up, and Paolo saw he'd forgotten to have anything to eat. "You want a hamburger and French fries and a strawberry shake on the way?"

"Could we?"

"Well, you could. But you know I don't care for the taste."

"I know." Lucius' palms lay flat against Paolo's cheeks. "You are what you are, and I am what I am."

It was one of those moments when Paolo was convinced the boy could not have been of his issue. The roles at this particular moment had been reversed, and suddenly he was student to his son, who was wise way beyond his years.

His need to protect his son was paramount. He knew that if he had to sacrifice himself to save Lucius, he would be doing his race a tremendous service. Paolo saw in the boy the future of the whole Golden vampire clan. He could feel the boy's destiny as surely as he could smell the blood of mortals.

Paolo felt ridiculous going through the fast food drive-through while driving Marcus's black Maserati, something Laurel and the other siblings back home in Tuscany would find odd. But this was Lucius's world, and it included drive-through, text messaging and cell phone games. He wanted the boy to have a normal upbringing, not living the gilded princeling days of the super-rich, which might distort his warm heart and avid mind. Lucius would be required to do great things in the future, Paolo thought. Time for being a king among Golden vampires would come soon enough. Now it was time to be a normal human boy.

They sat in the car while Lucius finished off his meal and wiped his hands and face with the moist towelettes he carried in his backpack. This also surprised Paolo.

"Where did you get these?" he asked as he held up the foil packet.

"Cook. She said using these would keep me from getting the flu."

"Ah." Paolo made a mental note to thank the cook, who was more a grandmother to the boy than his real grandmother, Aurora, that half-witch bitch mother of his fated female. Paolo found the reminder of the boy's mortal vulnerabilities touching.

He got out of the car and gave Lucius a brief hug so as not to embarrass him, and then watched him join several other friends. The cheerful gang of normal human boys ran together to their classroom just as the bell was ringing.

As he sat in his car, he felt another wave of Bella's despair. He'd seen Johnny's face and felt her mourn for him. It didn't make Paolo jealous. But he wished she would summon him. He could reach out and touch her with a message, but he'd given his word.

As he drove back to the Monteleone estate through downtown Healdsburg, he was struck with how normal the little town looked. Since it was a tourist Mecca, several large white busses were parked near the square. He pulled into a parking spot and went inside to get a cappuccino and hope he would feel Bella reaching out to him soon.

The screaming of the milk foaming machine was harsh, but not as harsh as the sound of sirens whizzing by. Perhaps there had been an accident on the freeway. Paolo's cell phone rang. It was Marcus.

"They've found Rory dead in an alleyway. Ripped the poor boy's head clean off."

Paolo knew Marcus was beside himself with grief. Since Rory was in California, and under Marcus' protection, this would be counted as a failure on their part, but would fall mostly on Marcus.

"I think the time for you to remain in California is limited, brother. You have to ask yourself if it is worth it."

"I'm not running from them. They won't defeat us."

"Maybe not us. Maybe we'll live for eternity, but what about our children, Marcus? Surely they don't have to pay the price."

"I'm taking measures."

"Simple when Ian is little, but I just dropped Lucius off at school. He'll be unprotected until I pick him up. I'm going daft with worry just thinking about it. As much as I hate to, I think I should bring him back to Tuscany, where we have the majority."

"That's your choice. What about the girl?"

"Sacrifice, brother. My primary goal is to keep you, your family and my son safe."

"She knows more than she should, Paolo. You perhaps should wipe her memory."

"That I can do." Paolo flinched inwardly about the difficulty of this task. He wasn't sure he could bear the look on her face when she saw him for what she would think was the first time. But it would be for her own protection. "There is other bad news, Marcus."

"Oh?"

"The girl's assistant was found dead this morning in her office at the University."

"Found dead?"

"From the sight of the face, I'm guessing he was drained. Neck ripped open and head ripped mostly off, though. Brutal. A dark executioner did this, I am positive."

"What's the scene like?"

"I haven't been over. Just what she saw, and she was scared brother. Almost catatonic. The office was ransacked." Paolo paused, and then said in a whisper, "We still have that gift, brother. I can feel her emotions, and hear her thoughts. Like a fating. And it's getting stronger."

"Is it a fating?"

"Sadly, it is not. Definitely not a fating. Although I have tried to tell myself it is. Wouldn't it be incredible if there was the possibility I could have two fated females?"

"Unbelievably lucky. But you say no."

"The physical attraction is there, no question. But not the animalistic, all-encompassing—"

"I get it."

Paolo had always felt guilty for bedding Marcus's long-time paramour. "This is different. The feelings I have for this mortal woman are growing. And with those feelings, the gifts are getting clearer and clearer."

"Interesting."

"And I have control, not that I don't want to be by her side, but I still have some control, not like with—"

"There has to be something of substance there. I'll consult with the Council next I am in contact. In the meantime, why don't you trace to her? Investigate the murder?"

"She hasn't summoned me, and I gave her my word."

Cara sat alone in the lecture hall, where her now-cancelled classes would have taken place, her head resting in her hands elbows dug into the black desk top. She gently rubbed her temples, and remembered how Paolo had done this, to ease her mind. She imagined his long fingers atop hers, imagined hearing his steady breathing and drawing in his spicy, lemony scent. She knew she could call him and he would be right there, in front of her. She knew she wasn't hiding anything from him by refusing to summon him because he knew what she was feeling. The ache she felt for him was growing.

You are still an addiction to me.

She was relieved that he left her alone. But was this smart? Somehow, she knew he had answers she needed.

The coroner and forensics team were done with the office, the body, and their questions for everyone who had been standing around the door, as well as the janitor, the school administration officials and several of her students who knew Johnny better than most. They stuck their heads into the amphitheater door and said their goodbyes. She had a tiny stack of their business cards in case she remembered or found something of interest.

She could not warm up, and a dull ache pounded in her thighs. Cara's bones were stone cold and she felt old. She wanted to be home in bed in her flannel pajamas, wrapped in the comforter her grandmother had made, with a cup of hot tea and a lemon slice on the side.

Lemons. Will I ever be able to smell lemons without—don't answer that.

The shock of the last few hours gave way as she finally allowed herself to grieve for Johnny. Warm tears streamed down her cheeks as she raised her head and stared at the sea of empty lecture chairs.

Why? Why Johnny? Had something happened at the dance she didn't notice? Did Johnny have some kind of secret life that she knew nothing about? Or, was it a random act?

'They're looking for something in a book, perhaps a book itself.' Perhaps it was time to show Paolo the book.

Should I be afraid of him? Who can I trust? He seemed like the only option available to her. Johnny's death left her feeling alone and unprotected in a world that suddenly felt very dangerous.

"Paolo?" She said to the room. "Are you there?"

I am.

I'm afraid. Johnny—

I have seen it through your eyes. You are in danger. Let me come to you.

I have a book I think you need to see.

Book?

Yes, I have located a book by Alasdair Fraser. And there is a letter in it. I think you should see it.

Yes. Cara, do not think about the book right now. Make no mention of it in your mind, either. Summon me so I can protect you. You are in danger, mi amore.

There it was again, that doorway to the unknown. He was asking her to believe in the fact that he was vampire and could be summoned. That perhaps someone else could read her thoughts. Did she really want proof of this?

Nothing can harm you if I am by your side. Alone you are vulnerable. He did sound urgent.

Okay. She remembered what she'd said in the bathtub, *Come to me, Paolo.*

And there he was, standing on the other side of the desk, all six foot something of him. Handsome, eyes ardent and studying her face, her neck, her upper torso, making her tingle and blush. He smiled as if he could feel what she felt inside.

Of course I can. It brings me unspeakable pleasure to do so.

Tears began to well up as her emotions exploded. It was too much for her to comprehend. Johnny was dead. Killed by some sinister person, probably a vampire, perhaps a vampire Paolo knew, which made it even worse. And there was an undeniable attraction to this tall male who could transport himself immediately from here to there, had fangs, and who had made her feel wonderful just yesterday afternoon—all afternoon, making her feel more alive than she had ever felt in her life. It was a strange combination of death and new beginnings.

I am at a crossroads.

You are, mi amore.

I am afraid.

You should be. There is a war brewing.

"Can you help me? Help me understand?" she asked him out loud.

I can, if you will trust me. He held his arms out to the sides, beckoning her to come to him. She had no choice but run to him, nestling her face in his chest, reveling in the feeling of his arms wrapped around her. Protecting her. Perhaps—something else too.

He held her face between his large palms. "Let me teach you about me and my kind. There isn't nearly enough time, and this isn't how I wanted to do it. But if you understand, I can teach you what I believe are some opportunities possible. Things neither of us ever dreamed could happen."

She placed her hands over his wrists and studied the strong face of the man she knew she had fallen deeply in love with. A man she had been searching for her whole life. Cara decided in that moment to embrace the new adventure like her life depended on it.

Because perhaps it did.

CHAPTER 28

The fluttering of warm wind all around Cara made her feel like she was floating in a cloud of butterflies. Pressed against Paolo's chest, as he held her there,
she laid her head to the side and listened to a heartbeat she hadn't known he had.
In a handful of seconds, the sensation stopped, the tracing was complete, and she
was standing in her bedroom, her arms up and about his neck.

She tipped her head back and willed him to bend his full red lips to cover
hers. It was delicious to moan into him, and feel the deep rumble of his chest
in response. He took everything she could give in the kiss, but she still needed
to give him more.

His fingers laced through the hair at the back of her head. He pulled, arching her face away from his, kissing the side of her neck. She pressed her lower
torso into his groin and felt his desire.

She needed him too. *Please,* she mentally sent him between kisses, now
becoming ravenously needy. She was starved for his ministrations.

Cara began to remove her blouse, watching as his eyes went to fire while
she removed her bra. He came to his knees and kissed each nipple tenderly.
She held his head, clutching at the loose curls, loving the feel of his mouth on
her sensitive flesh.

"You are a wonder, mi Carabella."

You awaken me.

He groaned and lifted her up, laying her tenderly on the bed. He removed
his clothes and then shimmied her skirt down her hips like tissue paper. Slowly

hooking her black lace panties with one long forefinger he slipped them easily down, the backs of his fingers smoothing over her thigh all the way to her ankles, and then off.

He parted her knees, tenderly easing two fingers inside her folds. She arched with the pleasure of his penetration, of the reassurance of what was going to happen between them in the coming moments.

"I've missed this," Cara said between sighs. She wanted to lose herself in the feel and scent of this man and forget the ugly scene from earlier this morning.

He twisted his head to the side, and with the lopsided smile curling up the corners of his smooth, full lips, said to her, "Bella, mi amore. It has only been one day. Already one day is too much for you?"

There it was, the honesty between them, though there was still so much she did not know about him. She was unafraid to show him how much she needed him to make love to her. "Yes. Already one day is too long without this." It was difficult to get the words out.

He covered her body with his, sliding his thighs beneath hers, lifting her bottom up off the bed with his hands and pausing at her opening. "It is the same for me, Carabella. I dream of this almost every waking moment."

He began to slide inside her, slowly. She lost herself in the dark pools of his eyes, the faint lemony scent of his chest covering her, making her feel safe and protected. Without speaking she was telling him how it felt, how her body ached to be possessed by him. He nodded and gently filled her to his hilt. Then he began to pump and drill deep inside her, pulling her chest up flat against him, pressing her breasts into the warmth of his hard body. She drew her arms up over his neck and he grabbed her underside, moving her up and down on his enormous shaft. His long, fluid strokes rocking her body back and forth on him made her insides explode.

She squeezed down on his girth until at last his spasms overtook him. He lunged deep inside her and held her buttocks in place so hard she thought perhaps she'd have welts.

I will kiss the pain away, if I've left a mark, he told her.

"I'll wear your mark with pride," she whispered. "I didn't want you to let me go."

I never will he said to her. "Mi amore," he whispered into her ear, kissing down the right side of her neck.

She knew he wanted to bite her. He was looking down, at the place where their bodies joined as their breathing hitched in tandem, as she admired his flat abdomen and the shadow that was their joining. She lifted his head, placing her palms under his jaw, and placed his forehead against hers. She relished the feeling of him between her legs, the rhythm of his breathing. His mouth was just out of reach, so she turned her head and mated his lips to hers, and then searched for the fangs inside with her tongue.

She allowed a pinprick from his sharp canine, and presented the drop of blood on her tongue to him, spreading it over his own. His breath became ragged, and labored like a runner. His cock inside her sprang to life and began to lurch. He rocked her body over his groin, burrowing deeper, in a circular motion.

"Take me, Paolo. Take me *your* way. I want to do this for you," she said.

At first he shook his head, but she held his face in her hands again and with firm resolve, nodded back, "Yes, I want you to take me in your way. Your custom."

"There is no custom for this. You are human and I am vampire."

"Please?" she begged.

"This is not wise, Carabella." He groaned as she clamped down on him again with her muscles.

"I need this. I need you to mate with me, Paolo, in the old way, the ancient way." She kissed the side of his neck and under his jawline. "The way of your ancestors," she whispered in his ear.

His eyes held questions. She was searching for some indication as to what he was thinking, but he had blocked his thoughts.

"Let me in, Paolo. Let me see what you don't want me to see."

He smiled. She could feel his will dissolving, and images started coming on strong. She saw herself naked across his big oak carved bed with the cream satin sheets. Torches lit the room and shadows on the heavy stone walls danced in the erotic rhythm of his heartbeat. Her arms were pinned above her head as he held her wrists with one hand.

You would take me to your bedroom?

That is my room in Tuscany. If I took you there, I would never let you go. Never, Carabella. He closed his eyes and the image was gone.

She traced his hairline with her forefinger, marveling at the tanned, smooth skin, the shiny dark hair and the dark, chocolate-brown eyes with lashes that made him look dangerous and demure at the same time. He'd told her he was naturally shy.

Do you blush when you recall what we've done? She asked as she kept her legs wrapped around his thighs, holding on with arms wrapped around his neck.

His warm smile told her everything she needed to know.

Take me now, Paolo. Here, on my bed. Take me and mark me and make me your own.

He bent to give her a brief kiss, then followed below her chin and then laid down a moist trail with his tongue, tracing over the vein pounding in her neck. He held her back with two strong palms beneath her shoulder blades. His eyes scanned her chest, paying close attention to her nipples as they hardened under his gaze.

Relax, he said to her, and immediately she was flooded with waves of pleasure. The touch of his skin against hers, inside her body, warmed her and she began to glow.

She relaxed her weight, trusting that his powerful arms would fully support her. His neck was exposed to her as well. She leaned forward and let her tongue wander and taste the salty goodness of his skin as he had done earlier.

He kissed her again, sucking and nibbling on her lower lip, making little liquid noises, and then inhaled.

Are you sure?

I am sure, Paolo. I want you to take me now.

The sound of her skin being breached was surprisingly loud. Like a bee sting, there was one moment of pain, and then euphoria traveled all over her body. His cock inside her began to swell while the muscles in his arms and shoulders tensed. He was trying to be gentle, but she could feel that urge to turn their lovemaking into a blood feast. He squeezed her flesh with his fingers, rubbing his thumbs over her afterwards to soothe the reddened skin. To his hardness she remained soft and giving. As he squeezed, she gave even more.

Take me. All of me.

She began to get light headed and saw large black spots in front of her eyes. The spots began to join. She lost her grip in his hair, and, without effort, fell back amongst her pillows, her arms raised above her head. Paolo followed her down, lapping the puncture wounds like he had done before, and then pulled away.

She could barely see him through the slits in her eyes, which were hard to keep open. Paolo gave her his wrist. "Drink, Bella."

"No, I don't want to hurt you."

"You can't hurt me. Drink. Drink for me."

"I don't want to bite you."

He smiled. "Very well." He placed two fingers inside her mouth and she tried to suck on them. "Open your mouth," he said as he pressed his lips against hers. "Open," he whispered.

Cara obeyed. Paolo's tongue slid over hers, and presented a few drops of his coppery goodness, blood that sent her ears buzzing. With his fingers, he rimmed her lips with his blood. She licked her lips and he suckled them. He repeated this process several times until her light-headedness subsided.

She suddenly felt like she could jump over the Golden Gate Bridge just using her own energy. A glow emanated from her insides out.

"What is this? Is this the fating I've read about?" she asked him thrilled with the way her body tingled.

"No, Carabella," he said as he traced a finger down her chest, between her breasts and then down to between her legs where he touched her lips and ringed their joining spot. A trace of a smile lit up his face.

"This, Carabella, is love."

CHAPTER 29

The bite and the rejuvenating droplets of Paolo's blood led to another tussle between the sheets, and a long orgasm that lasted several minutes, leaving her feeling wrung out and totally limp. She heard things happening outside in the park next to her complex—details she'd never heard before, like conversations between people and the tapping of a runner's feet along the garden pathways.

Her ceiling looked the same; however, the reflective light from car bumpers and shimmering leaves cast light and dark shadows on the smooth surface in greater detail. Light patterns seemed to dance all around her. Her entire world had shifted. She was in love, no, she was *consumed* by the love of a vampire.

They lay side by side, their thighs touching. Even her sense of smell was enhanced as she recognized the scent of their joint arousal. The droplet of cum she'd tasted from him during their lovemaking had sent curious jolts of electricity down her spine, jarring her and making her sex hungry again. She knew it was not going to be possible to get enough of him in the days and weeks to come.

I willingly am your addiction. I will host off your pleasure, Carabella.

His words send a shudder of pleasure through her body again. Everything he did sent her into a euphoric state. She turned, leaned onto her side, propped up on her elbow, and looked down at him. Her fingers traveled the smooth tanned surface of his muscular chest, up under his stubbled chin. She wondered if he had to shave. How often did he get his hair cut? There were so many questions she had now.

He'd blocked something from her. She knew he wanted it to be a private thought.

"Why keep certain thoughts from me?" She asked as she kissed his chest and toyed with his left nipple with her teeth.

"I don't want to scare you away."

"What would scare me?"

"The future."

That's when she realized that she was looking forward to her future with all her heart, and he was looking toward it with dread.

They dressed and made arrangements to get her car, which had been left at the University. Cara brought the book and the letter inside it, secreting it beneath some changes of clothes in a duffel bag.

"Does this mean you've invited yourself to what you call a 'sleepover'?" he said, his fingers caught in his belt loop. His hips were slung at an angle, and he was mind-numbingly bare chested. Cara couldn't decide whether she liked him in jeans and no shirt, or just plain naked. The effect on her body was the same.

"Hardly," she said as she turned and continued to stuff things into the bag. He moved to sit on the bed, watching her. "I didn't pack any pajamas," she said.

"I don't like pajamas. I like sleepovers without pajamas."

"Good to know. So, am I invited?"

"You are commanded."

She raised her eyebrows and formed an "O" with her lips. "Really? Commanded?"

He blocked another set of visions, but not before she definitely saw her own hands bound with black silk ties, and felt him filling her from behind. "Aha! You weren't quick enough."

He, blushed, and then smiled. A noise outside the window drew his attention. "Cara, we have to go. It isn't safe."

She was worried, so went to look out the window, but he grabbed her, pulling her back into the hallway. "You have the book?"

"Yes, right here." She held up her case.

"Then we are off. Hang on."

Again the fluttering of butterflies mixed with his scent carried her on a sensual cloud until she was standing in the grand room of the Monteleone estate in Healdsburg. An older woman was polishing an antique curio cabinet and jumped, startled, when they arrived.

"Oh, good Lord, Paolo. You nearly scared me to death," she said, clutching her heart.

"I am sorry. I needed the safety of the house perimeter and didn't have time to trace to the front door."

"Paolo, you're back," Marcus shouted out as he appeared from the study. "Cara? Does this mean you'll be joining us again this evening?" he said as he pointed to her duffel bag.

Cara looked back up at Paolo for the proper answer.

"Brother, I believe Cara is in danger, especially with the death of her assistant."

"A real tragedy, in more ways than one," Marcus said.

Cara stepped toward the older brother. "I've scarcely been able to get my breath," she said until she realized what she'd implied. Blushing, she continued bravely, "Do you know who has done this and why? I for one think it has to do with this book." She held up her bag.

Marcus squinted and tilted his head to the side, obviously thinking. Cara wasn't sure he wanted to have anything to do with the book, but Paolo took her bag in one hand, her elbow in the other, and lead her to Marcus' study. "Quickly. We need to act quickly."

Marcus stood at the doorway while Paolo zipped open the bag, which sat on Marcus' paper-strewn desk. "I'm not sure this is wise, Paolo." Marcus's long limbs carried him to beside Paolo in long fluid movements, just like Paolo's gait. The brothers looked remarkably alike, except for the slight difference in height. Marcus placed his hand over the unzipped bag. Paolo took a step back and clasped Cara about the waist from behind, waiting.

"This unlocks doors that, once opened, cannot be closed," Marcus said. "We are investigating something greater than the health and safety of this great family." Marcus's words of warning made her heart pound and her hands sweat.

What does he mean, Paolo? Help me.

Paolo gave her waist a squeeze. "Brother, perhaps you are saying Cara has to be brought up to date. It may be time for her to learn about our family and what she has unwittingly become involved in."

Marcus examined his knee-high black boots, his legs crossed in front of him as he balanced himself against the front of the desk. "My brother makes it difficult for me, Cara. I must tell you things he has not been able to, due to—"

"I know what he is," she said. "What you all are. I know you are a vampire coven."

Marcus winced. "No, not coven. We are a dynasty. A family. We protect and stand for one another. We don't feed off one another. Our family does not perform the hosting the coven families do. If you can even call them families."

"They are animals," Paolo whispered.

"No, not all. We have some who can be loyal, Paolo. Never forget that. Without them, we would have little information on what is happening in the dark world."

The shiver down Cara's spine forced her to move to the side, away from Paolo. "Dark world?" Cara crossed her arms across her chest and stepped away again when Paolo tried to encircle her shoulders with his arm. "I'm needing some interpretation here. I need some answers and I want them right now."

Marcus motioned to a red velvet settee and asked Cara to take a seat. Paolo wisely sat in an ornately carved chair beside her. At the tall windows of the study, Marcus stared out onto the vineyards below. Mists still burning off the remnants of morning fog sent tendrils of white swirling through the air, framing the handsome Monteleone brother's profile. "Paolo, this is yours to handle. You have to make a decision here, brother."

Paolo stood. The two brothers looked into each other's eyes before Marcus broke it off and placed himself behind the huge desk and collapsed into a wooden chair that groaned under his size. Paolo slowly faced Cara and leaned against the windowsill. He had the same impossibly long, lean legs as his brother, but his face that always looked like it had been kissed by sunshine was slightly fairer than that of his older, brooding brother. No matter what happened this grey morning, she would always love Paolo's face. It would be the face she would see in her dreams the rest of her life.

She hoped it wouldn't turn out to be a nightmare.

I can do this. Was she saying this to convince herself or Paolo?

"I know you can, Carabella. But there is much to share." Paolo stalked across the office from bookshelf to bookshelf, each burdened with more books than Cara had ever seen in a private library. These old books had been dusted and cared for. Some were wrapped in plastic covering. A couple of rolled-up scrolls lay on a reading desk built into the bookshelf, next to a white pair of gloves.

"This is but a fraction of the books we own. The library in Tuscany is second to none. It would probably keep scholars busy for centuries. It rivals some of the great libraries in Paris, the U.K. and the U.S."

Cara noticed Marcus had picked up a book and was letting his fingers filter through the pages, but she knew he was paying close attention.

"The library chronicles the works of our kind, the history, our genealogy, things Marcus and I haven't even had time to learn about. Cara, both Marcus and I are over three hundred years old."

He raised his eyes to watch her reaction. Marcus stopped perusing the book to look up as well.

Cara knew he was telling the truth. "How does that work?" she asked. She felt immediately it was a stupid question.

No, none of your questions are stupid. "We are Golden vampires, which are a different species than the dark vampire covens. We are able to live in the sunlight. We can appear human, just as any other mortal. We are not. Our children are human, and, at the age of puberty or some time beyond, each child is given the choice, one time only. Our choice is to whether remain mortal, human, or become Golden vampire. We can only mate," he blushed, and Cara loved him for it. "We can only produce offspring with our fated mates. Only then is the blood passed down."

"So you have had a fated mate, then," Cara felt the weight of her words falling into the pit of her stomach.

"Yes. Unfortunately, yes." Paolo's steady chocolate gaze poured into her chest, but it didn't lessen the burden.

She told herself it wasn't important. She'd not considered being a mother. She hadn't planned to consider it until she met the right man. And then she knew what had caused the pain in her stomach, what she was unwilling to believe about herself. She was staring right into the eyes of that man whose children she would gladly bear. She decided not to hide her disappointment, instead letting the sadness flow.

Paolo had frowned, furrowing his brow, and brought himself back the task of completing the story. "Our children are especially vulnerable, and, since they are very rare, cherished almost above all life."

As it should be, Paolo. You have a son and he will always be your primary responsibility. I understand this.

Paolo nodded, appearing glad she understood this. "So, until that time of choice, our children can be easily killed, just like any mortal child. It is for that reason we are so protective of our secrets, the secrets of the family."

Cara understood she was now the keeper of information few mortals knew. He trusted her, even if Marcus didn't.

"The fact that this is coming close to you means there is even greater danger than we thought, and certainly a lot less time than we thought we had."

"Time? Time for what?"

"Time to ready for the battle," Marcus added. "There's a war brewing between the dark covens and our kind. It will be a war of annihilation. Only one coven can survive."

"It appears they have chosen to embroil you in this war," Paolo whispered. "Cara, I didn't realize this until this morning. They are coming after you next. You are in grave danger."

"Is it because of us?" she asked.

"No, Carabella. I believe it is because of the book, and your knowledge of its existence. But the relationship we share will certainly complicate things," Paolo answered. "I did not want you involved in this. And now we have two choices, if they can be called that. We can either go forward and enlist your mortal support in this fight, or we can erase your memories and send you elsewhere."

"Elsewhere? You mean—"

"You would essentially become a different person. You could not study vampires. You would not be known as an expert. You could do and be nothing that would attract them to your scent. You understand?"

"You are joking."

"Wish I was. It is a valid alternative," Paolo replied. He walked fluidly over to where she sat on the settee and knelt in front of her. He took both her hands in one of his. "I would do nearly anything to keep you safe. The safest course for you in your life might be to stay completely away from me and my family."

"I couldn't—" she started.

"You could. It could be done. You could be made to forget we ever met."

Forget we ever met? Are you asking me to make that choice? I cannot.

"You remember when I told you, with the proper information, we might be able to do things we never thought possible before? This is one of the choices, Cara. But it would require you to move, to remove yourself from anything you ever knew of your past. Your life would start somewhere else. And trust me, you wouldn't be looking into vampires or the vampire culture, either. We can do that."

Cara felt sick to her stomach. What had she been thinking? She knew Paolo was concerned for her safety. He'd been blocking his thoughts ever since they left her place. The controlled, measured communication he'd just delivered hung over her like an axe. Any way she thought about it, her life, as she knew it, was over.

How could I have been so stupid?

It is my fault, my fault alone. I knew better, Bella. I should never have taken another mortal lover.

"Mortal lover? Am I that to you?" She felt like she'd been slapped. "Am I your pleasure partner for randy afternoons at the Inn, or early morning sex when danger is lurking around the corner? When those that are close to me are dying? Who's next? My students?"

She dropped his hands and pushed him back so she could stand up.

"Bella, I am truly sorry."

"Sorry? Sorry would have meant you wouldn't have involved me. For all I know, they are only interested in me because of you. You knew this—both of you knew this," she pointed to Marcus who was not smiling.

"You bed me, made me—do things," Cara frowned and shook off the sensual images of their sexual encounters. "I don't take risks. I like adventure, but I don't have a death wish, in case you—either of you—were wondering. I'd like to have my life back. I expect you will give that to me. No. I *demand* it."

"It isn't that easy, Cara," Marcus said through his teeth. The muscles in his jaw flexed as he spoke in monotone, choosing his words carefully. "I disagree with your conclusion. You involved yourself because you found something they want. If it weren't for us, you'd be dead already. But, make no mistake, you will have your life back, but you'll have to decide which life it is. Up to you how we handle this. We have limited options, but we will do what is best for our kind, there's no question about that. And Paolo will do whatever it takes to protect his son. Barring that, you can have it any way you want."

"Except I can't be Carabella Sampson, college professor, expert on the myths and mythology of vampires. No. I can't have that back."

Marcus traced over to her so fast it scared her. She could feel the anger boiling in his chest. "Why on earth would you want that if it meant you'd be dead in a day, maybe less? You just stood there and told us you didn't have a death wish, and now are pining like a sniveling child for a life that will mean certain death."

"Marcus!" Paolo inserted himself between his brother and Cara.

Marcus stomped away, then abruptly turned and faced Paolo. "You see now why having a mortal girlfriend is not a good idea? Now you have to make the decision for her, since she's incapable of deciding herself."

"How dare you—" She was going to run over to Marcus and scratch his eyes out, but Paolo held her back. "Let go of me. I want nothing to do with you. Either of you. You are keeping me here against my will."

"Bella, please. Listen to me," Paolo said while defending himself against her blows.

"I'm done listening to you. I'm—"

Marcus had traced behind Cara, placing his fingers at her temples before she could react. Spots appeared before her eyes as she sank to the ground. Suddenly the whole world turned black.

"What have you done?" Paolo said to his brother.

"I've erased part of her recent memory. I gave her what she wanted. Not that she will live long to appreciate it."

"Marcus, you fool."

"No, Paolo. You are the fool. Trying to live in both the mortal and Golden vampire worlds. Your indecision has nearly cost her the only life she has. It still may. You should have left her alone. I told you this would be a problem. She is too strong-willed, and now she knows too much. This is the only way. If she won't choose it, we will make the choice for her, for her own best interest. You will bring her back to her own place and she will not know anything of what has transpired today."

"But what about Johnny, and the book?"

"I'll want you to report on what she remembers. This isn't an exact science. We have to erase any of her memory of you, Paolo, and certainly the book. You understand this is only for her own protection."

Paolo's sadness eclipsed his need for her safety. For a brief moment, he thought about arguing with his brother. But he knew it was no use.

Paolo bent and picked Cara up with one arm under her shoulders and the other under her knees. One arm hung down and Marcus placed it gently on her stomach. Paolo looked down on the face of the woman he knew he loved and sighed. "I will take care of this. I'll take her back to her apartment and stay with her while she revives."

"And say what? She may not know you."

"I'll think of a pretense."

"And you have to be careful. You could be tracing into a battle zone."

"I'll stay to the outside first, then I'll enter. She will need to be somewhere where she feels safe and comfortable. Her office is not the right place."

"Good. Make it quick. I need you back here."

Paolo took a deep breath in and traced to outside the door of her apartment. A door down the hallway closed, but otherwise the floor seemed deserted. He opened her door, which was still unlocked, just as they had left it. He brought her to the bedroom. The smell of their tangled sheets was still in the air. But something else was there as well.

Dag.

He set Cara on the bed and strode into the living room to find the curtains drawn and Dag sitting on the lemon yellow leather chair in the darkened corner. It was the first time Paolo had seen a dark vamp in daylight hours, alive.

"Greetings, cousin. Are you quite done with her? If you don't mind, I might enjoy the leftovers." Dag smiled. It was the first time Paolo recognized the scar that carried from Dag's left brow down his cheek to the flair of his nose. Paolo's beautiful sister had created the same sort of injury to a mortal would-be attacker one dark evening in the alleyway by a theater in New York City. He and Marcus had arrived just in time to trace her away with her two children.

Even as a mortal, Dag had been a devil.

CHAPTER 30

Paolo cursed himself for not being more prepared, but he hadn't expected any dark coven interference, since it was still daytime. Of course the dark Supreme Leader would show up himself. Which also meant he knew about the Paolo's relationship with Cara. All the more reason he hoped his brother's erasure worked. He also hoped it erred on the side of erasing too much information, rather than too little.

He was careful to guard his thoughts from the clever coven leader.

"Tell me how it is you are out and about in daylight hours?"

"I've been feasting on Golden blood, cousin. You do know what happens when I drain a Golden?"

Paolo tensed, waiting for the identification he knew Dag would be only too pleased to provide.

"Young Rory was quite tasty, Paolo." Dag strummed his fingers on the arm of the leather chair, which sounded like drumsticks across a skin with Paolo's preternatural hearing. "He died badly. But he was quite generous with his blood, although he had not much of a choice. I promised to spare his sisters for a year."

Paolo felt his blood boil. The rage inside him was so strong he felt he could almost explode the whole building, killing them all. "You are an animal. You have no business feasting off innocents."

"Oh, Rory wasn't innocent. He'd have killed my new executioner—me too, if your thugs hadn't interfered. By the way, where is your protection detail?"

"Where is yours?" Paolo asked.

"Touché. So you can see I want to conduct business, since I have given you the advantage of showing up here alone."

"Her memory has been erased," Paolo informed him, hoping that would make the leader lose interest.

"Hmm. We shall see," Dag shrugged. He suddenly stood. "May I see her?" His dazzling blue eyes, which were a rare occurrence amongst dark coven vamps, contained swirls of deep navy smoke. Paolo knew that was the anger brewing.

"As if I could stop you. But be warned, she will not remember me or anything of what has transpired this morning."

"So she might not understand that she has been your lover, either. How sad for you."

"You assume too much."

"I'm giving you deference, just out of respect to your family, Paolo. Now, let me pass so I can check things out for myself."

Paolo knew Dag's Achilles' heel was his impatience. He decided to string things along a bit, to irritate the dark vamp.

"I will not let any harm come to her, even if she doesn't remember me. She is an innocent. Surely you would rather pester someone who is more important—a bishop, or female knight. Why go after a pawn when you can have a queen?"

"You mean Anne?"

"I didn't mean anyone. Just that this girl is unimportant now."

"Except that you will defend her to the death. I know you Monteleones. Very possessive of your women. Even if she doesn't remember you, I'm willing to bet a thousand mortal souls you'll remember every detail, every inch of her lovely body. And I'm also willing to bet you would protect her from me enjoying the same pleasures. Am I right, Cousin?"

"I abhor unnecessary involvement of mortals."

"Which is why you should never fuck them, Paolo. You see, you are more like me than your pompous brother would like to admit. I thoroughly enjoy fucking mortal women. I drain them, and let them die, too. You should try it. Very exhilarating."

"Isn't that sort of like killing or torturing your pets?" Paolo smelled Dag's foul mood oozing from the dark vamp's sweat. He wrinkled his nose. "Besides, if you smelled like that, how could anyone want to do anything but die after having you violate them?"

"It's the smell of my flesh rotting under the daytime sun. I don't smell at night," Dag said casually and appeared to be turning away. Without warning, he was on Paolo in a flash, hands clasped around Paolo's neck, scratching to tear at his jugular.

Paolo retaliated by tracing them both to the street corner in the center of downtown Santa Rosa, next to the park where the drunks and homeless camped out. Their fight would attract attention of onlookers who would never be questioned afterwards. Dag's flesh would start to burn and the fight wouldn't last long.

The dark vamp howled like a wolf as his skin sizzled and bubbled, turning black.

"You think you will win?" Paolo had pinned Dag's arms behind him, and had reopened the scar on his cheek under his eye. "I'm going to let you go. But she will be protected, and you will give the order, Dag. Or you will have the wrath of the Monteleone family come down hard on your twisted little coven. You prepared to start the war today? Over someone who cannot help you in any way?"

Dag yanked himself from Paolo's grip. He traced to a dark overhang between two tall office buildings, licking his wounds, cursing. Paolo watched him touch the open wound with fingers covered in his own spittle. The deep gash was healing, but left blood on his collar. Dag would need fresh blood to satisfy the healing requirements of his sun scorch. Paolo entered the alleyway and held his nose at the stench.

"Just be glad you didn't do that in front of my men," Dag hissed. "Your day will come, young Monteleone. Your family will mourn you, as they have all the children I have taken." He looked up at Paolo, who stood several inches taller than the dark vamp. "Your children. Remember your children. Is she worth that?"

Paolo wanted to grab the leader and tear off his head, but he didn't have the permission he needed. Once Dag's deeds could be verified, there would be time for a trial and his ending. Of that, Paolo was sure.

"Slither off to your cave, snake. I will see you in battle. Until then, pick on people who are able to fight you one on one. Not an innocent. Or, are you going to further prove dark vamps have no honor?"

"We don't live for honor. We live for revenge." Dag spat out. "Remember that when I take everything from you. It is revenge I fight for, and my rightful place above all the creatures of the world."

Dag disappeared, leaving Paolo in the darkened alleyway in front of a semicircle of homeless gentlemen and their shopping carts and puppies. Even the homeless, Paolo noted, didn't mistreat their pets. There were some things mortals did better than vamps, or at least dark vamps.

Paolo slowly began the walk back to Cara's apartment, rather than tracing, in case someone was tracking him. He wished it were nighttime, so he could have the benefit of the Jett brothers entourage. He didn't like the idea that he would have to be Cara's daytime protector, even if Marcus allowed it. He knew Marcus had plans.

The morning had started out so blissfully satisfying. It seemed as thought the God of vampires gave him one last gift of her body, before he would have to give her up forever. What was he thinking? Why had he not been able to stop from acting on the attraction to her at that dance? He was stronger than she was, and yet he couldn't leave her alone. She'd called him her addiction. Wasn't it really the other way around?

Marcus was right, of course. But it didn't mean he had to like it. Paolo could barely hope there was a solution to this mess that didn't involve one or all of them perishing.

Other walkers passed by him, on their way to meetings, work, or to a late breakfast or early lunch. He couldn't hear their thoughts, and he was grateful he didn't have those powers. But then, he wondered if he would be able to speak to Cara and she back to him now that her memory had been erased? Would that power disappear?

He walked a little faster, turning the corner onto her street. He was anxious to see her revived, to assess the damage, if any, and where he might have to fix things Marcus had done. It wouldn't be fair not to orient her properly so she wouldn't walk right back into the same situation. He'd have to help Marcus with this, deciding how much to erase and what to leave intact.

Perhaps she could still be a professor, studying myth and lore. Just not an expert on vampires. He wondered if this could be done. He wondered if he could enroll in one of her classes just to be near her. Would it pain his heart to have her answer a question he would pose in class, and have him think about how beautifully their bodies had mingled while she merely answered the question with no such knowledge?

He decided that, if it were required, he could do it.

But, Marcus, don't ask me to stay away.

He heard Marcus' booming thoughts. *Wake her up. We have little time, brother. I need you back here, not wandering around the streets worrying about someone you should not think about. Please be quick. There is news.*

Paolo did as he was told and traced to her door, knocking softly on the frame. He heard shuffling inside, and then heard a chain pulled across the door he knew was still unlocked. She opened it a crack, her hair disheveled, sleep still blurring her eyes. Her full red lips were beautiful and called to him.

"Yes?"

"Sorry, miss. I'm with campus security at the University. You are professor Cara Sampson?" He hoped she remembered who she was.

She looked puzzled for a moment. "Wow. I had one whopper of a dream and just woke up. But yes, I'm Cara Sampson. Is something wrong?"

Paolo decided to try a little glamour. He sighed, sending some of his breath her way. Right on cue, she reeled backward, her eyes crossing.

"I'm sorry. Feeling light-headed right now. Can you come back later?"

"Are you all right?" he asked. He wanted to touch her. He could steady her if he could touch any portion of her skin. He sent a suggestion she release the metal chain. She drew her brows down over the top of her nose as she concentrated on the chain, and then allowed her fingers to slip it loose.

She turned and walked down the hall away from him, which gave Paolo the opportunity to check out the empty hallway and close her door behind him.

"Here, please sit down. Let me get you a drink of water," he said as he took hold of her wrist. He could feel his calming powers spreading through her body. God, how he wished he could light a flame under her flesh again. He stuffed down the feeling.

Cara sat on the leather chair where Dag had sat no more than an hour before. She brushed the hair from her forehead and leaned back, revealing her long creamy neck. Paolo dashed to the kitchen, pouring a glass of water and coming back to present it to her. Their fingers touched as she took the glass. She jumped.

"Wow. Static electricity," she said as she took a long swallow. Paolo watched the delicate muscles in her neck move. He could still smell the remnants of sex in the room. He was getting hard, and he said a private curse to his errant body part. But it didn't listen.

"So, what does campus security want with me?"

Paolo didn't know whether or not to tell her about Johnny. She didn't appear to recognize him, so perhaps she didn't remember the dance. He decided to take a chance.

"When was the last time you saw your Research Assistant, Johnny Merrill?"

She took another sip of the water and set the glass on the coffee table. "Let's see, would be yesterday—no wait, maybe the day before. I'm supposed to meet him later tonight for a Halloween party."

"Halloween was two nights ago. Someone is having a party after the fact?" he asked, amused she didn't remember the party or spending intimate time with him at the bar.

"Something fuzzy is going on inside my head, like I've been sleeping for a week. Is everything okay? Is Johnny okay?"

"I'm afraid he's been found dead."

Her eyes got large and shimmered with tears. "What?"

"This morning, as a matter of fact. Forgive me if I impose, but you were there. You don't remember?"

She arched up and sat straight. "Don't you think I'd remember if I saw my best friend die? Where did he die, anyway?"

"Your office. He'd been murdered."

"Murdered! This morning?"

"We aren't sure. But you found him. You've already talked to the police. You don't remember any of this?"

She shook her head from side to side. "None of this." She held her head between her palms and began of cry. "What's happening to me?"

Paolo wanted in the worst way to take her in his arms. "I am so sorry, miss. I have seen this happen before. Sometimes graphic events do this to people and their memories. I'm glad I was here to give you the news. Wouldn't want you to find out on the news, or in class."

"My class! I am late for my class," she said as she stood and checked the large clock in the kitchen.

"No miss, your classes, actually all the classes on campus, have been cancelled, pending the investigation. The police I believe will have many more questions for you. So sorry." He tried to look at her with as little emotion as possible. But he couldn't help himself.

Do you feel me? He threw out the little thought, not sure what he would get back in return.

Cara stiffened, looking around the apartment, indicating she heard Paolo. "Anything wrong?" he asked.

"I just think I heard Johnny's voice. He—he talked to me!"

Paolo was warmed by her misinterpretation. It thrilled him that she was still so available to him, still. He took his time to savor the moment, knowing it would be the longest time he could be in her presence, for now.

"You are a college professor, Ms. Sampson. Surely you don't mean to say that you believe in ghosts, or people coming back to life after death?" He tried not to use any of his glam, just to see if she would respond to him all of her own.

It worked. She looked at her lap. "No. Sorry. That sounds stupid, doesn't it?" She laughed in that off-handed, unaffected way Paolo loved. She brushed her hair from her shoulders and cleared her forehead. Then she leveled a gaze at him that sent a jolt straight to his heart. Her wide green eyes were luminous; no doubt her body was feeling the effects of his presence, even if her mind knew nothing of it. He felt the same way.

"So you want to tell me why you are here? I never did see a badge or anything. How do I know I shouldn't be afraid of you?"

"Good. It is smart for you to be thinking that way." He produced a card he used on occasion to explain his presence. "This is my card. We don't have badges, or uniforms. We never carry guns. We are merely here, trying to look like everyone else, not stand out, to keep an eye on things. It's not every day that we have a murder on campus. In fact, I don't think we ever have since the founding of the University. You will be contacted again by all the authorities, and we want you to fully cooperate." He stood and she did the same. "I do not mean to scare you. Just checking up to make sure you are not being harassed here at your home."

"Thank you. I appreciate it." Her warm smile hit him in the middle of his chest. Her eyes traced there, as if it were a familiar place, a place where she had lay her head at one time. Or, as if she wanted to be comforted there.

Then she brushed past him, the electricity of their closeness sparking another current he tried to ignore. But he could see she felt it too. At the door, she opened it. "I appreciate your concern. Unlike earlier, I must remember to keep my door locked at all times. This little chain," she said as she touched it with her forefinger, "wouldn't really stop a bad guy, would it?"

"No, indeed." He moved past her, brushing her skin one more time. Her breath hitched. "Call me if anything comes up. Anything at all. I also have some psychic friends who could help you with the other thing, too," he said with a smirk.

She crossed her arms and aimed her glare at him. "No. Thank you very much, but I think I misunderstood something. Remnants of a dream I was having perhaps. No doubt something the police told me I had forgotten until you mentioned it."

"Well, anything at all. Anything I can do, just call me." He turned and walked down the hallway, feeling her eyes on his back.

"You never told me your name. Well, I guess I could look it up on your card," she called out, her voice vibrating down the vacant hallway.

He looked at her one last time. Would this be it, he wondered? The last time he would see her? Would he be able to keep her safe from Dag and his forces? It was everything he could do to simply speak to her. What he wanted to do was rush to her arms, and glamour her until she wanted him again. His heart was breaking.

"I am Paolo Monteleone, at your service, miss." He found himself bowing, as he had done for the past three hundred years.

"I've met you before. You're not from around here, are you? Originally? I can detect an accent."

"Tuscany. Our family is from Tuscany, and some are in Prague."

"Ah! The vampires I study are from those two areas as well."

"Really? I didn't know." Paolo became hyper aware of the vacant hallway, not wanting to be seen there talking to her. "But as far as meeting you before, I'm sure I would have remembered such a beauty." He looked down to allow her blush to be private. "Perhaps you'll have to tell me about your vamps some time."

"Perhaps. Thank you for your concern, Paolo Monteleone." Her voice wobbled a tiny bit from the thudding of her pulse. Paolo loved feeling how he affected her.

She turned and closed the door behind her.

Paulo's heart was ready to leap out of his chest. This mental bond with her, his need to focus on her well-being to the exclusion of the rest of the outside world felt like a form of fating. No way this attraction was ordinary, for human or vampire. It was something else entirely.

He didn't have time to figure it out. The God of vampires was giving him another gift. Just being close to her was going to have to be enough for now. The war was looming and Marcus was screaming in his ear.

"Yes, I'm coming. I'm ready to do battle, Marcus," he said out loud but sent the mental message as well.

CHAPTER 31

Paolo traced to Marcus' study, where his older brother was perusing the book from Cara's things. He looked up. "Good. I was beginning to wonder if I'd have to come get you."

"I thought it important to make sure she didn't suspect me in any of the morning's events."

"Good. And how is her memory?" Marcus asked.

"Spotty." He smiled, remembering his delight that she'd heard his mental question. "But all in the right places."

"Excellent."

"But brother, there is another problem. When I dropped her off, Dag was in her apartment."

"Bastard. And he knew you brought her back?"

"What else could he have deduced? I told him her mind had been erased."

"Under the circumstances, I would have done the same. Good."

"She hadn't come to. I took Dag for a little discussion downtown Santa Rosa. He won't stay away from her, that much is clear. Not sure he buys she has no memory of her research, or the book either, Marcus."

"I will get the security detail deployed. Waiting to speak to Lionel tonight." Marcus looked back at the book on his desk. "This is fascinating. Pull up a chair and let me show you a few things."

Paolo brought a nearly black lacquered chair around and sat down next to Marcus at the desk. The book was opened to an interior page. There was an image of a horned man carved into a large door. Paolo read the inscription underneath:

This horned man is one of a series of three, which adorn the front of the Banqueting House. The three men represent the emotions of Hatred, Malice and Envy. The Banqueting House was said to be built for the eating of desserts, but others have suspected its use as a place for human hosts to be fed upon by vampires who invite them to dinner. It was a reminder to humans and vampires alike, of their symbiotic relationship.

"Symbiotic relationship?" Paolo asked. "Vampires have always feasted off humans. I don't understand."

"He's talking about some grand legend of a joining between the vampire and human races."

"Vampires have had many pleasure partners amongst mortal men and women. What's so fascinating about these?"

"These Banqueting Houses appeared to be places where more than just blood was exchanged."

"Again, no surprise there, Marcus. I just don't understand."

"New vampires were born there, too. It is referred later to the *Place of Beginning.*"

"Someone took themselves a mortal bride, drained her, and turned her to be his forever. She was born there. That's all he's talking about, brother."

"Alasdair Fraser has uncovered the fact that there are halflings, Paolo. Half vampire, half human. They are another race, brother."

"That cannot be. The fating. It makes it impossible to have children unless there is fating. There is no fating except between species. Even dark vamps—"

Paolo's eyes grew wide as he looked into his brother's stern face . Marcus was nodding when he said, "Yes, Paolo. Darks are Halflings. Half human, half vampire. Some experiment gone horribly wrong. A mixing of the blood that was never intended to be mixed."

Paolo leaned back and stared at the carved walnut ceiling of the study. He'd spent decades studying the reliefs and the stories they told. He wondered what the person who carved the reliefs had been trying to tell them. Suddenly there were more questions than there were answers.

"*The Book of Spawn* this letter references here," Marcus took out the letter that had been embedded in the text, "was once a part of our library, Paolo.

It passes on the studies of this transformation, this experiment. I believe Alasdair Fraser found that book."

"This is the book Cara had?"

"No. She found and purchased Alasdair Fraser's book, with this letter in it. But I think the clues to where *The Book of Spawn* is located are in this book. I believe this is a map, a key."

"So the darks are looking for it because it contains the history of their origins as well," Paolo said.

"Exactly."

"Then they do not know about this book. They have no idea this book exists," Paolo guessed.

"I believe you are correct. They are after *The Book of Spawn*. They think that's the book she had. They wouldn't even recognize this one." Marcus was smiling as he stood, closed the book, walked over to the bookcase and placed it between two other older books. "It will be safely hidden in plain sight. If Cara doesn't remember the book, I'm not sure Dag and his dark coven hordes can find it. And I don't think she knows where *The Book of Spawn* is, either."

"Which doesn't ensure her safety, but means she is useless to them."

"That's right."

Paolo looked at the letter on his brother's desk. "What about this?"

"I'm going to take it to the Council. I've booked an audience with Praetor and the council for Wednesday. You want to join me? A little time in Tuscany could do you some good. Perhaps take Lucius where he would be safer?"

"I think he would like that. Would be good to see Laurel again, too," Paolo said, referring to their only unmarried sister.

"I'm going to make arrangements and break the news to Anne," Marcus started.

"You better take her, too. It isn't safe around here without your presence."

"I will be doing that. But you know how stubborn she can be."

They chuckled. After all, Anne was the one who had decapitated Marcus's witch/vampire lover and Lucius' mother within weeks of her turning. They learned never to underestimate her.

"I'll get with Lionel as soon as his sleep is over and make the arrangements for Cara's security detail," Paolo said.

"Good. Take Lionel's advice one hundred percent. He would never let us down. I consider him almost kin," Marcus replied.

"Wonder what the Jett brothers will do when they find out about all this."

"We'd just better hope we are the ones to tell them, Paolo. Be well. I'm off." Marcus took the folded letter, placed it back in the envelope and left the study, leaving Paolo to ponder the future he had not expected.

It was good that Cara should stay away completely, and they could achieve this. It was unfortunate today's findings made the impending war more likely. He thought about Dag and his belly full of hatred and resentment, and saw the dark vamp as if he was standing outside the heavily carved wooden door, not allowed to join the party.

Maybe the dark coven leader knew more than he let on. Maybe he was far more dangerous than any of them had thought.

CHAPTER 32

Dag traced to his bedchamber in San Francisco. Someone had left a sliver open between his blackout drapes, so his skin burned until he could reposition the fabric and find comfort. He cursed his staff. He'd kill someone for that lapse in judgment.

He ripped off his clothes, sniffing them. He was aware of the fact that dark vamps smelled when they were burning up. Who wouldn't? Burning human flesh was even worse. Had he not had a good dose of Rory's blood, pushing aside his coven cohorts like a pack of dogs, he could have been dead. His hatred of the Golden Monteleones and their powers boiled and burned the insides of his stomach to match the festering blisters on his skin.

He opened his bedroom doors. The house was quiet.

"I need blood," he screamed.

There was no answer. Of course there would be no answer. His daytime staff was worthless, and now he knew they weren't doing their jobs. They were probably out gambling or telling secrets. Well, they'd pay. And any who were unlucky enough to be loyal today would have to be his hosts. No one, not even someone who was grossly overpaid, would willingly share his bed and die for him. Fear him, yes, but sacrifice themselves for him like those ridiculous traitors, the Jett Brothers and their kin? No, none of his paid staff would do such a thing. "No one fuckin' cares."

"I care."

He smelled her before he saw her. The blonde from Starbucks and the cheap motel. His teeth ached as his groin went to granite. He was drooling on himself.

He lurched and grabbed her by the back of her head, forcing her lips up to his, plunging his tongue down her throat, sucking her tongue and then tasting one puncture wound he placed there. His surrounding saliva would heal the wound quickly. These were little love nibbles. But he desperately needed a whole meal, and fast.

"Need you," he heard himself say. *What the fuck is this?* He'd never said this to anyone in his life before.

"Dag take me. Take all of me if you wish. I am totally yours to do with whatever you want."

"Holy fucking nuns without panties. I don't need sex right now. Not until I can have blood, and I'd drain you."

"Then that is what I want."

He couldn't believe it. The woman would fucking die for him. Right here. How the fuck did she get inside his home, anyway? Was this a trap?

"Who let you in?" he whispered as he licked her neck. He pricked the surface of her impossibly smooth skin and lapped a trickle before he would waste a single drop. He began to shake and shudder as her delicious elixir coated his insides. His dick stayed just as hard as it always did. A brief thought flew through his brain. If he ever did die in the sun, his dick would be the last thing standing.

"Someone in an apron and little white cap."

"Why did she let you in?"

"I told her I was to be your sacrifice for this afternoon. When she started to send me away—" the blonde gasped as Dag had gone to his knees and had bitten her on her upper thigh, going for the femoral artery right through her jeans.

"Tell me, damn it." He insisted, licking his lips, growling at the growing red stain on her jeans. "And take these fucking things off."

"Thought you didn't want sex."

"The femoral artery. Bigger than the jugular. I need blood. Fast. Need. Your. Blood."

He allowed her to step back. The blood he'd ingested gave him the strength to wait until she slithered her jeans down to her ankles. Her white cotton top was all she wore. Her panties lay in the pile at her ankles.

"Off," he pointed to her top.

"Yes, Master."

"Quick. Make it quick."

"Yes." She ripped open the shirt, popping the buttons. Like depositing a tissue in the wastebasket she let her cotton top drop to the floor. All that remained was her bra. He liked the look of her bulging bosom all trussed and confined.

"Leave it on."

Her sweet smile drove him insane. He wrapped his naked peeling thigh around her perfect cool flesh. "Do I repulse you, with my burning skin?"

"Yes."

At first he wasn't so sure he liked that answer.

"I repulse you?" he said as he sunk his fangs into her thigh and slurped, blood squirting and spraying over the top of the stairway and cascading to the marble floor below.

"It is all I deserve. I would eat your scaling flesh if you commanded it."

This caught him off guard. He withdrew his fangs and looked at the little waif. "Eeewwww," he said as he scrunched up his eyebrows and wrinkled his nose. "Disgusting."

She did what no mortal or vamp woman had ever done to him before. She touched his flaking member, letting her fingertips travel over the lumpy, charred surface. She placed her palm under his ball sack and squeezed him while he stood there in shock.

She knelt and had him in her mouth so fast he didn't have time to respond. It felt incredible. She rubbed her bitten tongue all over his member and immediately it became smooth, albeit coated in blood. A trickle escaped down the right side of her mouth.

"Holy shit, Sheela,"

"Shirley," she said between sucks. "My name is Shirley."

"Shir—agh—"

She allowed her canine to drag along his shaft, scraping a tiny layer of skin with it. She must have gotten a minute taste of blood because she inhaled and almost swallowed him whole.

Dag traced backwards, looking with incredulity at the little vixen. "What are you?"

"Excuse me," she said, standing. She used her jeans to dab the blood draining from her thigh wound.

"Someone. Someone sent you. Who was it?"

"I believe it was yourself, sire."

"Don't fuckin' bullshit me. Who the fuck sent you?"

"Fate."

CHAPTER 33

Lionel Jett awoke to the sounds of someone else in his bedroom. Paolo had traced there, melding over the protection he'd placed around the perimeter.

"How'd you do that?" he asked his employer's brother.

"Marcus had the manuals at the study. I read them."

Lionel made a mental note to be more careful with the security literature. He stretched and began to stand, but realized he'd slept naked again. It was becoming a habit, as was the fact that he was making love to his sheets every night, regardless of whether or not he'd had sex with a date the night before. The visions in his head of the sweet green-eyed, red-haired hottie he'd screwed several times the night before, right next to his brother Huge, who had been screwing her sister, came flashing back and his dick boinked to attention. He immediately bent over to cover it up.

Paolo was laughing. It was not funny to Lionel.

"You guys had some fun last night, apparently"

"Still managed to call your brother first."

"And for your loyalty, we thank you. We are indebted to you."

"Thanks." Lionel grabbed a long-sleeved tee from the floor and covered up his groin as he shuffled to a dresser to retrieve some clothes. The evening sky had turned pitch black.

"So what do I owe the pleasure of your visit?" Lionel asked with his back to Paolo. He turned and caught Paolo eyeing his butt cheeks. "Fuck off, Paolo. I don't do guys. You know that. You go both ways now?"

Paolo was still in a good mood, and laughed it off. Lionel could remember a time when it would have cost him another humiliating fight that he was required to lose. Didn't mind the pain, which would heal relatively quickly. It had been about his pride, knowing he could kick young Paolo's ass and still had to take the fall, "for the good of the family." Still, it was his job, and he did it regardless of how he felt. He was glad Paolo had learned to temper his reactions. And he did seem happier these days.

"That's what I want to talk to you about."

"Going both ways. You honestly think you can have a conversation with me about going both ways." Lionel was close to tracing himself anywhere else, even though he was still naked.

"No, about protecting the love of my life."

"Love of your life or love of her—it is hope to God's hangnail a girl, right?"

"Well, yes, and she's mortal."

"A blinding flash of the obvious. How come you don't like female Goldens?"

"You forget what Lucius's mother did to me."

"Half my guys lusted after her too. Hell, you couldn't help yourself, everyone knows that. And most of the guys would have loved to have her abuse them like she did you. Paolo, time for you to grow up and be a man."

"So I've been told." Paolo's smile was getting thin.

"Marcus handled her for almost a hundred years."

Paolo wasn't jealous since he had no feelings for Maya. "But Maya loved Marcus. She barely tolerated me."

It was the truth. Everyone knew it. Sadly, though they were fated, Maya and Paolo would never have survived as a couple. They had enough animal attraction to produce an offspring, but as far as spending eternity together, it had been completely out of the question. It was fortunate her death saved him from the agony.

"Okay, man. Sorry. Tell me what you're here for, and I'll do whatever it is you want me to do." He started to step into a pair of boxers. "Within reason, of course," he added in a mumble.

"Of course."

Lionel put on his dark black jeans, a form-fitting t-shirt that made his muscles look twice a normal man's size, and thick black socks. He sat at the edge of the bed and pulled on his knee-high boots with the steel toe, stowing a KA-BAR on the side of one. Next he donned his shoulder holster, checked his Ultra Crimson Carry II with the 3-inch barrel, stowing it safely under his arm. His black jacket was fitted so no one would ever suspect he was packing. Which is the way he liked it. But one look into his eyes and they would know they were dealing with Dr. Death himself.

He liked that too.

Paolo grinned, glad he could call upon this lethal combination of brains, brawn and equipment sure to keep Cara safe.

"So where are we off to? And don't tell me it's a fuckin' hot tub party."

"Hardly. Call your brothers. We'll meet at that bistro by the square in downtown Santa Rosa. Tell them to be there in less than a half hour."

"I'll have them ready. Meet you there."

The three Jett brothers wore sunglasses, their eyes being extra sensitive, even to the votive candles on the little table they shared. The space was so small their knees almost touched, which meant that when one of them crossed or uncrossed his massive legs, the others had to do the same in tandem. Though it annoyed Lionel from time to time, it was a necessary evil, since they needed to be close together to discuss their plans so they wouldn't be overheard.

"Huge, you bring those magazines?" Jeb asked. He was referring to the fact that Hugh had a well-worn collection of girlie magazines they enjoyed looking at during long stakeouts. Sort of took the edge off their testosterone level for a bit. It never really helped Lionel at all. He found it extremely childish.

"Jeb, you have more money than God. Anything wrong with you buying your own smut?"

"Nah."

"Oh, I get it," Hugh continued. "You just like it free."

"Well, if you are offering and everything. Why not?"

Lionel pointed to Paolo, who was returning from the bar with four glasses of red wine. "Casanova here is on his way to Tuscany. Why don't you ask him to bring back some of those Eastern European magazines?"

"Those girls look young. Really young."

"Some of them are," Paolo interjected. "Big money these days in smuggling little girls into prostitution. You don't want to support them by buying their stuff."

Jeb looked up at the ceiling. Lionel could tell this was one of those times he felt impatient with their Golden vamp employer.

"Marcus over there, too?" Hugh asked.

"Yup. That's why we need your services," Paolo said, holding up his glass. "Cheers, gents."

They clinked glasses. Paolo sipped his wine, savoring it, while the brothers threw theirs back like it was a shot of whisky.

"They got absinthe here?" Huge asked Lionel.

"It's a French bistro. I'd say yes," Lionel answered him. "But let's stay off the green crazy stuff until we find out what's in store for us."

The brothers recrossed their legs in tandem again, Huge and Jeb crossing their arms as well.

"We have reason to believe the new dark coven Supreme Leader, Dag Nielsen, has his eye on a friend of mine, a college professor named Carabella Sampson," Paolo started. "I would be personally taking care of her, except I'm accompanying Marcus to Tuscany, where we have pressing business."

"We get to take care of her the same way, too?" Jeb grinned, demonstrating he had lost a tooth. One of his canines. Paolo frowned.

"What happened to your tooth?" he asked.

"Had it pulled. Was giving me some fits. I got an implant coming."

"How they going to do that?"

"Well Dr. Gervais—you know him, Paolo—done some work for Anne. He says he can give me an implant, but it will have to stay down all the time. The hollow point will be towards the back of the tooth so no one would be able to see it up close."

"Still, Jeb, gotta be kinda awkward walking around with a fuckin' straw sticking out of your lips all the time," Hugh added as he punched his younger brother. The ensuing tussle almost sent them all sprawling. They got temporarily entangled in the canvas curtain of the outside seating area, hitting the aluminum frame and alerting other customers to their presence.

"Would you guys stop with the horseplay?" Lionel whispered to them. "Some pair of covert ops you guys make."

Paolo finished off his wine and leaned into the table. "For the record, my brother doesn't approve of my involvement with the beautiful Cara, so he has erased her memory of me."

The Jett brothers looked like they were responding to a bad smell.

"For her own safety, she has to be kept in the dark. And that's where you come in. We need a detail on her 24/7. Marcus told me you have some brothers in arms you can trust during the day?"

Lionel nodded. "Retired SEALs. Bad ass dudes, for mortals."

"They available for hire?"

"Depends. They evaluate the situation first before they decide."

"No can do. This has to be kept strictly between us. No one outside the family and your family can know all the facts."

"Which are?" Lionel asked. The cat and mouse game was tiring him.

"This lady is a professor at SSU, an authority on myths and mythology, with a special emphasis on vampire lore. She had located evidence that a very rare book on our kind had surfaced again after centuries."

"Had? As in past tense?" Hugh asked.

"That's primarily why we erased her memory. But the other side doesn't know this—well, to be perfectly honest, they've been told, but they don't believe it. We believe this book was part of my grandfather's collection. It disappeared before I was born."

"And you have the book now?" Lionel asked.

"No. We have a book, a book Cara found and had shipped here to California, a sort of cryptic map written in journal form by a man who did find it almost two hundred years ago. That book is in safekeeping. We believe it will tell us where the missing tome can be found."

"And so what's the problem?"

"Dag Nielsen and his dark coven want that book, and they've been killing to get it. You know they killed young Rory Monteleone last week?" Paolo said.

Each brother silently nodded.

"And they got his little brother two weeks ago. They've been killing the Golden children like crazy. We're not sure why they've stepped up this geno-cide against our race," Paolo continued, "but Dag has something up his sleeve, and he desperately wants what's in the book."

"Makes me wonder too, Paolo. You got any ideas?" Lionel felt like his employer was hiding something, but he couldn't quite make out what.

"I'll give you specifics after I get them. Right now, we're going to Tuscany to get permission for a mission here. We're asking you just keep an eye on things until we return."

"You mean keep an eye on her?"

"Well, yes. We also have staff, loyal, trusted mortals who have served our family for generations. We cannot leave them unprotected."

"But you primarily care about her," Lionel dug deeper.

"I'm not lying when I say she matters a great deal to me, but her importance in this scheme is far greater than just my feelings alone. You've all felt the rumblings of war, right?"

The brothers nodded solemnly. Even Lionel couldn't look into Paolo's eyes. The smell of war and impending death was all around the little wine country community full of innocents who had no idea what was about to befall them.

"We are getting close to understanding what this grudge is all about. And looking for ways to stop the planned attack on us all."

"Why not round them up and take care of it that way?" Lionel wanted to know. He wondered why they were being so careful. "They aren't loyal even to themselves. Should be easy to get the information we need."

"Because we aren't sure they haven't discovered some weapon to use against us. And we don't know where their information is coming from." Paolo leaned back in his chair. "Brothers, we are trying to stop innocent lives from being lost."

The two younger Jett brothers looked at Lionel, who was stewing about a problem he suddenly had to express. "Just what am I supposed to tell the SEAL team? They don't even know we're vamps."

"Lionel, under the circumstances, I think you'll have to level with them."

"Suuuureeee. You fuckin' gotta be nuts, Paolo! They'll never believe it. What am I supposed to do? You ever try to convince someone about vampires? Someone who is absolutely an unbeliever?"

Paolo smiled. "Do what I did once."

"What's that?" Lionel asked.

"Disappear or trace them somewhere."

CHAPTER 34

Cara called the University and confirmed what Mr. Monteleone had told her. Classes had indeed been cancelled. It was all over the news about her assistant's murder. She spent the day in and out of bed, with long crying bouts in between.

It was odd how she had lost three whole days, just forgotten what she had taught, who she had talked to, what she had done. Though she tried to retrieve her memories, it was as if they were gone from her forever, not locked behind an iron wall. Just evaporated.

Something had been pressing on her, she could tell that much as she looked over the papers covering her desk. For some reason, just from the way her normally neat papers were splayed across the wooden surface of her home office, she got the feeling she had been looking for something. She started to organize the mess, hoping it would bring back at least a sliver of her memory.

She began to examine every slip of paper she could find, sorting them into piles on the floor. Bills, receipts for payments made, checkbook statements, professional magazines, and correspondence. She even had a couple of early Christmas cards from educational companies wanting her to purchase their teaching aids. There were several requests for donations to charity events coming up.

She'd made a decision skip any more faculty charity functions until next year. Although she made a decent income as a college professor, she was planning some trips—*what was that? Where had that come from?*

A trip? She'd been planning a trip?

She quickly scanned the travel brochures that she'd tossed on the pile of clothing and bedding catalogues she had planned to recycle.

She found a brochure with a post-it note inside describing a city tour and map of Prague. She read the note, which was not in her handwriting.

If you are in need of lodging, this hotel is very nice and not as expensive as some. My family and I live in a small flat above the bookstore and cannot accommodate you, although we would if we could. My store is quite close, within walking distance.

I am due to receive another crate from a monastery in Scotland in early November. If there is anything of interest there, I shall message you. Until then, please use my travel agent as a resource. She can find you some great airfare that could save you hundreds of dollars, if the tickets are purchased here.

Regards,

Tomas Novotny

Cara put the note down and stared out into the darkening sky. She hadn't even noticed she'd missed her lunch, and now was hungry for dinner.

As she prepared a salad, she thought about the note. For some reason, the name Tomas Novotny was familiar to her. Then she remembered where she had seen the name before. It appeared on her credit card statement as Novotny something. Novotny Travel?

Novotny Books.

She dropped everything in the kitchen and rummaged through her desktop piles and found the one for her credit card statement from two months ago. The single line item for August 15 read: Novotny Books. The charge was for $2,450, which meant it was a valuable book, or research material. She just couldn't remember what it was. Sitting behind the desk, placing her forehead to her palm, she concentrated.

What was this book? What was the book about?

She knew it must have been about vampires. And her upcoming trip to Prague was further indication of the connection she had with this particular bookseller. But why couldn't she remember the purchase?

She kept a stack of cards in her center desk drawer. Flipping through them, she came upon the card for a Tomas Novotny, rare bookseller. And there was a telephone number.

Before she thought about what time it was in Prague, she dialed the number but got no answer. The phone rang and rang. She hung up and retried the number. On the third try, an answering machine picked up with a man's voice speaking in broken English.

'This is Thomas Novotny. I am currently unavailable but will return your call if you speak slowly and leave your telephone number. Please also state the nature of your business, and what book or periodical you are interested in. Thank you and have a good day.'

The beep made Cara jump before she collected herself in order to leave a message. "Mr. Novotny, my name is Professor Cara Sampson and I am calling from California. I believe you sold me a book in August, and I would like to discuss this with you. You also mentioned you were receiving another shipment. I'd be most interested in what you have found, if anything. Thank you." Cara left her phone number and hung up.

Paolo was struck with a perplexing feeling. Something was worrying him. He concentrated on it as he rode with Lucius in the family limo to the airport. They were flying to his brother's home just outside Florence.

The persistent, perplexing sensation seemed to be generated from outside himself. He leaned back into the leather seat, resting his head and closing his eyes.

"Father, are you okay?" Lucius asked.

"Yes, son. I have a bit of a headache. I was trying to see if I could make it go away." He smiled down at his son, who grinned back, and snuggled closer to him. Paolo loved how just being with Lucius made him happy, and vowed he'd spend all his non-working time with the boy. "You excited to be going back in Italy?" he asked Lucius.

"Yes. I like the sunlight there. More yellow. Not as bright as California, more golden."

Paolo had never thought about that before, but Lucius was right. The sunlight in California did seem very harsh and often hurt his eyes.

The pain in his forehead came back. He could just barely make out a statement: *What was this book. What was this book about?*

Paolo gripped the leather armrest and sat forward, which nearly toppled Lucius. It was Cara's thoughts he was hearing. And she was thinking about a book. Looking for a book.

The limo driver was a newer employee, so Paolo dared not risk a cell phone call in front of him. He motioned to have the man pull the vehicle over. He got out of the driver's seat and opened up the rear door.

"Sir? You want something?"

"I just remembered. I forgot something at the house."

"But you will miss your flight if we return there now."

"But I have to go back."

"Sir, should I call the airline and see if you can take a later flight? I am quite sure you will miss your flight."

Paolo wished he'd taken his brother up on the offer to take a private charter, where he could show up late and they'd wait for him. Paolo had insisted on paying for his own way, taking a first class commercial flight.

The driver was waiting for an answer.

"Let's stop at Starbuck's. I need to use the rest room. I'll see if I can get hold of someone at the house. Perhaps they can mail it to me," Paolo lied.

"Very well, sir." The driver resumed his duties, pulling up to a Starbuck's within minutes.

Paolo didn't want to leave Lucius in the car, so he instructed him to accompany him inside. "You want anything?" he asked the driver.

"No thanks. We come stocked. I don't drink coffee, affects my nerves, not to mention my driving."

"Nasty habit. Lucius and I will be right out." He helped his son inside the shop and heard the familiar scream of the espresso machines. "You go first, Lucius. I'll get you, what, a hot chocolate?"

"Oh, yes. Thanks, Father," Lucius called over his shoulder as he skipped toward the men's room. He waited until he saw his son close the door behind him before he made the call to Marcus. His brother picked up on the first ring.

"Problem? You should be on your way by now."

"I just got an image, a feeling from Cara. She's looking for a book. Searching her memory, and she's a little frustrated with it, too. She's investigating it, brother."

"Damn." Marcus was not pleased. "You got the Jett brothers squared away?"

"All set. They should be all around the house. Marcus, what if they learn about the book?"

Paolo could almost feel the wheels turning slowly in his brother's head. "It's a risk we're going to have to take. I need you to get Lucius to safety. I need your help with the Council."

"But if she's beginning to put things together, won't she perhaps begin to regain her memories?"

"That I don't know. There is still only one course for you. You must get you and your son to Italy without any further delay. Let's have the Jett boys earn their salary. Is there a detail for the day?"

"Yes. Marcus, they are mortal."

"Who are they?"

"Friends of Lionel. Retired SEALs."

Marcus chuckled. "They'll do. If they believe in the cause, they're every bit as good as your ordinary black vamp."

Paolo reluctantly agreed to continue with his flight plans. He dialed Lionel just in case and was reassured that Cara had stayed home this evening, and was going through paperwork on her desk. No visitors. Nothing out of the ordinary. Nothing scented or sensed that caused them to worry. Lionel assured Paolo they were vigilant.

"And you wouldn't believe what my buds think of me now that they know I can disappear at will. They all want to learn the trick."

Paolo was glad for Lionel, who seemed to be able to fit into the human world as well as his own dark family, yet still maintain his loyalty to the Monteleone clan. He was indeed a rare warrior.

"They with you tonight?"

"We're training a few at a time. But yes. I've traced them to Murder Burger three times already tonight. They think it's pretty cool. I know it's not the hamburgers. It's the ride they love."

This brought a smile to Paolo's face, just as Lucius was coming from the bathroom.

Damn. He'd been so engrossed in the phone calls that he'd forgotten to order the hot chocolate.

They waited in line to order, holding hands. Then Lucius sat on his lap on the couch while they awaited their order. Paolo was glad he'd decided not to tell his brother the SEALs were going to be told about their Golden Vampire lineage.

He could see that the years of peaceful coexistence with the dark covens and the human world had left their family without their own protective forces made up of Golden vampires wishing to serve and perhaps lay down their lives for their families. That was a tremendous error in judgment. Relying on other species to protect the Golden families had left the dark covens with a distinct advantage. Just by their very nature, the dark covens had never ceased to maintain a fighting stance. And their numbers had been growing exponentially. Paolo intended to inform the Council of this.

The limo continued to the airport, where they got aboard the plane for Florence without a moment to spare. Paolo encouraged Lucius to sleep, but his son was avidly playing with all the gadgets available in first class seating. No doubt the boy would be halfway disappointed when they landed.

Paolo listened for another thought from Cara, but felt nothing. He smiled back at the attendant, who seemed determined to give him extra attention, leaning over him to serve his boy, making it hard for him not to get a whiff of the perfumed flesh between her breasts. It only made him long for Cara.

Paolo thought of Cara and wished that someday he'd get one more day with her. He'd even take a day where she didn't know him. He'd even agree not to glam her if he had to. Anything to be in proximity to her.

The attendant's breast brushed over Paolo's shoulder in an unmistakable gesture. Her peacock- blue eyes were lovely, he thought. Full pink lips that could no doubt do lovely things. But he sighed, careful not to sigh in her direction or she'd orgasm on the spot in front of the entire first class cabin. Perhaps he'd have to get used to this. But he would never forget Cara, or the wonderful music her body played for him. Her voice, her touch, the feel of her skin, were all something he needed, craved. And, unlike a true addiction, she was good for him. She granted him life and spirit. Strength and purpose.

For now, the need to protect his son and his family had to come first. He hoped the Jett brothers and their buddies would do their jobs like they had done for centuries. He prayed there would be time for love later.

CHAPTER 35

Dag awoke on his bed, but it was different. For one thing, he was spread-eagled. His wrists and ankles were bound with silver, making movement painful. Made not a bit of difference to his dick, however. It stood to attention like a telephone pole.

He was going to yell "fuck you" at himself, but decided his dick would take it as encouragement. The body part was so useful in so many ways, and so completely abnormal in others, and only a bit of that was fun for him. He liked control, and his dick always had a mind of its own.

There was someone else in the room. Suddenly the fact that he was restrained bothered him. "Hey. Who's there?" he said to the half-closed door to his private bathroom. The seconds ticked by and there was no answer. "I fuckin' said who is there? Come here right now and untie me."

Shirley, the little blonde waif, stood in the doorway to the bathroom, stark staring naked but covered with blood.

"What the fuck?"

"Look at your skin, master," She whispered. "While you were sleeping, I repaired you."

Sure enough, Dag looked at his formerly blistered and blackened skin and saw that most of the flakiness was gone. What remained was reddish and blotchy. Rather like blood marble.

"What did you do? And get me out of these cuffs. They're hurting me."

She smiled sweetly again. Something behind that smile alarmed him. Was the girl some species he'd not encountered before? A tiny shiver of fear coursed down his spine and, right on cue, made his dick lurch. She giggled. It pissed Dag off.

Shirley came over to the bed. Her wrists had been cut. She'd used her own blood to wash him, heal him. As soon as he got out of the restraints, he'd properly thank her. Or kill her. He'd decide later. Right now he was focusing on the juncture between her legs. He needed to feed, and that spot would work just fine.

"You want me?" she said as she outlined her left areola with her right forefinger. She held the finger up; there was blood covering the tip.

"Yes. Yes I do. Very much."

"That's not a very sexy way to get a girl to fuck you, Dag."

"Come here and I'll show you."

"You have enough energy? You sure?"

"Look at my fuckin' dick. That should tell you everything you need to know. I'm ready as hell. Come here."

"I want you to beg."

"What?" Dag pulled at his bindings but the burning from the silver chains made him stop. He considered severing his own wrist, since he'd regenerate in a day anyway, but he didn't want to experience the pain. But if he had to, he could do that.

"I said beg me. Be sweet to me."

"Please. Get me the fuck outta these restraints or I'll fuckin' nail your hide to the wall."

"That's not what I meant at all." She turned around, bent over and gave him a good look at her sex from behind. And her anus. "If you ever want to see these again, you're going to have to learn to speak nicely to me. Understood?"

"Whoa! Wait a minute. Nobody talks to me that way."

"I'm the one that talks to you that way. Until you talk nice." She began dancing, gyrating, smoothing the syrupy blood over her body. "You could lick all this off me, wash me. Then you could fuck me until I pass out. How does that sound?"

"Sounds nice."

"Just nice?"

"Okay, sounds like fun."

"Just fun?"

"What the fuck do you want me to say? Tell me what to say and I'll do it. Just get me out of these restraints. This is really beginning to piss me off."

"Tell me you need me. Like you did yesterday."

Did I do that? Holy shit, I did.

"I liked it when you talked to me like that. It made me come almost the instant I heard it."

"Look, Shirley, I have some very important things to do and I'm on a tight schedule. We can have a little fun, but you gotta get me out of these. There are people waiting on me."

"No one has come by the house. The phone hasn't rung. Your phone— where is your phone?"

Dag realized that in his blackened and painful après sunscorched state he had forgotten to look for his cell phone when he peeled off his clothes. "I think it's over there, in that pile of rags."

"What pile of rags? You mean the rags I took out and had burned?"

"You fuckin' did *what*?"

"I burned them. In your fireplace downstairs. Let me go see if the cell phone fell out."

She turned to go.

"No! Wait. Look, honey, this is real fun and all, but could you just undo me, please? I promise to be real sweet."

"I'll go check on the phone and *then* you can be sweet to me." She left.

Dag was livid. He'd never felt like he could have a heart attack before, but he was fairly sure he was on the way to having one now. It wasn't a whole lot of fun being restrained on the bloody sheets with his dick winking at him, taunting him in that unnatural way.

What the fuck is going on? Had everyone gone completely bonkers?

He heard screams coming from downstairs. That would be his staff, heading for the hills at the sight of the little twisted, bloody sister scraping through ashes in the fireplace. What a scene that must have been. He regretted missing it.

Dag searched for another solution. Severing his wrist was beginning to make perfect sense. Except he'd have to bite the damn thing off, and that would take too much time. If he had a knife, easy pezy. But no, that blade had

MORTAL BITE

been in his pants pocket, probably in the fireplace too, along with the phone numbers of his entire organization.

Whatever gave her the idea she had to burn his fuckin' clothes anyway? Some ritual sacrifice?

Uh, oh. He'd heard about some tribes who burned the possessions of their enemy before they ate them. Holy shit, maybe she was some freak from another world he knew nothing about. Were her people trying to get control of his coven by destroying him?

He was beginning to regret ever having met the little panhandler that evening in front of the coffee bar. No question about it. She'd been a plant. And boy, did he fall right for it. He'd underestimated them. Well, he wouldn't do that again. As soon as he got rid of his wrist, he'd show them how ruthless he could be with their vessel, their messenger of death and doom. No one was going to put that over on him.

Dag tried to take a bite up by his wrist and realized, to his horror, that he couldn't reach it and would have to eat through his elbow to obtain freedom. That presented a whole new set of circumstances. Big bones. Big arteries and lots of blood. He wondered if he should bite above or below the elbow joint. The skin above looked more tender, and didn't the lower extremity have two bones, not one? Or, was it the other way around?

Fuck! Where is my biology knowledge when I need it? He'd always hated that class. Served him right. He felt like murdering his old teacher just because he hadn't inspired him to learn better. He'd do it, once he got out of these restraints.

What the fuck was taking her so long? Dag sighed. Time to start biting.

The first bite hurt like hell. He'd nailed the soft tissue below his bicep. The skin tore off in ribbons and he spit it out.

This is disgusting.

He was about to take another bite when he heard heavy footsteps coming up the stairs, and the clanging of keys and metallic things.

My boys. Thank the devil himself!

Rhys and another of his men stood by the opened door and stared at the scene before them, appearing to be in shock.

"Don't you fuckin' stand there holding your dicks. Get me out of these things."

196

"Sorry, boss." Kevin, the one who was Sidney's nephew, hurried to one side of the bed and took out a pair of wire cutters from the toolkit he always wore on his belt. Dag had made fun of him, calling him "the gardener" all the time. Now he was grateful the dark vamp was so handy with his tools.

The silver stung poor Kevin, who whimpered at the blister for a long moment before completing the task on the other side.

"Would you hurry the fuck up?"

"Yessir."

While Kevin was undoing his ankle Dag asked about the girl.

"What girl?" the man asked.

"The one that did this to me. The little vamp slut I turned."

"There was no girl downstairs. Your housemaid called us, but she was hysterical. You don't think she did it, do you?"

"Of course not. But maybe she knows where the little twat went."

"They're all gone, sir."

Free at last, Dag leapt to his feet and ran for the bathroom to take a shower. Except he misjudged the smooth marble floor, slipped on the blood coated all over him and the floor and fell on his butt. He didn't even yell at the two guards who were having difficulty keeping in their laughter. He would have lots of time to get even, after he found the girl and made her pay for her crime.

But that would come after he got his hands on Paolo's girl, extracted the book information from her, and left her for dead. He had to kill something that meant something to someone else. That was the only way to soothe the pain inside him. He needed to even the score. It didn't matter who paid the price, but it made it more likely he'd be satisfied if it was someone who mattered to Paolo Monteleone.

Lionel Jett sat in a nest of yellow and white hamburger wrappers. Andrew, the SEAL he'd been training, had fallen asleep, probably due to the large globules of fat coursing through his veins from all the fast food he'd consumed this evening. Boy, those guys could pack it away, he thought. Almost funny.

He decided to let his buddy sleep, knowing that if he needed the man he'd be ready instantly, as ready as any creature on the planet could be. Since Lionel was always awake during the night, it was no problem for him. But he was bored.

He'd watched Paolo's woman sorting through all her stuff like they were sheets of delicate old books she was trying to preserve. Why was it women liked all this paperwork shit, he wondered? They liked to take care of little details that just didn't matter in Lionel's world. He dealt with the big things: life, death. That was about it. Honor was in there somewhere. Love was supposed to be there, too, but it was all lust right now, no chance for love.

Young Maria Monteleone had been like this lady, he thought. She liked to work on her needlepoint, sit quietly by the fireplace and listen. She'd hear things. Like the night she commented on his heartbeat. It happened every time he looked at her. He was grateful his member didn't make a sound or she would have picked up on that, too. Or, maybe she stole little glances at his groin when he wasn't looking.

She didn't belong to him, but it didn't stop him from having the kind of dreams any healthy dark vamp would have. Maria was sophisticated and kind. She didn't have to try to be nice, she was nice all the way through her core. But though his feelings for her ran deep, the fact that they were two distinct species meant that a mating could never occur without the punishment by death. The Council had made examples of other dark vamps who had been entrusted with the safekeeping of the Monteleone family, especially the women and children. Those who strayed and found themselves in an illicit affair with a Golden—and it happened only rarely—were swiftly tried and their lives ended. So sad that love should cause the death of a person. Lionel had always thought this should not be.

But the Council was everything. It controlled everything the Goldens did. It was the gatekeeper of their history, their rituals, the stories passed down from generation to generation. Unlike the dark covens, who were like wild rogue armies that came and went, leaving wreckage in their wake, Goldens enhanced the communities they lived in. And they cared for everyone who was loyal to them. They never sought out recognition, working silently for the good of the community of man as a whole, both vampire and mortal.

Lionel saw she was getting tired. She'd had coffee, and that kept her awake for a couple of hours, but now, past midnight, she was fading. Her sheer, dogged determination kept her poring over the paperwork. She took notes. She leaned back against the tall wooden chair and he could see the beautiful chest of Paolo's woman. Her graceful neck. Her blood would taste sweet, he thought.

Paolo, you are a lucky man.

Paolo was allowed a mortal bride, a pleasure partner. Lionel would have to defend her with his own life if need be. Yet Lionel would never be allowed to have this for himself. It wasn't fair, but it was the way of it. Lionel knew it didn't do anyone any good to dredge up those latent feelings that perhaps there could have been another future for him. If he'd taken another path.

He knew Paolo regretted his choice to become vampire. It had weighed on his mother heavily. She'd wanted to remain mortal, though her husband wanted the change. But Maria, beautiful, full of life Maria, didn't want to live forever. Lionel couldn't understand that. Who wouldn't want to live forever?

She bore all eight of her children as a mortal woman. Back in those days, women died in childbirth all the time, but Maria was blessed with a strong body and an even stronger will. Lionel had to admit, it was her will that he had loved, even as he lusted for her body. He could have gladly married her, even if he could never touch her, just to be close to her.

In the end, he had to be satisfied with being her personal bodyguard and most trusted companion, and later most trusted advisor as her health deteriorated, as she was left alone, as the children she bore adopted the vampiric life and had children of their own if they met their fated mates. She didn't want to live to hear all the stories, she said. At the time of her death, Paolo, Laurel and Marcus were unmarried and had never felt the fating.

He wondered if there ever could be a fating between Golden and dark. Was that the secret she bore? Why she wouldn't take the turning, even when her children begged her? Perhaps as a mortal woman she could bear the children she would not be able to bear as a vampire lady. Perhaps she was not fated to her husband. Perhaps she was fated to—

Lionel heard a sound and shook the snoring form of the SEAL.

"We have company, I do believe," he whispered to Andrew.

"Roger that." The SEAL woke up ready, just as Lionel had expected. He radioed his counterpart on the other side of the building.

"They haven't seen anything," Andrew reported back.

"There's something out there. I can smell it," Lionel breathed He motioned a zipper to his lip, indicating they'd be doing hand signals from now on.

Andrew donned his night vision goggles and then switched to infrared. He tapped a thumbs up and passed an extra pair to Lionel. A torch of deep orange was gliding, floating across the street and up towards the window of Cara's bedroom. It was the heat sig of a tracing vamp, but it was in slow motion, as if the individual wanted to be detected.

Curious, Lionel motioned for caution and continued to watch the torch blend through the walls and stand in the bedroom beyond. Lionel decided he didn't want to wait any longer to get between this creature and the woman he was hired to protect.

He motioned to the SEAL, who slipped an arm around Lionel's shoulder so he could trace them both to a spot in the hallway beyond. As they landed, a flash of light temporarily blinded them. The tracing vamp had been wired to explode, and if they had been in the same room, would have been killed. As it was, Andrew had suffered a head injury. He lay on his back, blood draining from both ears. Lionel examined himself and determined somehow he'd been unscathed. He heard Cara scream, and immediately he dashed for her home office.

Cara was wrestling with a dark vamp who turned and gave Lionel a bloody smile. He had taken a bite out of Cara's neck and was trying to wrench her head from her body.

Dag.

"Too late again for the party, Lionel. You can have seconds, if you like. I know you love mortal flesh."

Lionel's fury overtook him. He grappled with the coven leader, sure that others were going to follow. Andrew came to his feet, assisted by another SEAL teammate. Jeb and Hugh took hold of Cara.

"To the villa," was all Lionel could say before he was thrown against and through the wall of Cara's apartment. As he landed on the ground outside, he briefly saw his two brothers trace Cara away, hopefully to safety.

"Still doing the Monteleone's dirty work, Lionel? Can't seem to get a woman of your own, but you'll die defending theirs? That what your life's about?"

"What would you know about my life, you miserable creature? You've lived a third of my lifetime. I've killed more of you than I can remember."

"Your own kind. You've killed your own kin, for what? For them? You think they understand you? Care about you and your needs?" Dag was smirking, circling Lionel with lethal intent. Lionel realized he was waiting for something. He didn't have to wait long to find out what it was.

A silver net fell over Lionel's body, encapsulating the guardian and denying him the ability to do further harm.

Before they injected him with the sleeping serum, Lionel saw the face of Dag's new executioner, who was wearing heavy gloves to protect his hands from the silver netting. He aimed the pistol containing the tranquilizing agent at Lionel's heart, and laughed.

CHAPTER 36

Cara looked around her at the band of men who stood as if they were going to take orders from her. She was unclear what had just happened. But somehow she had been transported, *flown* here at a high rate of speed. She must have passed out, yet she had no sense of losing consciousness. Something about the two-second ride was familiar to her. It felt like her skin had tiny pinpricks all over it. And she *knew* that it wasn't the first time that had happened.

She looked from the face of one man to another, one by one. Until she found the man who had grabbed her by the waist and had done the flying—if that is what it could be called.

He was handsome, and huge. Sandy brown hair covered his camouflage-painted forehead. He didn't flinch as she stepped toward him. "What exactly just happened, you want to tell me what you just did to me?"

"Ma'am. You were in danger. We brought you here to safety." The giant then pointed to her neck, which suddenly hurt. She placed her fingers on the sore spot, and they came back bloody. Black spots began to form in front of her eyes, and even they seemed familiar, but she fought the urge to sink to the ground. One of the men stepped forward to help her steady herself and she pushed off the tattoo-covered arm.

"Just how did you do it? You grabbed me and the next thing I knew we were here. I want answers and I want them right now."

Several of the men began to smile, but others solemnly nodded their heads.

"And I want to go back to salvage what's left of my apartment."

"They've got Lionel, Huge," one of the men said to the gentleman who had carried her. The big man looked angry.

"You've been placed here in protective custody until the Monteleones can return home. Until then, you are to stay here with us," he said.

"Like hell I will. Monteleone? Did you say Monteleone? As in the head of security for the University?" she asked.

The band of men laughed. White teeth, dimples, bulging chests and war paint. They didn't look like killers from the way they laughed, but they were sure dressed for it.

"What's so funny? I'd be able to show you his card, except my apartment seems to have been blown up. This the security office?"

She realized how stupid she sounded. There was no mistaking the fact that the two-story room with carved ceilings was the great room of a grand estate, and not a security office.

"You'll want to freshen up until they return. It's been a long night, but you're safe here, honest." The big man held our his hand, "My name is Hugh Jett. This is my brother, Jeb, and these are our team members. We are the private security force of the Monteleone family, your hosts, and owner of this villa."

One by one the men peeled off from the circle, leaving Cara alone with Hugh and Jeb Jett. "This way, ma'am," Jeb pointed to the iron stairway leading to the second floor.

"Do I have a choice in the matter?" Cara asked.

"Not if you want to live." Hugh Jett answered her from behind. She hung onto the handrail and began the long climb. It began to be too much for her and she started to faint.

Hugh Jett was right there, as he had been before, with his arm around her waist. Before she could protest, he had lifted her up and carried her up the stairs as easily as she might carry a pillow. He brought her to a set of double doors, which he opened, revealing a dark chamber with a roaring fireplace. A large bed with satin sheets stood against the wall opposite the fireplace. The room was warm. The bed looked inviting. Cara suddenly felt very, very tired.

"I will have one of the girls come get you ready for bed. We will provide some bedclothes for you, and some clothes for the morning. But tonight you must stay here, for your own protection, understand?" Hugh looked down on her like he was talking to a child. She felt like a child.

"Of course," was all she could think of to say. Although she wanted to take a shower and get clean, she desperately needed to sleep. There would be time enough tomorrow for fighting.

"Ma'am. I have some things for you, plus a nice bowl of warm soup." A young girl in maid uniform brought a tray with a soup bowl and glass of water. Tucked under her arm was a fluffy flannel nightie. "This is mine. I think it will fit." The girl set the tray down and whisked the two giants out of the room.

"Whose room is this?" Cara asked as she accompanied the girl to the light brown marble bathroom. A man's robe hung on a brass hook shaped like a palm. She noted a slight lemony scent to it.

"This is the guest room, currently occupied by Mr. Paolo Monteleone. His brother owns this villa, and the winery.

"Ah. He runs the security company that Sonoma State contracts with, is that right?"

"I'm not sure what the nature of Mr. Monteleone's business is here. He lives in Tuscany, ma'am."

"And where is he this evening?"

The girl blushed as she tested the shower water she'd just started. "He left for Tuscany this evening. You'll not be disturbed. Don't worry."

Cara looked in the mirror at her ruined clothes, the blood that had seeped down the side of her blouse. The skin around the wound was getting pink and swollen. "This is going to need some attention. Perhaps after my shower I should be taken to the Emergency Room."

"No, ma'am. You are safer here. We have a healing balm that will take care of most of the pain and the infection."

"You have no idea what just happened to me. I was bitten, by this man—"

"Yes, I understand. I can see as much. But, trust me, we have a very effective salve we use for all injuries around the estate. There will not be anyone available to take you to the hospital until tomorrow. But, we will see to whatever you need Please?" she motioned for Cara to come toward the shower.

Cara allowed the girl to remove her blouse. She was becoming stiff. Her back ached from the jarring she took as she—

Flew?

Cara thought she was losing her mind. First Mr. Monteleone told her she'd forgotten about the death of her assistant, and that police had questioned her and she had no recollection of it. Now she was standing in a stranger's bedroom, about to disrobe, and be treated for a bite wound?

And what about the rare book? The book about—

Vampires. Ohmygod, this is all about vampires. Did one bite her?

"You have to get me out of here," she whispered to the young maid.

"No, ma'am. You must stay here. It is for your safety. Trust me when I tell you there is no safer place than this home. You are in danger. There has been already loss of life."

"Yes. My assistant was murdered."

"And Jeb and Hugh Jett lost their brother tonight as well. They lost him while rescuing you."

Cara could see the girl was speaking what she believed to be the truth. She wondered if the girl would answer her next question truthfully.

"I need to ask you something and I want you to be honest with me. Do vampires exist?"

The maid turned her gaze to the ground and nodded. "Under the Monteleone's care there is no greater protection."

"Are they—?"

"No more questions. Everything will be explained tomorrow. Tonight you must shower, I'll apply the healing salve and someone will discuss all these things with you in the morning. Fair enough?"

Cara stepped into the shower, which had filled with steam. The lemony soap was exhilarating on her skin, gave a little lift of hope to her insides, the feeling that perhaps the nightmare was about to end, that there was a new chapter beginning in her life.

And everything in her life was about to change forever.

Again.

CHAPTER 37

L ionel was trussed and hung from the rafters in the old warehouse Rubin the executioner used as his own private torture palace. A perimeter security current prevented him from tracing out to a safe place. His strength had waned. When the dark guards and soldiers went off for their daytime sleep, a mortal brute was brought in to continue waking Lionel up, whipping him, dousing him in vinegar, and making fun of how fast he healed from his injuries, which prompted spurts of more cruelty.

The senior Jett brother was growing weary of the game, and knew that unless a vital organ were hit, he could continue on this way for centuries. In fact, there were stories about this kind of sacrifice, a dark prisoner outliving several lifespans of his mortal torturers. Lionel wondered if he, too, would someday be looked upon as a fixture on the wall, no different than one of those ugly, buzzing fluorescent lamps no one ever looked at. His groans and moans would be background noise to an otherwise busy day, or lost in the dusty corners of the abandoned warehouse.

He actually liked it when someone was present, even if it meant torture. The boredom of hanging, reacting to every strange sound, the wind jangling the chains that held the doors shut or the scurrying of a tiny rodent was mind-numbing. But even if he wanted to, Lionel knew he could and would not end himself. As long as he was alive, his mission was still to live, protect and give witness to the mighty Monteleone clan.

The executioner had brought a couple of curious girls to the warehouse, no doubt to prove his manhood and cruelty, something Lionel thought Rubin felt a bit self-conscious about for some reason. He talked them into the leather restraints. He whipped them with a crop, and if they didn't cry out enough, he'd whip Lionel, causing a ribbon of flesh to fly off his body. They'd scream just watching Lionel suffer.

Later on, Rubin brought someone else who definitely was not using drugs and was a whole octave higher on the intelligence scale. Lionel could sense she was a dark vamp, and a recent turning. Rubin's bloodstained fingers massaged the little tart's breasts from behind as she stood in front of Lionel, watching every ripple and movement of muscle his body made. She was naked and had nice skin. She revealed a sullen smile when his pecker rose for a salute, not that she deserved that. He just couldn't help it.

The executioner had seen her arousal at another man's dick and cried foul.

"Shut up, sweetheart," she replied to him. "I'm the one you're going to fuck. Let's do it right here, in front of him. Maybe he'll come in my face."

Rubin grunted and got to work, bending his knees to make up for their difference in height. He wasn't light on his feet and was having positional difficulties. The little vixen sighed, grabbed Lionel's thighs and bent herself forward, balancing on the bloody prisoner. This gave Rubin full access to either orifice and he got to work, until he noticed she had licked Lionel's cock and began licking the old sticky blood from his body.

"Hey. Not. Sure. I. Like. That," Rubin gasped between thrusts.

She wiggled her eyebrows up and down and mouthed *whatever*, then got back to work, teasing the prisoner to the point of making him pop.

Lionel had to admit he wanted to push her head into his groin and smother her, but his hands remained tied high above his head. He tried to focus on her face and where her tongue was going, rather than what was happening behind her. She had a nice touch. He could almost say she was gentle.

"I want your cum, lover boy," she whispered between licks. She took a couple of steps closer and enclosed him with her mouth, no longer teasing but working on him with in a very skilled and professional style.

Rubin didn't seem to notice. The executioner's eyes were squeezed shut as he grunted his release, probably thinking she was referring to him.

Lionel let her have it, all eight fuckin' ounces of it or however much it was. He'd never measured. She got most of it down, and her breasts were creamy and covered in his sticky seed that had leaked from her lips. He could tell she would be gagging soon, but instead, she rammed him deeper, all the way down her throat, which sent a new wave of cum from him in response.

Holy shit.

If he ever made it out of here, he'd have a hard time getting his brothers and the Monteleone boys to believe what had transpired.

Not that he had any choice in the matter than to relax and allow himself to become a tool.

Rubin was done and he began to wipe himself up with a dirty rag. The blonde righted herself and smeared the cum over her breasts. She was breathing hard as she studied Lionel. He saw a question there, but had no idea what she really had on her mind. Just that she was the most twisted lady he'd ever met. Her eyes had gone dark. Lionel could tell she was enjoying the pleasures of his preternatural sperm. She licked her lips and gave him a wicked smile. He knew he was in for more sex if he didn't get out of this warehouse. Maybe he could use her arousal to his advantage.

"I'll show you a real good time if you untie my hands."

"I don't need your hands. I need your cock."

"Hey, missy, you've had cock," Rubin objected. "Give me a little time and I'll be right back on your little ass so fast—"

She turned and cut him off with a slap across the face. Lionel was instantly alarmed. He didn't like to see a fight erupt when he was unable to do anything about it.

"Why you ungrateful little bitch," Rubin lunged after her, going for his preferred method of killing women: strangulation.

But she was fast, much faster than he was. Her lilting, teasing laugh echoed throughout the building, making a couple of trapped pigeons fly up and hit the metal ceiling. Rubin lost his balance and fell on his stomach.

She pulled a gun from her bag. Lionel judged the thing to be a Raptor II. He hoped to God she'd put silver bullets in it, or she was in for a nasty surprise when the executioner got up and continued chasing her.

Lionel watched her breasts bounce as she pranced around the room, brandishing the gun. The executioner was livid with rage. Lionel just hoped she'd get on with it, but no, she seemed to want to tease the fat vamp until he had to stop, bending over to brace himself on his knees, out of breath. He shook his head.

"Okay, okay, missy. You win this round. Come on, let's kiss and make up." He massaged his limp dick a few times and almost got it to salute for her when Lionel heard the gun go off. Sure as shit she'd shot the vamp and only a silver bullet in the middle of his chest could have stopped him clean like that.

She blew the barrel of the gun like a gunslinger from Hollywood. But she certainly didn't look like any gunslinger he'd ever seen before.

Forgive my evil thoughts. He'd never wanted a woman more in his life. He thought about begging her to get right to it, not even untying him first, he was so hot for her. But then reason came flooding into his brain, and he remembered the mission.

"Untie me."

"And you'll do what?"

"I said I'd make it up to you. And I will."

She cocked her head to the side. Her gaze dropped to his groin and, sure enough, he was ready to perform for hours on end. He was twice the size he had been when she had him in her mouth.

"How do you guys do that?"

"This?" he said, looking down. "I have no fuckin' clue. I just know that I like it."

"Aren't you afraid of me?"

"Should I be?"

She nodded very slowly. "I almost killed Dag."

That did earn a little respect from Lionel. "How the hell did you do that?"

"Tied him up with silver when he was sleeping. Your employer left him in a terrible shape. Disgusting burned flesh. I think that's why he came over and got you. After I healed him, of course."

"So why aren't you with him now? Why choose his man?"

"Because I wanted to see you. And besides, Dag wants to kill me now. So you see, we are a match made in heaven. He wants us both dead."

"Wanna celebrate?" Lionel was trying to sound casual, maybe a little sexy. He was starting to get alarmed that perhaps this little lady only liked to torture her conquests. That he had grossly misjudged her, as had Dag.

"Thought you'd never ask. Beg me."

"Please."

"Not good enough. I can wait all day, but you can't. You haven't much time. They'll be over here for Round Two."

"If you and I were alone together, and I had my hands, I'd first explore every inch of your body. I'd scrub your sex so hard you'd come in my shower. I'd remove any trace of that filthy disgusting slimeball excuse for a vamp, and then I'd replace it with some good clean cum and make you glow from the inside out. You'd want me so bad you'd keep me in a darkened room and fuck me 24/7. And I'd make you come, baby, every conceivable way possible. There. How's that?"

She jumped his bones, wrapping her legs around his waist, which pulled his restraints and hurt like hell. But he'd made a promise, and if she kept hers, he'd keep his. She whispered in his ear, "I can't wait."

She ran buck naked to search through Rubin's pants until she found the restraint keys, then ran back to unhook each wrist.

Lionel was grateful.

"Thanks, sweetheart. I can trace us somewhere for a quickie, but I got things I need to do, and I sure as hell have to get out of here, and I think you do, too."

She nodded her head. She was going to be putty in his hands.

"I keep my word. You let me go, and I promise to come back and send you to heaven a few dozen times, but not right now, honey. You understand?" He lifted her chin with his fingers and placed a sweet kiss on her lips.

She began to wrap her arms around his neck and he ducked out. "Nope. Sorry. Just hold that thought. If we both survive the next few days, I'll be back."

"Take me with you. I'm an ally now. I've fought your enemy. I've aided your cause."

"Doesn't work that way. I don't make the rules. You're going to have to fend for yourself for a bit until this is all over."

"Did I tell you I qualified expert?"

Lionel began taking Rubin's clothes. The pants he had to cinch up with the belt high above his waist. His shoes were about five sizes too small.

"I can believe that."

"Let me be a member of your team."

"I don't get to choose that."

"Let me try out."

He thought about it for a moment and then decided yes; he had room for one more, especially if she was a crack shot. "Okay, get your clothes. We gotta disappear right now or it will be too late."

She was quick. He took her hand and they opened a side door to the night. "Hang on, sweetheart," he whispered in her ear. Lionel traced them to the Monteleone villa, dead center in the living room, like he'd done dozens of time before. She stepped clear of Lionel and they both studied a cadre of muscled and well-armed men grinning from ear to ear. Some had been playing video games, some were lounging in front of a big screen TV. Pizza boxes and fast food wrappers were everywhere. Lionel knew the Monteleones would be royally pissed if they saw the scene in front of them.

"Holy cow. Lionel's brought the cavalry," someone said.

"That's right, boys," she said with a twinkle in her eye. "I'm the inspirational speaker for tonight's meeting."

CHAPTER 38

Cara awoke to the sounds of cheering coming from down below. She slipped out of the luscious, buttery sheets and padded barefoot across the room to the double doors. She was pleased when she found them unlocked. On the landing she could hear lots of chatter and movement down below. Music was playing, and she could smell sweat and something else besides the left-over aromas of fast food. A glance to the corner by the front door explained it all. A small arsenal was leaning against the plaster walls of the grand house in case any intruders chose to come uninvited.

There was some raucous party happening in the living room. Waves of laughter erupted. Someone wearing a shirt and no pants disappeared into what looked like a hallway guest bath.

No pants?

The music sounded like a home Karaoke machine and the male singer was horrible, flat and off key. But a female singer took over to the whistles and catcalls of the audience. She was singing a song Cara had seen on old Marilyn Monroe films. But this singer was better than the the great lady herself.

Cara retreated to the bedroom. Beside the door she spotted a wicker basket with a set of clean clothes and a pair of shoes. She quickly dressed. Grateful that the maid had provided tennis shoes, she tiptoed down the hallway and found a rear exit leading to the back yard of the house. She opened the back door and began to run like hell.

Paolo didn't like airplanes. He usually traced. But the tracing always scared Lucius to death, so this time he sat back and allowed himself to be transported more slowly, enjoying quality time with his son, and politely fending off the attendant who kept inserting her body parts everywhere.

Lucius waved a generous goodbye to her as they were deplaning. "I think she liked, me, Father."

When Paolo turned to look back, she winked at him.

"You know, son, I think maybe you're right."

Paolo and Lucius were picked up at the airport by Marcus, who drove an armored Suburban. It surprised Paolo he was not taking more precautions.

"How was your flight, brother?"

It was morning in Italy, and Paolo wished he could go straight to bed.

"It was awesome, Marcus. I played video games, and we watched three movies."

"Oh, my." Marcus picked up Lucius' bag and slung it over his shoulder. "You get any rest, then?"

"Not a wink."

"Well, I'm afraid to say you'll not get any for a bit longer. I have to get over to the Council chambers within the hour. There's just time enough to drop Lucius off."

"Where's your driver, Marcus?"

"I needed to speak to you in private, if you know what I mean."

"Problems?"

"Complications. And I'm having trouble with some loyalty issues."

Paolo paused after he deposited Lucius in the second seat and made sure he was strapped in. "Not the Jett brothers?"

"No. God, no. They're golden."

Paolo looked back at his brother who chuckled, "Well, not Golden, but no, no problems there. Dag made a raid on Cara's apartment about an hour ago. She's safe; Jeb and Huge traced her to my house. But they captured Lionel."

"Not good."

They sped along the freeway, Lucius becoming engrossed in the movie playing behind the driver's seat on a portable screen. The countryside was greener than he remembered. The farms and olive orchards they passed, nestled amongst old stone ruins, looked smaller after living for a while California, where the scenery was similar, but with larger open spaces. But Tuscany was his home, and he was glad to be here at last. He wished Cara were at his side.

"I've alerted the local authorities," Marcus began. "The SEAL embedded with them said Cara was sorting through lots of papers last night. And she made a couple of calls. We're trying to track the numbers now."

"Surely you don't suspect Cara of—"

"No, brother. But I think she's beginning to piece together her last forty-eight hours, not that she remembers any of it, but she's re-tracing her steps."

They got behind a tractor pulling an enormous tiller. Marcus had to reduce speed. He checked the clock on the dash. "We have to hurry to make our allotted time slot."

"You should have brought the driver, Marcus," Paolo said.

"I can see that now. But, we need the privacy."

"So what else is going on?" Paolo asked.

"The Council is very concerned about the missing book. They hold the family partly responsible for its disappearance. Praetor says they have already had one meeting."

"No way we could have known. I think we told them as soon as we found out. It's not like we were hiding things from them."

"I agree. We have to make the Council understand. They can impose sanctions if they feel we have mismanaged things, brother."

"That would be so unfair. We have all risked much."

"And complacently underestimated the gathering forces of the dark coven leaders."

"Leaders?" Paolo knew about Dag. But the Monteleones had a long history of coexisting peacefully with the dark coven lords, helping them through tough times on occasion. They had been generous with their time and their money.

"The leaders are uniting. There is a scramble. Word is, the book contains something so powerful it could affect us all."

Paolo had felt such a shift in the temperature of their world.

"So I was right, she was looking for the book last night," he said to Marcus. "Perhaps it wasn't wise to erase her memory. We might have needed information she had stored in her head."

"I admit, perhaps I acted rashly."

The tractor pulled off on a dirt road and Marcus gunned the Suburban. They tore down the narrow country road until they saw the villa mounted high atop the hill, like a crowned jewel amongst the pale olive trees that had been in their family for nearly a thousand years. Was all this at stake, Paolo wondered?

"Whatever happens, I am with you till the very end. You will not have to suffer for any of my misdeeds, as has happened in the past."

"Love. Always complicated. Sometimes fleeting, and for us, usually dangerous."

"Very dangerous. I should have been more careful, Marcus. I have much to make up for. First Lucius, nearly costing you your life, and the life of your Anne. Now Lionel, who has been loyal to this family since before we were born. I pray to the God of vampires he will be returned to us safe."

They rounded a sharp corner and Marcus nearly lost control of the vehicle. Paolo held on to the handgrip bolted into the ceiling.

"In a sad way, your becoming involved with Cara has perhaps saved us. Had we not known about the book, the coven leader and his designs, we might not have been as prepared. So don't take that guilty tone with the Council. We have to convince them we have done all we could. I fear the day they would take the power away from us to act on the Council's behalf."

"If not us, who?"

"I don't know. I have been away this past year. Laurel doesn't involve herself in politics, so I have no clue, brother."

They drove up to the stone pillars that meant home. It was bittersweet—he was so grateful to see the apricot colored stucco of the family villa, but he faced the possibility it all could be confiscated, or worse yet, lost in a dark coven war that might claim them all.

As soon as the vehicle stopped, Paolo dashed out and ran around to unstrap Lucius, carrying him into the house. Marcus came behind with the luggage.

"There you are, young prince," Laurel said as she ran to her nephew and lifted him in her arms, twirling him around the kitchen. Laurel was wearing flowers woven into her hair, and her blouse was frilly, with a big collar that fluffed up in the breeze coming from the kitchen. "Let me look at you. Oh, so handsome." Lucius blushed and giggled under his aunt's affections.

Laurel addressed Paolo, giving him a hug. Paolo could feel her shaking. His sister was scared. So was he, for the first time in centuries.

"Marcus tells me there is a new love in your life. I am so happy for you." Laurel was Marcus and Paolo's unmarried sister. She had served as a link between Paolo and the rest of his family while he was living out his fantasy of a normal, mortal life in the States, as he said farewell and buried three wives.

Paolo had loved spending time at this house, where she had entertained him over the years, talking about Marcus and his investments and adventures. Laurel was the one who kept Paolo informed about family business, the marriages and births, and occasionally the tragedies, making sure he stayed loosely connected in case he ever wanted to return to the fold. And now perhaps it was too late. He could see it in her eyes.

It was in this house, Paolo remembered, that he learned the fragrance of the orchard as it bloomed in the spring months. As a young boy his mother had taken him through the warm sunny hillside, back when he was mortal. When everything was perfect. He still missed that idyllic life, even now.

"You are lovely, even more beautiful than before I left."

Laurel's caramel-colored hair and fair complexion were similar to his own. They'd been mistaken for twins growing up, and they were the closest in age. However, Laurel took the turning two years before Marcus and Paolo, anxious to be done with her mortal life and ready to begin a family.

But time had not been their friend, and so neither of them had married. Laurel had never met her fated mate, and Paolo hadn't wanted anything to do with his. Because they all believed Marcus had fathered the child, Laurel made it her job to look after young Lucius for her bachelor brother. "Laurel," Marcus said to her, "we have to trace to the Council immediately. You will see to it Lucius gets settled?"

"I will, certainly. Safe journeys."

Outside the villa, Paolo asked a question he'd been wondering about for the past half hour. "Any idea what number she called?" Paolo was curious to see if someone else had gotten close to Cara and was directing her actions.

"A number in Eastern Europe."

"Give me the number."

Marcus gave Paolo a slip of paper with the number written in Marcus' scrawl.

"We have no time for that. Let's meet with the Council, and then we'll make plans," Marcus said.

They both knew the way, having traveled to the little Council headquarters numerous times. Their tracing appeared with practiced precision at the steps to the chamber building. The brothers entered, and the tall copper doors with copper bas-relief designed by Michelangelo himself, shut behind them, sounding like the boom of a cannon.

In the anteroom, a robed novice greeted them. She was a beautiful girl, probably not quite twenty and not yet the age of choice, for she had porcelain features and appeared to be affected by the two handsome brothers. That was a mortal trait.

Paolo cursed under his breath when he saw her.

Careful, brother, Marcus mentally warned.

The Council, made up of aging Golden vamps of legendary lineage, always surrounded itself with younger girls, and it was well known that Council members occasionally bedded them.

Paolo checked his attitude, inhaled, and set his mind on the task at hand, not quite knowing if this would be the last day he would wander around Italy as a free man.

The lovely novice opened the doors to the inner chamber and they stood before the dais of the Council. Paolo recognized almost all of them. But a few newcomers were present who did not smile. Two members were hunched over in wheelchairs, red IVs dripping into their arms. He'd always thought it was odd some members would waste their lives on things that would make them weak and sick, and wondered why their advice could be valued considering their aged, addicted state.

In the center of the council sat Praetor Artemis. At last Paolo had something to feel grateful for. He knew the Golden vamp to be an honest man who had helped Marcus out of the predicament of the murder trial. But since most the Council were made up of men who were clinging to power, Paolo wondered how much of a tightrope his old friend had to walk to stay on as Chairman.

"Welcome back," Praetor began. "You've had some adventures out in the Wild West, I'm told." Someone at the end of the dais sniggered.

The brothers bowed in tandem, as they had done for decades. They both made sure the bow was long, and low.

"Thank you for agreeing to see us at such short notice, Council," Marcus began. "We have urgent news we felt the Council needed to hear from us directly, and in person."

One of the members Paolo did not recognize slammed his fist on the table and yelled, "Where is the book, Marcus? That is all that matters here."

"We are trying to locate it—"

"I'm told you had it in your possession, and yet you allowed a mortal woman to take it away with her? How can that be?" another member demanded.

"Not true, sire. We have never seen this book. Only heard about it. To my knowledge, no one has seen this book since it disappeared in the fire before we were born," Marcus replied calmly. "It could very well be destroyed, for all we know."

"Then why the hell are all the darks revving up for war over it?" another Council member asked.

"I don't have an answer for that." Marcus was running out of room to maneuver. Paolo could see his brother shaking slightly. So much was at stake. They'd had little time to plan for this. The sudden accusatory tone of the Council distressed him as much as it did his brother.

Paolo stepped in front of his brother. "Members of the Council. I am the one responsible for this series of events. I came to be acquainted with a young woman, a college professor in California, who is an expert on vampire mythology. During this casual conversation I discovered that, while she did not believe in vampires, she had followed a lead to a rare book on the subject that she was able to purchase from a bookseller in Prague."

Several members nodded. Two muttered something unflattering. Paolo paid little attention. He focused on Praetor Artemis as he completed his statement. "What happened next was a lapse in judgment, something you are all aware has happened to me before."

The room fell silent. Paolo knew no one could argue with the logic of his statement. "It was my error that I became too obviously curious about her studies. But, in the course of the conversation, I learned she had found this book, which claimed to have been written by a British explorer who studied early vampire legends. He traveled throughout India and wrote a book about the Temples of the Vampires in the Sind, dating back to a few hundred years after the death of Christ. She found references to a joining, an apex of races.

I believe he may have discovered the book, or information about the origins of our species."

"This is blasphemy!" the member who had slammed his fist on the table. "There is no such history. There is no apex."

"Oh, but there is," a voice behind them said smugly Paolo and Marcus turned to see Dag Nielsen standing just inside the doors. He was the first dark coven leader to ever be allowed entrance into the Council chamber.

CHAPTER 39

Dag sauntered to the front of the room, and began pacing in front of the dais. Paolo wanted to wipe the smirk off his face, but he struggled to tamp down his emotions so as not to give the dark leader something else to gloat about.

Marcus appeared to be in shock. Praetor was searching the table from side to side. "Who gave this man entry?"

"I did," the angry council member responded sweetly. "It seems we've been blinded by the legendary Monteleone family and their secrets. I call it a fatal case of hero worship." The robed member leaned back in his chair, studying the brothers, then abruptly turned and addressed Praetor. "And since you are friend to these two, I call for a vote of no confidence. I believe your judgment has been colored by your affection for this family."

"Nonsense. No dark coven leader has ever been granted admission to our halls. Never in thousands of years."

"But, with all due respect, you've never faced the extinction of your race," Dag inserted himself. Several on the Council gasped. Groups of two or three members whispered and muttered amongst themselves.

Paolo swallowed hard. His light-hearted thought about this being the last day of his freedom came back to haunt him, turning his stomach into a pit of oily black rage.

"As I see it, we have two items on the floor," one member spoke up from the opposite side of the table. "First we have a vote of no confidence which has been leveled at Praetor Artemis, a man I have found to be exceedingly fair and just in all the years I have known him. But it is Capuro's right to request a vote. The timing is what I find unclear."

Artemis leaned forward. "And since I am not yet the unseated Council member, the other item on this floor is the admittance of a dark coven leader to our halls. And for that, I do not give my permission at this time."

Capuro leaned back and stared at the ceiling, extending his hands out to the sides as if he'd tried his best and was giving up. Dag began to turn beet red at the attempt to muzzle him. Before he could spew out something venomous, Paolo stepped toward the dark leader and grabbed him by the elbow.

"This man is a traitor—not only to himself and his own family, but to the entire race of dark vampires. He is amassing an army. He is killing the Goldens' mortal children. I now formally accuse him of also planning the destruction of this great body. He is not your ally nor your friend. He does not seek peace. He cannot be trusted. He is dangerous, and he is my sworn enemy. As well as yours. If he remains here, then this body, this Council, will no longer speak for me."

The collective gasp that erupted from the dais surprised even Paolo. He continued to hold Dag by the elbow, taking care to make sure the dark leader remained in a small amount of pain.

"You would listen to the man who has ordered the killing of young Rory Monteleone and his younger brother, who was only a boy of ten?" Paolo shouted over the commotion.

Artemis stood. "And I have knowledge of three other children of this house who have perished at the hands of a dark guard. They were not accidents. There is a systematic attack going on, consuming the lives of some of our youngest and brightest children. This has never happened while I have been a member of this Council."

No one said a word. Dag had inhaled to shout something, but Paolo twisted his arm up at an angle and thought perhaps he felt a small bone break. The pain set Dag off, just as Paolo knew it would.

"You! You and your stuffed hedonistic bodies and your sanctimonious attitudes." Dag jerked himself free and swore as his arm hung at an unnatural angle. "Who are you to tell any of the dark covens they are not your equals? Just because you have the privilege of walking in daylight, doesn't mean you have the right to claim dominion over everyone and everything else. I'll personally watch each one of you burn in the fires of Hell. And I'll do it while fucking your wives, your girlfriends and your daughters. I will spread my seed and spawn throughout the Golden vampire race and will create a lineage that will last forever, the lineage originally denied me. I claim dominion! Mark my words. I will prevail."

Marcus and Paolo glanced at each other.

Guards traced to surround Dag as he struggled to free himself from their confinement. As quickly as it had begun, it was all over. Dag had traced himself away to a safe location.

Paolo cursed to himself, wishing he'd grabbed the man and traveled to the middle of the sun-baked deserts of Death Valley. He wanted to smell the burning flesh of this animal and watch until he had withered to nothing.

The guards were looking around for signs Dag was still in the room.

"You. You are a traitor," Artemis pointed to Capuro. "You allowed him entry without Council permission, nearly costing all of us our lives." Artemis gave the order and guards took the former Council member away in silver chains.

The whispering amongst Council members subsided. Praetor Artemis sat back down and straightened his red robe. He was not smiling. He showed Paolo and Marcus no friendship, no mercy. "This changes little. All the facts are still the same. The book must be found and if you can't do it, then we will and you will be stripped of your holdings, you will be denied the protection of the Council, and you will be left to your own devices."

Paolo and Marcus both bowed. He hadn't given them a time limit, which was good, Paolo thought.

"One more thing," Artemis said as he stood up. "You have twenty-four hours to produce the book. And bring the girl here."

"Cara? Here?" Paolo asked. "Why—"

"You wish to argue with my lenient proposal? In twenty-four hours the fates of everyone in this room will be sealed. If I thought I could do this any faster, I'd have you in chains and would go about it myself. But if you test me, if you fail, everyone you care about will pay dearly. Some with their lives." He sat down. Looking from side to side he came upon a sea of nodding heads and one who had fallen asleep in his wheelchair and was snoring.

Artemis leaned forward on one elbow, braced his chin on his arched fingers, and said with icy clarity, "I suggest you get going right away. You now have less than twenty-four hours left."

Marcus and Paolo didn't bother to take the time to bow. They looked into each other's faces and traced away. They had both been thinking about home, the villa in Imprunetta. That's where they went.

Lucius was giggling in the yard outside the tall metal and glass doors to the kitchen. The kitchen smelled of freshly baking pies, which was a custom in the Monteleone household, since Lucius still ate as a mortal child. His favorite was blackberry.

Laurel was gathering flowers in the garden. Paolo sighed as he looked at them both. Marcus capped his shoulder with his palm. "They will be safe. Somehow, we've got to make this work."

"Brother, I—"

"Nonsense, Paolo. Your instincts were perfect. You assessed the situation far better than I could, and your actions probably saved our lives, possibly the life of Artemis as well. I'm beginning to believe in divine intervention. Your meeting her has turned out to be a godsend. Just think what would have happened if we'd had no warning? Lucky for us, we have her safely stowed away at the villa in California. Otherwise, I'd be willing to bet we'd be thoroughly screwed."

CHAPTER 40

Paolo wanted to trace to California to see her again, but the urgency of the mission to learn more about the bookseller in Prague eclipsed his desire. At least he felt it was desire that prompted his need to see her, and he was learning how to do the right thing, rather than the first thing that came into his head.

When he arrived in Prague, he was greeted by an early afternoon sun that warmed his otherwise cold flesh. He walked down the designated street and stopped in front of the bookstore, troubled to see that it was boarded up.

He looked at the slip of paper Marcus had given him and dialed the number. He was rewarded with the sound of a phone ringing inside the store. No one answered. He redialed and again got no response.

He tried calling the bookstore once more. This time an answering machine answered with a message in a heavily accented, guttural man's voice. He decided against leaving a message, and against calling the local police.

He scanned the area around the little shop, looking for someone on guard, and saw none. He stepped closer to the once hand-lettered windows of the bookstore and peered between the shards of broken glass and pieces of metal and scrap wood keeping out the public. He saw that some books remained, and that someone had been packing them into crates. He needed to investigate further. Checking to make sure there was a clear spot inside the store, he stepped into the alleyway and traced to inside without being noticed.

He was immediately assaulted by the smell of death and decay.

Saturated by the distinct iron smell of blood, he walked carefully around the concrete floor, which was littered with papers and remnants of books torn asunder. When he accidentally stepped into a nearly dry pool of blood, his boots almost stuck to the floor.

Paolo knew the police wouldn't be investigating this scene. There was no evidence on the outside that a crime had even been committed here. That was both good and bad. Good that he would be allowed to rummage through the contents of the store without being disturbed. Bad that he had little time in which to do it, and since he was alone, it would use up precious minutes they could ill afford to lose.

Where to begin?

He walked over to the crates. They were all being shipped to a bookstore in San Francisco. It was clearly Dag's handiwork . Paolo sniffed the air. No trace of the dark vamp remained, if he'd even done this himself. Probably Dag had assigned the executioner and the other dark guards he used to do his bidding.

Paolo's boots made crackling noises as he stepped on more broken glass. Protective bookcase doors had been shattered. Even reading lamps and tables had been upended. A cash register, the old fashioned kind without a digital anything, was yawning open. Its vacant drawer hung down like the tongue of an old prospector.

Towards the back of the store was a narrow stairway leading up. Paolo stepped quietly, but the boards underfoot groaned anyway due to his size. He wasn't sure what he'd find there, so, although he needed the element of surprise, his need for safety was primary, so he did not trace.

A few precious moments later, he found a young, pregnant woman lying dead, next to the bodies of a pudgy little boy and his dog. It was an execution killing, done several days ago, and the stench consumed the room. No trace of the bookseller, but from the size of the pool of dried blood below, Paolo didn't doubt he was dead as well.

He was sure the perpetrator had wanted information and didn't shrink from using innocents to obtain it. However, if they had found the information they sought, the place wouldn't have been ransacked. Cara's office had been similarly ransacked.

Holy God of vampires. They don't yet have the book!

Was it too much to hope?

He glanced around the little family living space. He was looking for the phone, so dialed the number again. It rang next to a bed that had been ripped apart, and the mattress stuffing strewn all over the room. Drawers were ripped from the dressers and their meager contents dumped on the floor. Under the phone sat a square device with a blinking light. Paolo pushed the red button and heard the familiar voice of the women he now knew he loved.

He listened to Cara's message. "You also said you were receiving another shipment. I would be most interested in what you found."

Another shipment?

Paolo was about to go downstairs when he heard the end of Cara's message, and another one left after it.

The man was speaking in broken English. Paolo could barely make out that the man was from a trucking company, and was asking for instructions for delivery of a crate of books from overseas. Paolo was ecstatic.

He ran back to the machine and replayed it again, jotting down the phone number and address. He hesitated, but then decided to erase the tape, just in case he was being followed.

Once outside the shop, he ran through several alleyways until he came to the dirty riverfront. He could see the name of the warehouse across a delicate metal span bridge. He ran across the metal planks on the walkway as little cars buzzed past him.

At the office of A. Novak & Company he spoke softly to the shipping clerk who sat behind metal bars, sending some glamour her way. Her eyes fluttered, crossed, and then she promptly fainted, her plump legs resting on the swivel chair cushion she had been sitting on.

Damn it.

He took a chance and traced into the little office. In the back he heard the sound of workers and machinery, including forklifts. He decided she would make a good front for him to gain entry.

"Scusi," he said, using his practiced pigeon English/Italian dialect. "The signora has fainted. Please. Come. You must help me. She is too heavy for me to carry." He pretended to nearly drop her and several workmen came running over to give him a hand.

A clerk with a clipboard and without a hard hat addressed him. "You see what happened?"

"I was jes talking to her. She fell over. I think she hit her head, maybe? I don't know. So sorry."

The man looked Paolo over carefully, ending with laser focus on his shoes. It occurred to Paolo he might recognize his $1000 leather pumps. "My brother-in-love is a shoemaker in Napoli. He gets me the very finest at a good price."

That seemed to satisfy the man.

"Scusi, but I am sent here to pick up a crate for a mister—" Paolo dug the slip of paper from his pocket. "Tomas Novotny." He showed Marcus's note to the man. "I was to be here yesterday, and I am so sorry. I have car trouble."

The man frowned. "Hope you have something bigger than a car. This crate is full of books."

"Perhaps I will find a truck for taking crate back to Napoli."

"Thought you said it was for Tomas Novotny."

"Yes, yes, it is. But I am to sell for him in Napoli at the book festival. You've heard of it perhaps?"

"All right. You can come this way."

Paolo walked behind the man just as he heard the woman beginning to talk. He was glad she had not been hurt by the fall.

The crate for Tomas Novotny was about four feet cubed.

"You want to inspect it?"

"Sure, sure. Yes, I can do that."

The workman pried open the top with a crowbar. He removed some shredded pine packing material to reveal several antique book covers.

"Ah! Molto bello. I can look for a moment or two?" Paolo asked.

"Fine."

"I also call my friend and see if he has right truck."

The man walked away without saying a word.

Paolo took out his cell phone and dialed Marcus.

"I think I've found what they were looking for," he said.

"You found the book?"

"I found a crate that was destined for Novotny's bookstore. I don't think anyone else knows about it."

"You know what you're looking for?"

"Help me out a little bit, brother. Or, do you want to send a big truck and we'll take them all?"

"That would take too much time. It will be pretty damaged, probably flaking. I'm trying to remember what color the rest of the books were."

"You saw them?"

"Yes, when I was little. This was part of Grandfather's set, and he showed me the books before the war. I wish I'd paid more attention then. God, if only they were still alive."

"We are the old ones now, brother. Would you recognize the book if you saw it? Why don't you trace here and help me look?" Though Paolo was whispering, he felt his voice was carrying too loudly throughout the warehouse. Several of the men surrounding the woman had turned to look at him. And she was pointing right at him. "Um, I'm afraid I've run out of time. You best not do that—"

Marcus appeared right next to him and cleared his throat. Paolo darted a quick glance at the crowd of onlookers and several of them crossed themselves. Well, if they were afraid, that could give the brothers a few extra minutes. He'd have felt much better if they had one of the Jett brothers to help out. Marcus was doing a stare-down with the man Paolo thought was the foreman.

"Don't look at them. Let's get to work," Paolo said to his brother.

Incredibly, under the second layer of books was a light greenish-brown book that had been covered in green plastic archival wrap. There was no title on the outside, which Paolo thought was odd.

Marcus untaped the wrap and opened the interior of the book. There were diagrams and charts, sketches and celestial maps for navigating the oceans. A hole had been carved into the pages of the book without damaging the text. Inside the hollowed-out pages was a tiny skeleton key.

"What's this? Did grandfather ever speak of this?" Paolo asked.

"No. Never." Marcus put the key in his pocket and re-wrapped the book in the green plastic. The group of men began to descend upon them, but by the time they were close, Marcus and Paolo had traced back to the family villa in Imprunetta, taking the sacred text and the key with them.

CHAPTER 41

Paolo and Marcus were ecstatic with their find until they got the call from Lionel Jett.

"Lionel! You escaped, thank the God of vampires. Good to hear your voice. We had feared the worst," Marcus said.

"Prepare yourself, Marcus. I have some bad news."

Paolo couldn't help but overhear the conversation. He instantly thought of Cara. He had not felt anything coming from her for some time. He'd thought perhaps her altered memory had made the physical distance between them more significant than it had been earlier.

"Cara is missing."

Paolo grabbed the phone. "Lionel, was she taken?"

"No, Paolo. I am sorry to say we misjudged her and she slipped right out, when we were distracted."

"Distracted?"

"It's a long story. I must bear the responsibility myself."

"When?"

"Sometime this evening. She had been put to bed. The maid brought her some fresh clothes and a nightgown, and watched her fall asleep. When she checked on her later, Cara was gone. Sometime between midnight and two."

"Who do you have looking for her?"

"Just about everyone."

"I'll be there shortly. Let me make arrangements and I'll come help out."

"Thank you. And Paolo?"

"Yes?"

"I am so sorry for my poor judgment. We were sort of celebrating. All my fault."

Paolo didn't want an apology. He wanted Cara back. She was at huge risk, being out there by herself. But he also knew Lionel would even lay down his life if necessary to save her.

"Let's concentrate, Lionel. We need to be sharp, or we won't find her."

"That's affirmative."

Paolo handed Marcus back his phone. "No matter what, you stay here with Anne and the baby until all this is over. Protect Lucius. I have to go find her. If you have to, go before the Council with the book and give it to them. Explain this to them. I wish I could stay and study it with you, but I think I can still feel her emotions, and that gives us an advantage."

"And you are also doing the Council's bidding. You forget that they want to see her tomorrow."

"No, Marcus. I haven't forgotten the stakes. I will not fail you again."

Paolo peeked outside the kitchen windows and saw Lucius and Laurel in serious conversation about something on the patio. He walked over to his son and hugged him, inhaling the boy's fresh scent one last time. This wasn't the kind of war he'd expected to wage, chasing after a mortal woman down a dark alley. Waiting for the dark forces to rain down their wrath on all their innocent women and children. On his son.

"Lucius, you mind Laurel. I have to go away for a little bit."

"How long?"

"I'll be back very soon. I promise." He hated to make a promise he wasn't sure he could keep, and a glance at Laurel told him he was a bad liar. She was fighting back tears.

"You are going alone?" she asked.

"We have all the guys back in California. Marcus will stay here with you, Anne, the baby and Lucius. Cara's escaped."

"Oh Paolo, I'm so sorry. Don't be foolish. We need you. If she has a death wish, don't let it cost—" she stopped because Lucius was hanging on every word. The boy's lower lip quivered.

"Be brave, Lucius. Can you do that for me, for auntie?" Paolo asked.

Lucius sullenly nodded his head.

Paolo picked up his duffel bag, gave the boy's hair a tussle, kissed Laurel on the cheek. As was his tracing routine, he inhaled, as if taking the last breath of the land he loved so much. He arrived a moment later in the living room of Marcus and Anne's house in Healdsburg.

Lionel Jett was waiting for him. Paolo noticed Lionel wouldn't look him in the eye. He could tell the man was filled with remorse.

"You've got to get a grip, Lionel. Things happen."

"But I let you and the family down, sir."

"No, you've been our loyal, trusted bodyguard for centuries. We owe you our lives from so many occasions in the past. This is a complicated mess. We must concentrate. Can you do that for me?"

"Affirmative."

"Where should we start? Know anything about what she was thinking before she left?"

"No. I didn't speak with her. I was otherwise occupied," Lionel blushed and squeezed his eyes shut. He briefly told him what had transpired in the warehouse.

"And she is with your men, looking?"

"Yessir."

"You trust her?"

Lionel was having difficulty answering. "I just don't know who to trust anymore, sir, and I needed the manpower. The woman is fearless, Paolo. I don't feel she means to do us any harm. She could have done that easily already." Lionel blushed again as he looked at his feet.

"Lionel, I thought you were smarter than that. For all we know, your little lapse in judgment wasn't that, but a carefully orchestrated plan to draw Cara out into the open so they could snag her."

"I've thought of that."

"Where is everyone else?"

"Where *aren't* they? We're in radio communication. Since Cara doesn't have a vehicle, we're all over Sonoma County."

"Do a check-in with everyone. See if there are any new leads," Paolo directed. He walked into the study, scanned the bookshelf and satisfied himself that the book was still where Marcus had placed it. He wanted to touch it, knowing it was something Cara had touched, but he didn't want to leave his scent anywhere it could be detected by a dark vamp.

Cara was freezing cold, which only added to her confusion. She was running away from a house full of armed guards into the night filled with who-knew-what crazies. What was she running from? But her instincts had demanded she get out of that house. Something else internally told her she didn't have much time to get her hands on that book before it fell into the wrong hands.

Though she had on a long-sleeved shirt and jeans, they had not provided her with a jacket. She was going to have to find an all-night restaurant that served hot coffee, and had a decent bathroom. Then she'd sit down and think about what her next step should be.

Over and over in her head she thought about the dark, handsome campus security staffer, Paolo Monteleone. Hadn't she seen something in that face she could trust? Why was she not surprised when she slid into that bed last night and felt his presence? Was that the room he stayed in? Surely the master of a house that size would have a lavish master suite. And the maid had said it was a *guest bedroom*. So Mr. Monteleone was a guest?

She scanned the pebbles along the dirt pathway that shone in the moon-light. It helped to keep moving. There was, thankfully, no wind. She would need some money in case she wound up on the road for a few days. She cursed the fact that she had no cell phone.

She remembered her old phone, which was in a box at the apartment. Perhaps it had survived the bomb. She had planned to give it to Johnny. She stopped, frozen in space.

Johnny. Suddenly she was filled with images of him lying in a pool of blood in her office, his head ripped almost completely off his body. She remembered the police and rescue crews. She now remembered the questioning she had undergone.

So, Paolo Monteleone, whoever the hell he was, had been right. She had forgotten all these things, temporarily. Now they were coming back in layers.

Cara headed further down the dirt path along the country road she knew led to the square in downtown Healdsburg. There might be a coffee shop open somewhere nearby. Someone who might give her a free cup, since she had no money.

Paolo Monteleone. Something in her heart called out to him.

And she felt the warm response in return. *I am here, mi amore.*

Cara stopped and turned around. The street was deserted. An oncoming car's headlights, though distant, scared her. She jumped behind some hedges and waited for it to pass.

Her mind was racing as little pieces of memory began to stitch themselves together. She remembered the smell of the lemon shower gel, the way the robe in the bathroom had left a tingling sensation on her skin when she brushed against it. Sliding into the almond-colored satin sheets had been like sliding into—

Then she saw the lovemaking. Paolo leaning over her, kissing her, filling her with his love. Hot tears began to slip down her cheeks. How could she have forgotten so much? Or were all these just vivid dreams?

Are they dreams, or did I live them? What is happening to me?

She started to run, seeing lights of a gas station directly in front of her. Checking her surroundings, she saw a car full of men waiting in the shadows. Grateful they hadn't noticed her, she detoured around the bright lot, heading down Healdsburg Avenue toward the square.

The bar crowd was letting out, and several couples lingered under twinkle lights of the square, gazing into shop windows. She pretended she was one of them. A bar was still open on her right, so she entered.

Grateful for the darkly lit room, she motioned to the bartender she wanted to use the restroom and was granted a nod, as he pointed to the back. Locking the bathroom door behind her, she collapsed to fetal position, leaning against the wall covered in graffiti. The tears came. She felt hunted. Trapped in a strange bathroom. No money, no help. And there was something else; something dark and sinister had formed around her.

Her eyes had been shut. When she opened them, a man she recognized from her apartment, dressed in black, stood before her in the women's rest room.

It was not Paolo.

Instinctively she held her neck.

"That's right, little one. I nearly separated your pretty little head from your luscious body."

His hungry eyes perused her body like he owned her.

"Paolo should be shot for keeping you all to himself."

"But I am not with Paolo." She tried to sound brave. It didn't work.

"And good for me, then. Does this mean I won't have to beat you to submission?" Dag stepped closer and yanked her to her feet, gripping her by the upper arm. "Or, do you like it rough, my sweet?"

His foul breath sickened her. *Paolo. Help me. He is here.*

Dag cocked his head to the side. "How nice. You speak to each other nonverbally. I get to eavesdrop on the lovers. This is a most unexpected pleasure."

Cara was terrified she'd committed a fatal error. She was hoping the fact that Paolo wasn't answering her back meant that he was trying to locate her without being detected. She could tell he was close. God, she needed him and his strong arms.

"When you and I are having delicious sex, your lover boy will be able to enjoy the festivities as well. How nice for you both." Dag smiled and Cara could see the pink healing scar on his cheek from the wound Paolo had given him. Dag grabbed her by the hair and forced her face against his. His tongue plunged down her throat and made her gag.

"I'm going to enjoy this. I shall kill you slowly, as I fuck you to death, Cara. Or, excuse me if I call you by the very apt name he gave you, *mi amore*."

Dag hauled her to the hallway and pulled her through the bar. She looked with alarm at the bartender, who frowned. He bent down and reached for something from under the bar. Dag turned on him before he could stand up.

"Not wise, unless you want to sacrifice your life for hers."

The bartender stood back and raised his hands in surrender. "No trouble, please, no trouble," he babbled nervously.

"That's what I thought. Good choice," Dag said and continued to haul Cara out onto the street. A black van pulled up with its rear doors flapping open. Dag threw Cara inside and into the arms of several men, then slammed the door shut.

She was assaulted by the rotten cabbage smell first. She tried to move and accidentally kneed someone's foot. That someone was huge. He howled like a wolf. As the van began to take off, in the streetlight glare she could see a large, protruding, festering toe and what looked like a thoroughly rotten toenail sticking out from a hole crudely cut into a boot. The toe began to bleed.

"Sorry," she said, out of reflex.

She was rewarded with a slap across the face that made the whole world go dark.

Paolo lost her location just prior to arriving with Lionel at the square. The only opened structure on the block was a bar. He ran over to the bartender.

"Have you seen a brown-haired woman, about twenty-six—"

"Yes, she was just here. A guy dressed in black broke in the women's rest-room and took her. They took her in a black van." He pointed outside. "They went down towards the freeway."

"Shit." To Lionel's wounded face he said, "They've got her. Damnit. Must have done something to her, because I can't get a read on her. We were that close," he held up his thumb and forefinger.

"I'm going to call on Huge and Jeb and some of the boys to meet us here. We can trace the SEALs anywhere you say.

"Come again?"

"They dig the ride. Again, Paolo, long story. We don't have time for this."

"Your little distraction will be among them?"

"Fuckin'-A, she will be."

"You be careful. She could turn on you. Or be a secret ally of Dag."

"Not likely. She's killed his executioner, just remember that."

Lionel radioed the rest of the teams, and a crowd of armed men in dark glasses traced, arms in arm, to the nearly abandoned streets of the square and quickly separated upon arrival. Paolo could hear a couple of *wa-HOOs* erupt from the crowd as he felt the sizzle of their energy, pumped and ready for war.

In the middle of the group was a stunningly beautiful blonde warrior woman, covered in camouflage face paint, wearing a skimpy top that showed her flat, muscled midriff. She also wore a pair of cutoff jeans revealing long, tanned thighs and muscular calves narrowing into steel-toed boots. Paolo was taken aback.

"I'm Shirley," she said, extending a leather-gloved hand. She wore an ammunition belt buckled over her shoulder, and gripped an H&K MP5 semi-automatic assault rifle like she was balancing a toddler on her hip. Paolo could feel Lionel's testosterone level spiking off the charts, as well as that of the rest of the team.

"Welcome to our war," Paolo said and was rewarded with huge grins all around the group.

Then he caught an internal image of a warehouse door being slid open. Cara's vision was blurry, but he saw what she saw. She was sending him the images with great detail.

He turned to Lionel. "Warehouse, greenish silver on the outside, near a chain link fence, like a school."

"I know right where it is," Lionel replied. "Men, we're rolling in, and hot. Shirley, you stick with me and Paolo."

"Yessir," came the group reply. Arms were clasped. Paolo found himself being hugged by a couple of really huge mortal guys with tattoos covering their forearms and necks. Linked together, they traced to the warehouse.

The team spread out. Lionel was whispering orders in his Invisio. Paolo wondered where he had gotten the training, but he was also very grateful the men seemed to know what they were doing. Shirley stayed by his side the whole time. He made a point to stay out of her way, too.

He wondered if he should telegraph to Cara he was here. He decided it would be too dangerous for her. But the visions he got next speared him through his core. Cara was chained by the wrists. Her clothes were being stripped. She was standing naked in front of a room full of dark henchmen. Through Cara's terrified eyes, he saw the images of every one of their faces, and he counted the numbers, grateful she had her wits about her.

"I count fifteen at least," Paolo turned and told Lionel. Jeb and Hugh Jett each took five men and planted them outside the other two entrances.

"You stay back. You're a primary target," Lionel said.

"Nope. I'm going in with the rest of you."

"That's what they want. That's why they have her."

"Not an option."

Lionel sighed and spoke into his microphone. "On my mark."

Before he could give the order, Paolo heard Cara's scream and then the distinctive shrill voice of Dag Nielsen.

"Oh lover boyyyyy. She *needs* you. Come in and she won't be harmed, any further, that is. Your lovely beauty has just lost her right eye."

Paolo was furious and immediately traced to inside the warehouse. He saw Cara's face, with both her eyes intact. But her neck had been sliced open and her blood was spurting in a light fan spray all over the concrete floor. Dark vamps around the warehouse were smacking their lips.

"Oops. I lied," Dag said as a net of silver with a restraining charge fell over Paolo's body, immobilizing him.

The SEALs led by the Jett brothers traced inside and began engaging the dark guards.

"Stop!" screamed Dag. "I have Paolo and the girl. What are you fighting for?"

Dag was hit with automatic machine gun fire and he laughed as he saw smoke erupt from his chest. "Silver bullets? You found silver for those?" He was distracted momentarily by the fact that the person who had fired the shots was Shirley. "Well, I guess you didn't miss me, then."

Shirley fired off another set of rounds but Dag had traced to right next to her. This allowed Jeb to overcome the guard next to Dag and release Cara's bonds.

But Dag was not going to die. "You'll pay for that, and slowly," he said to her. Dag traced several feet away, dragging Shirley by the hair. He landed next to Paolo's net before any other rounds could hit him. Shirley was on him, was carving up his stomach with a KA-BAR knife she'd pulled from her boots.

"Fucking little twat," Dag said as he got hold of her neck. Shirley's arms and legs were flying around wildly, trying to find something to connect with. "Go ahead," Dag said calmly while he battled with Shirley with one arm. "You see, it isn't as easy as you thought to kill me. And if you do, you'll kill Paolo too, and this little lady, although I'm tiring of this game." Dag swung Shirley's body through the air, slamming her against the corrugated metal of the warehouse, where she lay motionless until Dag kicked her aside.

Lionel began to take a step toward him. "Oh please. You want the Council knowing you ended the life of the handsome Paolo Monteleone?" Dag smirked as he gave a signal that triggered the sounds of guns cocking and safeties being disengaged.

A forest of barrels pointed right at Paolo's head.

Dag was smug. He'd thought of everything, Paolo brooded. Though the silver netting was heavy, it didn't burn his skin like it would dark vamp's. It was the anti-tracing charge that was the problem. Paolo was powerless to do a thing.

"I can have him eliminated with a click of my fingers. You will please drop your weapons, and stand down," Dag said, especially to Lionel, who nodded, and the men lowered their weapons.

"No, I said Stand Down! That means you drop your fucking guns," Dag screamed.

The men complied as Paolo heard the crashes as weapons hit the concrete floor.

Cara hid behind Jeb's muscular frame. Paolo could see she hoped Dag would be so focused on the battle, he'd forget about her.

But Paolo's hopes were dashed when Dag strode over to Cara and pulled her by the hair into the center of the warehouse, several feet in front of the security webbing where Paolo was confined.

Blood had poured down her chest in thick, four-inch ribbons. Paolo could tell she might very easily bleed out if they didn't resolve things quickly. Even worse, Dag held her head back, throwing her slightly off balance, and increasing the flow of her blood. They were about out of time.

"Stop. I have what you want. I have the book," Paolo heard himself say. He couldn't believe he'd offered it.

"No, Paolo," Cara sobbed. "Don't believe him. He's lying to protect me."

Dag was interested and leaned closer to the netting. "Come again?"

Cara was starting to pass out. Paolo could see the Jett brothers were tensed and ready for action. Lionel was fixated on the little blonde's body near the dark corner. Then each of the brothers nodded almost imperceptibly, staring at each other. Paolo could tell they had formed an unwritten, unspoken pact.

"Please, don't interfere," Paolo said to Lionel. "Let me do this. I have the book, Dag. It's at the house, just down the road."

Cara was literally being held up by her hair, but her face had gone grey and her eyes were closed. Her mouth hung open and blood drooled slowly down her chin and breast. Paolo tried to revive her mentally, but he did not get a response.

Dag dropped Cara's torso and started over to the netting. "Good boy. Just what I wanted to know."

In a burst of speed, Jeb Jett grabbed Dag and tried to trace out of the warehouse, but the protection barrier held and they fell to the ground. One of the SEALs picked up a grenade launcher and blasted a hole the size of a truck in the wall of the warehouse before Dag could right himself. Jeb lunged at the dark coven leader again, and they disappeared out the opening into the night air.

The battle between the dark guards and the Team guys never began because their leader was gone. The dark coven guards faded away, some quickly, some walking backward, slowly.

And suddenly the room was full of sorrow. Lionel and Hugh hung their heads over their brother's sacrifice. Paolo was grief-stricken at the enormous sacrifice of life. Then he threw an anguished look at Cara, lying dead nearby, and wished with all his heart and soul that he could join her right now in eternal sleep.

Hugh and the others removed his netting while Lionel kneeled beside Shirley's crumpled body. "She still breathes!" he said triumphantly.

After extricating himself from the security webbing, Paolo ran to Cara's side. She had no pulse. He grabbed her body and held her tenderly, screaming his rage and despair. Cara remained limp in his arms. Everyone waited.

She continued to turn paler, and her skin began to feel clammy and cold. Her lips were turning deep purple. Paolo kissed those lips, tried to breathe life into them, but it was no use.

"You have a decision to make, Paolo," Hugh said as he put a hand on Paolo's shoulder.

"No. I cannot do that."

"She is gone to us now, Paolo. She is entering death's doorway. You would rob her of her immortal life because of your loathing for your choice? She cannot make a choice. You must make it for her."

"I cannot take her humanity away from her."

"It's done. Dag did that. Jeb sacrificed himself for you, and for her. Don't dishonor his gift."

"No, I am responsible. I killed her by loving her. I am her executioner as surely as if I'd carved open her neck myself." Paolo buried his head in Cara's chest. He knew he would not be able to endure a lifetime without her. He swore he'd take a tracing to Death Valley, where he assumed Jeb Jett had gone with Dag. He'd end himself before the next sunrise.

And then an image of his precious son intruded on his grief. The choice and the path became very clear.

"I am so sorry, Cara. Please forgive me." He bit his wrist and placed it over her lips. The blood from his vein ran down the side of her cheek. He opened her lips, kissed the little pillows of flesh he'd loved, tried to empty a few droplets onto her tongue.

Cara, please forgive me. Come back. Please, if you want a life with me, please come back. I promise to make the rest of your days filled with everything you desire.

The men began to fidget. Paolo knew they wouldn't let him sit there and grieve all night. At some point he'd have to stop working on her. Not every turning worked. Not every life could be saved. Only if they were compatible, but God of vampires, how Paolo wished they were compatible, how he believed—no, knew—they were.

And then Cara began to breathe. At her first raspy gasp her hand gripped her own throat, as if she was suffocating again. Paolo held his wrist to her lips and she finally bit down on him, and began to suck.

She fed ravenously as her cheeks turned pink, and her grip on his arm actually left welts on his flesh. Delicious welts. Welts he blessed and celebrated. The wound in her neck began to close, and all that remained were stains of red, which dried and began to flake off.

Cara looked up at Paolo and, yes, he could see that she was confused, but looking to him for guidance. She *trusted* him. He hoped in time she would forgive him for the choice he had made for her.

He bent down, pulling aside his wrist as she kissed him, almost as if by instinct, and closed his wound with her tongue. With his own blood still on her lips, he kissed her, feeling her little shaking body melt into his strength.

Inside him a bonfire began to burn. It wasn't the fating he'd experienced years ago, but it was something else. Something wonderful.

CHAPTER 42

Paolo and Marcus entered the anteroom off the great hall of the Council chambers with Cara between them. They'd been told to wait for their summons. Marcus held the old book they'd found in Prague, and Cara held the book by Alasdair Fraser. Paolo had insisted she carry it, since she was the one who had discovered its existence.

She'd asked a lot of questions about her making while they prepared for this meeting. How her life would change. What would she eat? All the little basic things Paolo hadn't thought much about, since his routine had been established almost three hundred years ago.

Marcus had been so distracted over the upcoming meeting that he hadn't engaged in much conversation, certainly no small talk. Therefore, Paolo was as worried as well, but did his best to cover it up. There'd be time for celebration, he decided, once they fulfilled their duty to the ruling Council. He hoped there would be no surprises.

So, they waited in the anteroom. No one attended them. For all they knew, they awaited an execution, but Paolo was careful not to think about that for fear Cara would hear his thoughts. He tried to think about sunny days in the orchard in Tuscany, and picking apples with Lucius.

He decided suddenly that it was time to set aside his fears and focus instead on life's beauties. He'd begin by being more attentive to Cara as she snuggled against him, so he wrapped his arm around her shoulder and kissed the top of her head. Marcus watched the demonstration of affection, and smiled.

"It is good to see you happy, brother," he finally said.

More minutes passed. They were now beyond their time limit of twenty-four hours. The large, carved wooden doors opened with a sucking sound, and two novices in white robes emerged. They each linked elbows with Cara and asked that the men wait outside.

Cara turned to give the book to Paolo and one novice instructed her to keep it. At the last moment, she looked back over her shoulder at him, alarm filling her lovely countenance.

Love you, Paolo.

Love you, mi amore. All will be well. You'll see. Just answer their questions.

She bravely stood straight and focused ahead as she was led through the doors. With a heavy boom, Paolo and his brother were cut off from any hope of rescuing her. It was now in the hands of the gods.

"What do you think they will ask her?" Paolo muttered as he stared at the doors.

"Hard to say. What her background is. What she thinks of vampires. Does she bleed."

"Does she bleed?"

"They asked that of Anne."

"Why on earth for?"

"To see if she was fated."

"But Cara does not bleed, at least I don't think she—I have no idea. I have never asked her."

"You've not even known her for a full cycle, Paolo."

"True."

"Women's private things. They are so confusing. But the Council will focus on the blood, the blood lines, the possibility she could be useful in some way, like to bring offspring into their world."

"You say their world, like it isn't yours."

Marcus hesitated. "I read nearly this whole book while you were in California. I now know why the darks wanted it."

Paolo watched the hand of his brother as it smoothed over the blotchy and peeling surface of the old book with reverence. "This book has cost many, many lives of our kind. It will cost more."

"Tell me."

"The human condition? It was an experiment, brother."

"I don't understand."

"Someone had the bright idea to mess with God's handiwork. Perhaps it was devil-inspired. But the bible is correct. Humans were created, except they weren't created by God."

"Who created them?" Paolo asked.

"We did, brother. We are the original race."

"Not possible." Paolo's heart thumped loudly, seeming to echo in his chest cavity.

"I'm not sure the Council knows this fact, Paolo. I'm not sure they need to know."

"The book spells this out?"

"Yes. We were the result of natural selection, until a small group of our kind began to mess with our DNA. They created two sub-races. One was mortal but could live under the sun and the moon. The other was immortal, but could not go out in the sun. It was believed that because of humans' limitations, we could hold dominion over them. It was a failsafe mechanism built into their bloodlines."

"So how can a turning occur?"

"Our blood is stronger. Our blood will prevail. I think Dag was trying to eliminate as many of the Goldens as he could, and then would rule supreme over the whole world: human, dark vampire, Golden vampire. It's just a theory, but I think he wanted to force one of us to turn him so he was free from the limitations."

"Where did he learn of this?" Paolo asked.

"That's an excellent question, and one we must investigate."

"In secret."

"If we live long enough. If they let us live."

The doors opened. Marcus leaned to Paolo and whispered, "Continue thinking of Lucius picking apples, brother."

Paolo was heartened to see Praetor Artemis down on the main floor, smiling and discussing something with Cara, who sat in a carved chair, unharmed. *Thank the Gods.*

She had been given one of Laurel's white fluffy blouses with the low-cut neckline, and he noticed Artemis was drawn to the way she looked. Paolo unconsciously made a fist, but Marcus placed his palm on his brother's forearm in warning.

Artemis greeted them warmly, winking at Paolo, which was something that had never happened before. "She's lovely," he whispered to him.

"Thank you."

"Distinguished members of the Council, I give you the two heroes of the day, Paolo and Marcus Monteleone."

The brothers bowed. Cara sat directly behind them.

I especially like the view, Paolo heard Cara say. Marcus winced like he'd been slapped.

Shhh.

Paolo experienced a flood of liquid dreams of them making love on the cream satin sheets. He was starting to get hard, and it couldn't be a more inappropriate moment for it to happen.

Marcus stepped on his foot. Hard. It jarred his attention back to the Council. He heard Artemis snigger.

Is my whole life an open book for anyone to read? Cara silently asked him.

He hears my thoughts only. But I'm sure that was enough, Bella.

"Excuse me, Council members. I must speak to Cara for just a moment." Paolo didn't wait for permission. He grabbed her elbow and led her to a corner. "You will stop this. Right now. It is not appropriate."

Cara looked back at him and swung her body from side to side, her sultry eyes at half-mast. "But I love the way my new body feels, and I'm anxious to try it out. Can you make it quick? I can be good for a few minutes, but only a few."

Paolo looked at his brother, who awkwardly tried to come to the rescue by inserting a comment. "Members of the Council. My brother is having trouble with his, his—"

"Fiancé," Cara shouted out. The Council went aghast. A gavel was pounded on the table. Paolo scowled and Praetor Artemis nearly doubled over with laughter.

"Well, that's what he promised me, anyway," she added with conspicuous innocence.

Paolo looked at Marcus, who shrugged. There was no help from any quarter, so Paolo began stuttering as if he'd been caught in a lie to gain sexual favors.

"You must forgive what I've said in the heat of passion," Paolo told the Council. Cara slapped him, but Paolo smiled, "I say many things, and I don't always agree with all of them, or remember what has been said, or promised."

Several members of the Council laughed. The oldest member woke up from his sleep and asked if the meeting was over.

Marcus tried to hide his giddiness at the brilliance of the deception. Even Praetor seemed anxious to keep things on a very light and celebratory note.

"Then let it be said, Paolo Monteleone," a gray-haired Council member stood and delivered, holding onto the tabletop, "you are to wed this woman within the next thirty days, as punishment for your insolence. The debt for your turning her will be satisfied if you make her an honest woman."

A cheer went up. Even some of the novices at the sides of the room clapped. "And you, Carabella Sampson, shall honor and obey your husband-to-be, and shall submit to him whenever and whatever he desires. Do you agree to this?"

Cara crossed her arms, feigning some slight disagreement, but then ran to Paolo, put her arms around his neck and said, "I will. Most certainly I accept your terms."

Congratulations were given generously. Within a matter of minutes, Praetor said he would accompany them home, in his private limo. As they left the chamber hall one member of the Council shouted out.

"The book! What about the book?"

Marcus turned and bowed. "I shall return it to my grandfather's study, from whence it came, for safekeeping, of course."

"Excellent," the member said. "Make it so."

Cara found it very hard to behave herself during the limo ride. Her hormones were raging. She wanted to strip off her blouse and skirt and ride Paolo's cock all the way home, with or without an audience. She slipped her hand around Paolo's side, and between the leather seat and his waistband, managed to slip a couple of fingers under the fabric, feeling a bit of flesh at the top of his thigh.

Marcus was engaging in conversation with Praetor, but Paolo's constant jumps and twitches wheneverCara tickled and stroked another inappropriate and extremely private body part finally elicited a comment from him.

"You two. There will be centuries for that. Trust me. It never gets old, Cara. No reason to rush into things."

"I am starved."

Praetor's eyes sparkled at the blush of her lust, which filled the whole vehicle.

"She is charming," Praetor had said to Paolo, but was staring right at Cara.

Her bra felt two sizes too small; her panties were wet with her juices. Crossing and uncrossing her legs only pressed her lips against her nub and made her shudder. It was an ache like she'd never experienced before. She had become a wanton woman, and not afraid to show it.

"Five minutes, Cara. We'll be home in only five minutes," Paolo said to her, but he too was grinning.

Cara feigned impatience and swiveled around, presenting the men with her back. Her arms were crossed and she looked out the side window at the cobblestoned streets of the village, gleaming wet with rain. Paolo found a way to move his palm up under her skirt. He slid two long fingers around and under her lace panties and found her core.

Cara hitched her breath as he sunk the fingers inside her. "Better?" he whispered in her ear.

She moved her pelvis against his palm, rubbing herself and pulling his fingers in deeper by way of an answer. She barely heard even dribbles of the conversation the three men were having.

"And so I want to spend some time studying every chapter in this tome. Just the three of us," Marcus said.

Praetor agreed. Paolo mumbled a "yes" into Cara's hair.

"Until we thoroughly analyze it, we say nothing to anyone else, can we all agree to that?" Praetor asked.

The plan was formed. Marcus and Praetor would begin work on the project in the morning. Paolo would begin work whenever he would manage to escape from the bedroom.

With the doors closed behind them, the fireplace roaring, Cara felt a little timid, now that she was going to have her first encounter with the man she loved as a vampire female. A Golden vampire female. Though she'd studied the myths and legends in her teachings, she never in her wildest dreams thought she'd be preparing for a night like this.

Every minute she remained untouched by Paolo was painful to her. The desire to couple with him, to mate in the old, ritualistic way Alasdair Fraser described in his lovely book, was stronger than any other need. Stronger than breathing. She was burning up with lust. Her ears buzzed. Her neck pulsed and her breasts shook with the pounding of her heart.

He came up behind her and whispered, "You were very naughty today."

The feel of his warm breath on the side of her face and in her ear sent her spine tingling, and the little sparks of passion found their way all the way to her toes. "I hope I can make it up to you," she whispered in return. She helped his palms find her breasts and she moaned and rolled her head back on his shoulder when he squeezed them.

"I've been told I have to make you obey."

"Do you want me to fight?"

"I want to let you do whatever you want to do."

"I want to please you."

"But you do, my Carabella. You do."

He slid her blouse over her shoulders, undid the zipper at the back of her skirt and slid the fabric down over her thighs as he came to his knees behind her. She'd worn the black high-hip panties that showed off her full bottom and he hissed, and then kissed her flesh, one cheek at a time. He turned her around to face him, still on his knees.

A lazy forefinger traced down the crack between her buttocks while his hand palmed her mound from the front. He drew her to his mouth, slipped the lacy fabric to the side with his tongue and found her labial lips. She felt a nip as he bit he there and drew blood.

"So sweet, Carabella," he whispered. "I want more."

"Yes," she said as she looked over her shoulder at him. His tongue had found her folds, ridges, and then her insides. His saliva tingled on her skin, healing the first wound before he bit harder, creating another one.

She groaned and bent over, giving him better access. She entwined her fingers in his as he gripped her thighs, his face buried in her sex. From out of the corner of her eye she could see the growing tent in his pants.

"I want to taste you too," she whispered. "Show me how it is done."

"Very well."

He took her hand, led her to his bed and let her remove his shirt. She knelt before him and undid the old-fashioned silver clasps of his waistband and snaked her hand inside to feel his shaft and balls, giving them a gentle squeeze. Paolo arched into her hand. "Yes. That is how it is done."

"Can I bite you there?" She asked.

"Um. No. Well, I've not done—"

Before he could say anything further she had slipped his pants down over his hips and had bitten him on the upper thigh next to his balls. She sucked the wound and then sucked his cock, spreading his own blood all over the shaft. Paolo bent over her, smoothing his palms down her back, down over her buttocks, squeezing them.

He angled himself so she took him in her mouth and pressed her breasts into his thigh as she sucked, scraping a canine over the surface just enough to draw a little blood. The tiny droplets made the lips of her sex swell, made her nipples hard and knotted.

The bra was getting uncomfortable, so she stood and removed it. They were man to woman, completely naked, and hungry.

"I want to do it the first time the way your ancestors do it."

Paolo nodded. He pointed to the bed. She lay back and he covered her body, licking the side of her neck, kissing her from her earlobe to her shoulder.

"You do what I do. You follow me."

"Yes," she sighed. She licked and gave sucking kisses to the hard muscle running down the right side of his neck. She tasted the saltiness of the skin near his shoulders.

"Your tongue will soften the sting, like this." He traced a trail along her jugular. She could feel her body defer to him, as the vein pushed itself to the surface of her flesh for easy penetration.

Cara did the same to Paolo, and yes, his skin became soft under her tongue. She could smell the blood thumping there.

"We become one plus one." He kneed her legs apart and thrust inside her, making her arch back at the feel of his huge cock stretching and filling her. He stroked her insides with circular motions, coating her with fire, setting her aflame. Deep inside her, he stopped.

"And now we take the bite." Paolo cracked the skin of her neck and all she could do was push up against him, the need for him to take all of her was so strong. "Take me, Cara," he begged.

She found the warm flesh of his neck and pressed her teeth against it. Her new fangs slid into his skin without a sound. She tasted his elixir and instantly needed more.

She felt ancient. She felt powerful, stronger than ever before. He rocked her body with his powerful hips. She raised her knees folding her legs over his shoulders, and he took her deep.

When at last he shuddered his release, she began to explode as well. Her body glowed from the inside out. The delicious ripple of her orgasm traveled up and down her spine, sparking at every nerve ending. Her fingertips were covered in pinpricks. She moaned her pleasure into his hungry lips.

"Yes, I want all of you," he said. "Give me everything, Carabella. Mi amore."

They stilled but he didn't pull out. Breathing heavily, he balanced part of his weight on one elbow. She loved the feel of him pressing on top of her, inside her. She traced along his hairline, gazing into the deep chocolate of his eyes. His full lips came down and planted a delicate kiss, and then deepened.

"Thank you," she said.

"For what? I thank you, mi amore. I have never felt such ecstasy."

"Thank you for showing me."

Paolo chuckled.

"What's so funny? Did I say something wrong?"

"Mi amore, I have only begun to teach you. This, my sweet Carabella, is only the beginning of your beautiful immortal life."

The End

OTHER BOOKS BY SHARON HAMILTON:
The Guardians Series

ALL AVAILABLE ON KDP & AUDIBLE!

The Golden Vampires of Tuscany Series:

OTHER BOOKS IN THE
SEAL BROTHERHOOD SERIES:

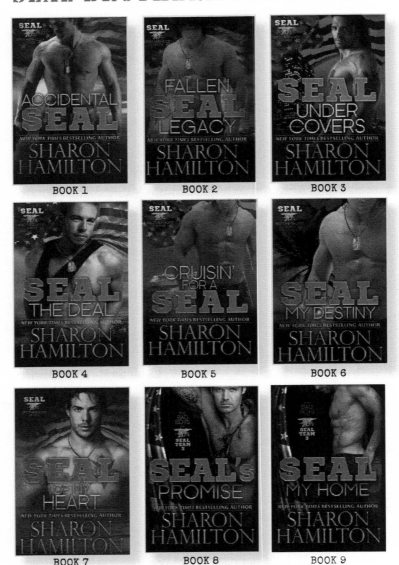

BOOK 1   BOOK 2   BOOK 3

BOOK 4   BOOK 5   BOOK 6

BOOK 7   BOOK 8   BOOK 9

ALL AVAILABLE ON KDP & AUDIBLE!

BAD BOYS OF SEAL TEAM 3:

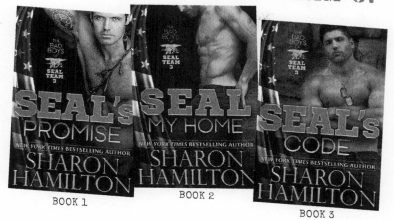

BOOK 1

BOOK 2

BOOK 3

BAND OF BACHELORS:

BOOK 11

Connect with Author Sharon Hamilton!

www www.authorsharonhamilton.com

f facebook.com/AuthorSharonHamilton

t @sharonlhamilton

http://authorsharonhamilton.com/contact

29625756R10154

Made in the USA
Middletown, DE
21 December 2018